DONATI BLOODLINES PART 1

BETHANY-KRIS

Published by Bethany-Kris

www.bethanykris.com

ISBN 13: 978-1-989658-42-0

Cover Art © London Miller
Editor: Nina S. Gooden

For London.

Because you just couldn't love Calisto enough.

CONTENTS

PREFACE

Calisto Donati

She was just a woman. That's what Calisto wanted to tell himself; that's what he wanted to believe. Emma was nothing more than a woman. There were other women for him to want. To obsess over.

It couldn't be Emma Sorrento.

Not for Calisto.

She was taken.

She was claimed.

She was not his.

In a few days, Calisto would hand her off, and that would be that. He wondered why it wouldn't be that easy to let her go.

What good had saving her done?

He had simply taken her from one monster to give her to another.

Emma Sorrento

Emma slid on her mask. All someone would need to do was look close enough to see what was really beneath the sheer falseness of her smile.

At the other end of the table, Emma found her lies staring her right in the face.

He smirked.

And winked.

Calisto Donati was her worst mistake, her greatest shame, and the one thing she still wanted more than anything. Emma could still feel him all over her, long after his touch and kiss was gone. In thirty days, her entire world had changed—he had changed her.

1

Emma had a feeling that if she played another game with Calisto, she would surely lose.

She had already lost once.

Wasn't it enough?

1.

"Duty" was the first word a *Mafioso principessa* learned growing up. Be good to the family. Bring them no shame. Smile for the crowd.

And when the time comes, do your duty.

At only twenty, Emma Sorrento was not ready to do hers.

"You look wonderful, Emmy," Maximo said.

Somehow, Emma managed a smile for her uncle. "Thank you."

Maximo waved her closer. Emma followed his unspoken demand until she was standing in front of him with her hands clasped behind her back. Maximo looked over the silver, flared dress that fell just above Emma's knees, and the black pumps on her feet.

"Your hair is down," Maximo said.

"You asked for it to be like this, *zio.*"

"I did. I like it better this way. I'm sure Affonso will appreciate it as well. And your mother made sure you toned down the red lipstick, I see."

"*Sì.*" Emma swallowed back the disgust rising in her throat. It burned like bile on her tongue, acidic and full of shame.

"Smile, Emma. That frown does nothing for your pretty face."

Her uncle's words had been spoken lightly, as if he were amused, but a heavy ring of warning lingered right behind them. Immediately, Emma fixed her frown to a smile.

Fake and bright.

Enough to distract a man.

She could do this.

Right?

"She's a little nervous," came a voice from behind her. "It's a big day for our little Emma."

Emma found her father, George, leaning in the doorway with a cigar dangling from his fingertips and a glass of brandy in his other hand.

Maximo chuckled. "How much of a fight did she put up this morning, brother?" A single finger ticked under Emma's chin, making her stare up at her uncle's face. "What is there to fight about, hmm?"

"Nothing," Emma said.

"Surprisingly, very little," George said.

Maximo smiled. The sight was almost predatory in nature. Her uncle had always treated her well, especially considering that she was the only daughter in their small family. George had no other children but Emma, and the other Sorrento brother had died in a childhood accident when he rode a bicycle out onto the street and was hit by a car.

The Sorrento family was one of many Italian-based organized crime families in Vegas. Over the years, the Sorrentos and other syndicates across the country strengthened their ties by mixing their names and blood. In Cosa Nostra, girls were fodder to a bigger plan. That plan being a man, the one with the best last name for a contract, the family to push them higher, make them safer, or earn them business.

Because that's all her life was worth.

Emma knew this day was coming.

"It's just business," Maximo said as if he could read Emma's mind.

"Business," she echoed.

"The Donati family had a long night getting here. Some issue with the plane caused them a layover. It ended up connecting them to a redeye. I expect you to be pleasant and respectful, Emmy."

Emma felt the spark of anger stab through her heart. She had done all that she could to ignore the lingering rage simmering in her blood, never mind the resentment burning through her soul.

Maximo didn't give her a chance to voice her inner war. Her uncle left the large office. He passed by his brother in the doorway without so much as a goodbye, and disappeared into the hall. When Emma was sure that she couldn't hear her uncle's footsteps anymore, she finally took a real breath.

For two months, Emma had felt like she couldn't breathe. Ever since her uncle had visited her parents' home one evening, sat down at the dinner table, and calmly explained that she would be married off to a man nearly thirty years her senior.

Affonso Donati was forty-nine, but his fiftieth birthday was right around the corner. Apparently, the man's wife had passed away a few months earlier after three separate battles with cancer. Every good Cosa Nostra Don needed a wife and so, Affonso went shopping for one.

Emma's father and uncle—without her knowing or giving input—had placed her name, picture, and pedigree directly in Affonso's path.

It pissed Emma off like nothing else. The Donati family certainly wasn't the biggest or best syndicate for her uncle and father to marry her off to. They were small-time in New York compared to the Marcellos or even the Calabrese family. Affonso could be her father, for Christ's sake.

Emma forced back the sickness beginning to rise again. She took a deep breath, needing to calm the torrent of panic starting to well all over again.

Duty.

That stupid word kept ringing louder and louder.

"Your mother is waiting for you downstairs," her father said.

His voice reminded Emma of George's presence.

"Thanks," she said, spinning around.

"You know I appreciate how good you're being about all of this, don't you, Emmy?"

Emma refused to even grace her father with a smile. The man knew how angry and disgusted she was over this entire agreement between the Sorrento and Donati families. "Yes, I know, Dad."

"Good."

George smiled, taking another step into the room. Her father reached out and snagged Emma's hand, drawing it away from her side. He glanced over her bare ring finger and said nothing about the slight tremor rocking her hand. Then, her father's grip tightened to an almost painful point. His fingernails dug into the skin of her palm with enough pressure to leave marks behind.

Emma sucked in a sharp breath. "*Ouch.*"

"Remember that feeling, sweetheart. I hear Affonso has a taste for pain where his women are concerned. At least, he does if they don't behave."

Oh, God.

"And the ones who do behave?" she asked quietly.

"He treats them like little queens." George smiled again. "I have given you everything you have ever wanted, Emmy. You have been spoiled rotten, treated like a princess, and handed over every bit of respect you deserved as a Sorrento daughter. It's time for you to repay me for that. Be a good girl, and do this for your family without issue."

Emma had never been particularly close to her parents. Both George and Minnie Sorrento had been far more focused on their social lives and *la famiglia* business, than they had been about Emma as she grew up. Her parents' way of making up for neglecting her of love and attention was by giving her things.

Lots of things. Love couldn't be bought. Emma ignored the pain in her chest. Her screaming mind was louder.

Loyalty is bought all the time.

DONATI BLOODLINES: PART 1

Her parents were the perfect example of how people attempted to do just that. They'd birthed a daughter they didn't really know, gave her a glamourous life that placated and tricked her into comfort, and now she didn't have a choice but to do what they wanted. Emma had no money of her own, no status to keep her safe or provided for unless she did what her parents demanded. Even her apartment and car were not hers to keep unless she did what she was told.

Emma hadn't realized how controlled she was by her parents and Cosa Nostra until a choice was placed on the table. A choice that wasn't really a choice at all.

"What is Mom waiting on me for?" Emma asked her father.

"She brought along your birthday gift. The diamond and pearl set she wore for our wedding. She wants to see you wearing them for yours. Happy twentieth, sweetheart. Another month to go, and you'll be a married woman."

Emma stifled her shudder.

Barely.

"Smile," George reminded her sharply, his fingernails cutting into her palm again.

She did.

And blinked back her tears at the same time.

Her life was not her own.

She didn't get to choose.

Emma had always known this.

It didn't make it easier.

• • •

"Emma."

Spinning on her heel, Emma came face-to-face with a gentleman who was taller than her by a half of a foot. His black hair was peppered with gray just behind his ears, and his easy smile spoke of kindness and grace. His eyes, however, were an emotionless, cold brown.

Affonso.

Emma reminded herself that people were watching the exchange. A whole houseful of people, actually.

"Hello," Emma said, offering the man the best smile she could muster up. She held her hand out and Affonso took it instantly to press a feather-light kiss on her knuckles. "I'm sorry there was a problem with your plane yesterday."

Affonso raised a single shoulder in response, like he didn't give a damn either way. "Me too. I was hoping to get a decent night's rest before meeting you and taking you to church. But *non è importante.* You, however, are very important, *bella.*"

Emma wished the man's charming smile and his sweet words was enough to lull her into some sense of comfort around him. They didn't. She didn't know Affonso from a goddamn hole in the ground. She was thirty years younger than his nearly fifty, and she couldn't forget that she had essentially been sold to the man like cattle.

The price for her hand was still a mystery.

Affonso moved closer, tugging on Emma's hand at the same time. He drew her just inches from his tall frame, slid a finger under her chin, and tilted her head up. "You don't seem happy, my dear."

His words had been spoken far too quietly for anyone else to hear.

"I am," Emma lied.

Affonso chuckled. "Well, you're a good liar. I will give you that. You'll certainly need that, being my wife. I was promised a girl who knew her place as long as she was kept and spoiled properly. Can you turn your cheek as well as you can tell a lie and smile, *bella?*"

Emma blinked, stunned. "Why?"

"I didn't ask for a question. I suggest you learn quickly to answer what I do ask, and without any other frilly nonsense to waste time. I hate wasting time, Emma."

8

DONATI BLOODLINES: PART 1

A sliver of dread drove into Emma's spine.

"Okay," Emma said, looking down to drop the man's gaze.

"I simply want a good, young wife, Emma Sorrento. Nothing more. A young woman who can birth me the healthy boy my first wife didn't give me, and my mistresses seem unable to produce. I have daughters galore. No boys. Give me the boy, and you can live your life in a spoiled, peaceful bliss. Does that sound good to you, *bella?*"

Emma's air caught painfully in her chest.

That's what this man wanted from her?

A *child?*

A boy, for that matter.

Was that all she was worth to this man? Her ability to carry him a child, one with the gender of his preference? Didn't he realize that the man decided the sex of a baby and not the woman?

Affonso's smile faltered for a split second. "You're overthinking, Emma. I can see it in your face. Your father and uncle have gone through great hoops to get one of theirs tangled in marriage with a New York family. You're not going to ruin it for them, are you?"

"I don't really have a choice, do I?"

The man sighed.

She'd asked another question. "I mean no. Of course not, Affonso," Emma said quickly.

"Well done. You're young, and so I will give you a pass on your behavior. I imagine this is still a shock to you. A huge change. Am I right?"

Emma's emotions thickened in her throat. "*Sì.*"

"*Povera ragazza.*"

Poor girl.

She glanced away from the man and the softness in his tone. "I'll do what you need for me to do, Affonso."

"You really are just a girl, hmm?" he asked. "Twenty is still a child in many ways."

Maybe to him and his nearly fifty years.

Emma didn't feel like a girl. She was simply trying to let her mind and heart catch up to this awful day and begin to work together.

Even still, she didn't answer the man.

Apparently, Affonso wasn't looking for an answer. He dragged his gaze from the heels on her feet to the bareness of her legs, and up to the swell of her breasts.

"I like this dress," he told her.

Always thank a man when he gives you a compliment, her mother used to say. *Smile for him, sweet girl. Men need to feel respected.*

Emma's lessons over the years came rushing back to her like a tidal wave of memories. Whether she wanted to admit it or not, she had been groomed for this very moment ever since she was just a young child.

"Thank you," Emma said with a smile.

"I'll have you a dozen more dresses like this one waiting in your closet at home."

Home.

The one word was enough to make Emma sick.

"As I was saying," Affonso continued, smiling slyly as his leer traveled over her body again. "… you're still young in many ways, but you're old enough in all the ways that count, *bella*. I hope you know how to use those ways. I'm not interested in teaching and, let me just say, you wouldn't enjoy the way I would teach you."

Emma felt her cheeks pink. Was he asking what she thought he was? That he hoped she wasn't innocent to a man and sex?

She bit the inside of her cheek before muttering, "I don't need to be taught."

"Wonderful."

Stepping away from Emma, Affonso spun on his heel to face the waiting people. His hand hadn't released Emma's, and he pulled her with him. She found the familiar faces of her family and a few of her uncle's men watching the exchange with curious, but wary, expressions.

DONATI BLOODLINES: PART 1

"Maximo," Affonso said, "are we just about ready to leave for the church?"

Emma was shocked that her uncle was going to church at all. He hadn't returned to the Catholic church since he divorced his first wife. Maybe it was another way for Maximo to extend a hand to Affonso in friendship. She wasn't sure.

Her uncle nodded. "Yes, we are. The cars are waiting."

"We'll catch up in a minute," Affonso replied to Maximo. "I want a second alone with Emma, if you wouldn't mind, old friend."

Maximo passed Emma a look as if to silently ask if she was okay with the request herself. Emma didn't see how her opinion of things mattered at all. It hadn't before, so why would it now?

Before long, the house had cleared of people but for Affonso and another man standing at the bay window. The color streaming in through the glass bathed him in bright light, showcasing a tall frame and broad shoulders hugged by a tailored suit. His dark hair was cropped short, but it was still long enough for him to run his fingers through as he lifted a glass of water in his hand to take a drink.

"Now that we're alone," Affonso said, turning to Emma.

She shot the quiet man with his back turned a look. "Um—"

"My nephew always stays close by. Ignore him. As I said earlier, I was promised a girl who knew her place, Emma. I want to make sure you understand everything that means."

"I think you explained it well enough."

"Then why are you trembling like a little leaf?" he asked.

Emma stilled on the spot. She hadn't realized that she was still shaking. "I'm nervous."

Affonso frowned. "Calisto?"

The man at the window turned his head slightly, just enough to stare at his uncle and Emma. Dark brown, almost black, eyes and a strong jaw framed the man's face. His sharp cheekbones and unsmiling lips hardened his features, but it still stunned Emma.

It stunned her because he was … beautiful.

A hint of something dangerous and sinful wafted from the young man as the corner of his mouth tugged upwards into something resembling a smirk or even a sneer. She couldn't be sure. Long fingers wrapped tighter around the glass he was holding, drawing Emma's attention to the fact he wore no wedding band and his hands seemed strong.

She could clearly see the resemblance between the younger man—Calisto, Affonso had said—and his uncle.

"*Sì?*" Calisto asked.

"*Cal, ottenere vino.* Fill a glass. Hurry, before someone comes back and bitches about her age and drinking."

Calisto chuckled deeply. The sound came out dark and heavy, and his tall, fit frame rocked with movement. Emma thought he sounded almost musical, even if the man looked entirely bored with the situation and day.

"Whatever you need, *zio.*"

Then, Calisto was gone.

"Wine?" Emma asked.

"It'll take the edge off for you," Affonso said, smiling widely. "As long as you're a good girl, Emma, I will always take care of you."

A good girl.

Emma felt sick again.

"And of course, Cal will always be around to keep an eye on you when I can't," Affonso added. "He's closer to your age, at twenty-seven. Too bad, really. Had he wanted what I wanted for him, then I wouldn't need you at all, Emma."

What was that supposed to mean?

"I prefer Emmy," she said.

It was the only thing that came to her mind. She felt stupid for even saying it, but it was better than spitting out how disgusted the man made her.

"Emmy," Affonso echoed. "Sounds a bit girlish and young, doesn't it?"

Suddenly, a presence was behind Emma. She knew Calisto was back before he'd even said a thing.

"Here," Calisto said, handing Emma a glass of wine.

Her fingers brushed his and warmth spread up her arm. She pulled her limb and the wine glass back as fast as she could, but not before dropping her gaze.

"Thank you," she said.

"I prefer Emmy," Calisto said quietly.

Emma's head jerked up, finding Calisto watching her curiously.

"Pardon?" Affonso asked.

"Her name. Emmy. I like it."

Emma tipped her wine glass up and gulped down a mouthful just to keep from smiling. Who was this man? A few minutes ago, he seemed like he didn't care who she was or if she was even breathing.

"It's got a nice ring, *zio*," Calisto added. "Rolls off the tongue, if you know what I mean."

Affonso scowled. "You would think so, Cal. Hurry up with the wine, Emma. We have things to do and people to see. A good Don doesn't keep people waiting. You've spent enough time around Maximo to know this."

Emma drank her wine a little bit slower.

2.

"Our church isn't quite as big as this one," Affonso said from beside Emma in the pew.

Emma didn't know how to respond to that. For the last two hours, Affonso had been dropping hints and information about New York during the drive to the church and during Mass. He spoke about his two daughters from his dead wife. Michelle was the youngest at fourteen and Cynthia was the oldest at sixteen.

Emma was sure the man had said he had a "handful" of daughters. Apparently, the ones born from his mistresses weren't important enough for him to talk about. She didn't press him about the children he might have made outside of his first marriage. Even the two children he did talk about were quickly discussed and then dropped before he moved onto something else. Emma did learn that the two girls spent most of their year away at boarding school.

The two girls would likely hate her.

Jesus.

She was only four years older than the oldest one.

Holidays would be awkward, if nothing else.

"I know your uncle hasn't attended church since his divorce from his first wife," Affonso said.

"He hasn't, no," Emma agreed quietly.

"But you do, yes?"

"Every Sunday."

When she had been home to go, that was. While she was away at boarding school, church hadn't been a very important thing. Emma didn't add that information in. It'd been two years since she graduated high school, anyway. She'd messed around with some college courses but never settled on one particular area of study.

Now, she wouldn't get the chance at all.

"Good. Then explaining to you why you'll continue to attend in New York is pointless. You already know."

Emma glanced up at him. "I enjoy church. I think it's peaceful, in a way."

Affonso's lips flattened into a grim line. "I find it boring, but it's a necessary evil. Confession is even worse."

Maybe if the man didn't have a lot to confess, his confessions wouldn't be so daunting. It wasn't Emma's place to point that out to her future husband, so she stayed quiet.

"You won't have to worry about convincing me to go," Emma said.

"Wonderful."

The progression of Mass continued. Emma, like she usually did on Sundays, watched her family and the familiar faces surrounding her in other pews. Her gaze caught the rays of early January sunlight filtering in through the stained glass windows. Prisms of light danced across the altar, down the aisle, and over the congregation. Shuffling clothes and the squeak of shoes echoed throughout the building as the people stood, prayed, and sat back down, over and over.

It was familiar.

Almost comforting.

Peaceful, Emma repeated silently.

"How do you feel about a private lunch after Mass?" Affonso asked.

It wasn't really a question.

Emma smiled falsely. "That would be nice."

"Your uncle has some kind of dinner party planned later, as far as I know. The arrangement for the marriage will be announced then and I will hand over your ring. I'm sure you'll like the piece. Your father said you have a taste for anything that's princess cut, an interesting color, and more than a couple of carats. Was he telling me the truth?"

Shame rested heavily on the back of Emma's

tongue. It tasted a hell of a lot like disgust and anger. She wasn't feeling those things for Affonso, but for herself.

She hadn't minded the life of a spoiled mafia *principessa*. Being respected and adored by *la famiglia,* simply because she was someone's daughter and had a good last name had lulled Emma into a false sense of security. Her sheltered life and foolishness had put her in this position.

A position where she woke up one day to the rug being ripped out from under her.

Emma wondered if she deserved this. She had rows and rows of beautiful clothes, shoes, and bags at home, bought for her by her mother and father. She had jewelry galore, a penthouse apartment in a Casino hotel, and a Benz with her name on the license plate.

She had always been stupid.

Spoiled into submission.

Tricked like an idiot.

And now she was the one being used.

"Emma?" Affonso asked again.

Drawing in a slow breath, Emma said, "My father didn't lie. He's been spoiling me with diamonds for years, Affonso."

Emma was only now realizing the game her father played.

And she had lost.

"What's wrong, *bella?*"

Emma blinked down at her hands clasped in her lap. She knew from her earlier discussion with Affonso that he didn't like it when others questioned him. He certainly didn't seem to like it when a much younger woman, one he essentially considered to be a child, questioned him.

Even so, the words still spilled out.

She couldn't stop them.

"Is that what you want?" Emma asked.

"Pardon?"

Emma caught Affonso's eye from the side. He was

watching her with a hint of amusement in his otherwise cold gaze, but the ghost of a smile shadowed the edge of his mouth.

"Am I what you want, Affonso?"

"I would say so, considering you're the woman I chose."

"A silly, young wife," Emma said, not bothering to hide her contempt or bitterness. "A stupid, spoiled, and easily placated wife. One that will brush off the awfulness around her when you buy her a new car. One that will overlook your whores when you fill her closets with new dresses and furs. Am I supposed to hide the unhappiness with all the jewelry and makeup, too?"

Affonso smiled slowly. "Well, well."

Emma didn't wish for a second that she could take her words back. She'd meant every single one of them. Frankly, her father, uncle, and Affonso were lucky that she had made it to the church without spilling her true feelings.

Up on the altar, the priest asked the congregation to stand once more for another song and yet another blessing. Emma stood like she was supposed to. Affonso quickly followed beside her. She placed her hands on the rounded edge of the back of the pew in front of her.

One of Affonso's hands covered hers.

She felt the heat of his palm, but it did nothing. The weight of his fingers and the gold bands he wore rubbed against her skin.

Again, nothing.

"You're exactly what I want," Affonso murmured.

He never once took his eyes off the altar.

"I married for love once. In twenty-five years of marriage, she gave me two daughters, a well-kept home, and a warm bed. She was neither spoiled, stupid, nor easily placated, as you said. But like you will, Emma, she learned her place in the hierarchy of *la famiglia* and took her seat like all good wives of bosses do. The quicker you take yours, the easier this will all be."

"I don't want to be married," Emma said, harsher than she first realized.

Affonso chuckled. "You mean to say that you don't want to be married to *me*."

Was there a fucking difference?

Emma didn't see one.

"Nonetheless, you will be my wife in a month's time," Affonso added. "You'll have another few weeks here with your family before you fly down to New York, and settle into a new life with a much better status than you have now."

"I don't care about status."

But she had.

Once.

The truth choked her.

Emma despised herself for even knowing that at one time, she had soaked in the attention as a boss's only niece, reveled in her family's position, power, and wealth, and at the same time, ignored what it would mean for her in the end.

Stupid girl.

"I wondered how long it would take," Affonso said, more to himself than her.

Emma watched him from the corner of her eye, wary and unsettled in her heart. "Take for what?"

"For your anger and fight to show. A tiger can't change or hide its stripes, after all. Your father and uncle did a damn good job this morning of dressing you up, prettying your face, and prepping you for the first meeting. But it was when you were alone and without them that I knew you wouldn't be able to hold up the mask. And it's fine, really. Better for me to see it than them."

"Why is that?"

"Because I know that no matter what you feel or believe, you're still going to be my wife. Your father and uncle want you to take the easy road down the altar with no muss or fuss."

Emma swallowed hard. "So?"

"Honestly, *bella*, I don't give a good goddamn if you fight your way down it."

Great.

• • •

"I've hired a moving company for your penthouse apartment," Affonso informed her.

He had done it at the right time, considering Emma had her mouth full of steak and couldn't respond. In just the few hours she had spent with the man, Emma had quickly learned that Affonso Donati was shady and sly.

It left behind an icky feeling. Like the man couldn't be trusted.

Swallowing the bit of meat, Emma said, "I can take care of packing my own things, Affonso."

"Perhaps, but you won't be bringing much down to New York at the end of the month. Most of your things will be given away or donated. I'm sure you have a few knickknacks or treasures that mean something. You can keep those, of course. And your clothes, shoes, and whatever else you females enjoy dressing up in. As long as it's appropriate, a good name, and stylish enough for the wife of a boss, then you are more than welcome to pack it up and have it sent to the mansion. One of the maids will sign for it and I'll let them know which room to put it all in. You can go through it again with me when you're home."

Emma's frustration made her drum her nails on the tabletop. "You're not staying here?"

Her words had come out as irritated and sharp as she felt. She wished the nervousness and unease from earlier in the day would return for long enough for her to do what she needed until Affonso left Las Vegas.

Then maybe she could plan.

Something …

At that moment, Emma didn't know if there was anything she could do to get herself out of this situation and arranged marriage.

Affonso's brow lifted. "No. I'm flying out tomorrow afternoon."

"Huh."

"You don't look disappointed."

Emma didn't even try to placate or lie to the man. "You're upending my life. You're making rules, taking away my things, and forcing me into compliance because you know I have nothing to fight against you with. I'll get a month without you looking over my shoulder before I have to stare at you every day for the rest of my life. Do you really think I'm going to be disappointed that you're leaving without me?"

Dry, deep chuckles echoed from Affonso before he lifted his glass to take a drink of white wine. Emma wondered if the Don had a taste for alcohol. It was only noon, after all, and that was his fourth glass.

Affonso's gold pinky ring hit his glass as he tapped his finger along the side. Sitting across from her at the small, cozy table, Affonso radiated an aura that churned with his aloof attitude and cold demeanor. The few lines at the edges of his eyes deepened when he was annoyed, but that was his only show.

Turning his head slightly, Affonso watched Emma from the side. Silently, unmoving, and calculating. A shiver raced down her spine.

Affonso wasn't exactly old, but he wasn't young, either. Emma had a feeling that Affonso's age made him more susceptible to people's bullshit and lies. His profession, on the other hand, taught him how to deal with those kinds of people.

Emma didn't want to be one of them.

"Are you quite finished?" he asked.

The deadly calm tenor of his tone reminded Emma

of a slow-moving river. It looked safe enough, but once a person caught the undertow, they were dead and gone.

Emma quickly decided not to irritate the man more than she already had. Affonso had been promised something from her—a proper, young wife who knew how to behave. One that could give him exactly what he wanted in his personal and professional life. She could be the perfect public image of a housewife, while also being the respectable persona of a Cosa Nostra Don's wife.

He clearly expected her to understand that, too.

"You're quite a combative little thing, aren't you?" Affonso asked, smiling slowly.

"I—"

"Don't argue the point, *bella*. It's clear to me that your spoiled nature occasionally bleeds into your personality more than you realize. I can only chalk that up to age for so long before that is no longer an acceptable excuse."

"I wasn't going to argue it," Emma said.

"Oh?"

The genuine surprise on Affonso's face almost made her laugh.

Almost.

Emma held it back, somehow.

"No, I wasn't," she said. "My father regularly tells me to cut the attitude. I'm aware that I can sometimes be …"

"I think *bratty* is the word you're looking for."

Ouch.

His words felt like a slap cracking across her cheek.

Emma let out a quiet breath, and put her rudeness in check. The last thing she wanted to do was anger Affonso and end up in a worse position than she already was by having to marry the man. "My apologies, Affonso."

"That's better," he murmured. "As for your things and the movers, I'm sure you will have no problems."

"I thought you were leaving. How am I supposed to

know what you consider appropriate for me to keep or wear, without your input?"

"Just because I'm leaving doesn't mean you will be left alone, Emma. I may be a couple of decades older than you, but that doesn't make me a fool. And I certainly won't give you the chance to make me look like one, either."

What?

Emma's brow furrowed. "I don't understand."

Affonso tipped his glass in the direction behind Emma. Turning slightly in her seat, she caught sight of a familiar presence. Calisto sat two tables away with his head down and cup of coffee in his hands. He raised the cup high enough to take a sip. The curve of his mouth, tipping into a smirk that felt laced with something unknown, said that he knew she was watching. The strong lines of Calisto's face were darkened by the corner he sat in.

Tilting his head up, Calisto's dark eyes found Emma's green ones almost instantly. His expression was passive, uncaring even, but his gaze burned straight through her.

Instantly, she wondered who he was beyond Affonso Donati's nephew. She knew better than to let her curiosity climb higher than it already was. Calisto lifted his cup to take another sip, and he cocked an eyebrow at her. Something wicked twisted in her gut.

Sexy came to mind.

So did *sinful.*

Her interest was undeniable.

And *unobtainable.*

Jesus.

Emma turned back around in her seat. "Is he my bodyguard?"

Affonso barked out a laugh. "God, no."

"Oh."

"My nephew will stay behind and keep an eye on you, but once we get back to New York, he'll go back to working as my consigliere," Affonso said. "God knows I could use a break from him for a month. Believe it or not, but Cal can sometimes be even more difficult than your bratty attitude, Emma. He's made his place abundantly clear to me—unfortunately—but I'm sure he won't mind the break, either."

"And what is that?"

"Hmm?"

"His place. What it is?" she asked.

Affonso set his glass to the table, and rested back in the chair. "As I said earlier, if my nephew would do what I wanted for him to do, then I wouldn't need *you* at all. Despite your age, you're a smart girl, Emma. I'm sure you can figure it out."

3.

Calisto

Dragging a hand through his hair, Calisto leaned back in his seat and observed the two people talking a couple of tables beyond his. His coffee was long gone, his plate empty, and he itched for a cigarette.

The nagging voice of his mother wasn't too far behind his craving for nicotine. She'd always hated his habit, and never failed to point out how unhealthy it was.

Calisto had never been able to explain to his mother that when he smoked, his problems drifted away with every drag and exhale. Like a foggy cloud that he blew into the air, his stresses floated off his shoulders.

He'd cut back on the cigarettes since his mother died a year ago. Even his mother's heart attack hadn't been enough to scare him away from the little death sticks. More often than not, he found himself digging out the pack he kept inside his jacket and lighting up. He could forget the blood on his hands, the demands of his uncle, and the expectations of *la famiglia* for a brief while.

Simple.

Easy.

Calisto blew out a heavy breath, trying to tamper down his restlessness. Keeping an eye on Affonso and his new fiancée was boring as hell. It wasn't like he'd expected the trip to Vegas to be particularly interesting, but he'd hoped that the Sorrento *principessa* might give his uncle a decent run for his money when it came to getting her down the aisle.

Something to make this trip worth his time.

If there was anything Calisto enjoyed, it was watching his uncle squirm. Affonso didn't find himself in awkward positions very often. The man's middle name was control. When Affonso mentioned the marriage arrangement a couple of months ago, Calisto thought his uncle was a fool.

Nothing good could come from the Sorrento Cosa Nostra, female or not. Hell, even Maximo Sorrento's only son had been a useless fuckup before his death, known for his hothead and heavy hand. Calisto didn't understand his uncle's reasoning for wanting to tighten their ties with the Vegas syndicate, but it wasn't his place to question Affonso on that.

As consigliere to the Donati dynasty, Calisto simply had to keep Affonso happy. A happy Affonso was a happy *famiglia*.

And when his uncle was happy, he stopped pestering Calisto every chance he could. There were things his uncle wanted from him—things Calisto refused to do. If he trusted his uncle, it might be a different story.

Out of the corner of his eye, Calisto caught sight of his uncle's jaw clenching. That was never a good sign. Anger didn't look good on the Donati Don.

The Sorrento *principessa* was twenty, to Affonso's almost fifty. Knowing the girl's age and family, Calisto went looking for more information on her. Curiosity was a killer. Calisto knew about death better than anyone. A little looking and a few questions filled him in on everything he needed to know about the girl and where she came from.

A spoiled woman.

Kept and pleased.

Primed and waiting.

The girl didn't seem to have much direction in her life. She'd taken a few college classes, but mostly she enjoyed the Vegas nightlife, her status in one of Nevada's most elite families, and her free-range lifestyle that wasn't actually free at all.

Calisto hated a wasted effort.

He figured that was exactly what Affonso's arrangement would be with the woman—a waste of damn time. Affonso wanted an heir of sorts, a boy specifically, but if the man hadn't yet produced one with his dozen mistresses and his twenty-five-year marriage, he probably wouldn't ever have one.

And now Calisto was going to be stuck babysitting his uncle's soon-to-be bride while the girl worked her anger out on whoever she could for the next month.

How *fun*.

Emma Sorrento, however, was proving to have a wide spectrum of personalities. In just the few hours that Calisto had been shadowing Affonso and Emma, he'd watched the young woman go from quiet and reserved, respectful and jittery, to having peeks of fire in her eyes. At this very moment, she had a back so straight it spoke entirely of anger and indignation.

Don't worry, dolcezza. *Affonso has that effect on everyone.*

Calisto chuckled dryly.

Maybe the girl would even grow to like it after a while.

Or maybe not.

Either way, it wasn't Calisto's problem.

The rapid beat of fingernails against wood brought Calisto from his partly amused but mostly annoyed thoughts. Emma drummed her manicured fingernails on the table in quick succession as Affonso looked her over. From his position, Calisto could see the young woman's heel beating against the floor. Her other hand balled into a fist at her side.

Affonso looked entirely bored but somehow irritated at the same time. The man had little patience for women, and his reserve lessened the younger the woman was. In fact, he had such little desire to deal with younger women—barring the bedroom—that he even sent the daughters he publically recognized away to boarding school, just so he wouldn't have to manage them.

Whims were fantasy, after all.

Didn't women like that sort of thing?

Affonso had no time for it.

DONATI BLOODLINES: PART 1

This is not going well.

With a flick of his wrist, Affonso silently dismissed the woman across from him without even saying a word. Emma stood quickly from the table, grabbed her bag and tweed coat off the back of the chair, and bolted in the direction of the front of the restaurant.

The flyby of the woman's dark brown, wavy hair, the grim set of her full lips, and the flash of heat in her green eyes was all Calisto caught before she disappeared around the partition. He wasn't entirely sure what had happened, but it couldn't have been good.

"Good God," Affonso groaned.

Calisto watched his uncle rub at his forehead, squeeze his eyes shut, and clench his teeth.

"Trouble, *zio?*" Calisto asked.

"Oh, don't start, Cal," Affonso snapped without opening his eyes.

Calisto smiled to himself, knowing damn well what the issue likely was. Emma Sorrento was not bowing to his uncle like most women did when faced with Affonso Donati. Usually, women found themselves entranced by Affonso's handsome features, curious about his lone wolf personality, and then were surprised to see the monster behind the mask.

Affonso had hoped to easily ensnare Emma so that the transition from Vegas to New York would be a simple one for the girl and the families.

"She's … frustrating," Affonso muttered to himself. "Combative. Argumentative. Young."

"You picked her. You thought she had a pretty face, if I remember correctly."

And she did.

Emma was a beautiful young woman, there was no denying it. Her trim, petite figure held sweet curves that would make any man feel like he was protecting her just by holding her. Her pixie-like features and wide eyes only added to the appeal. Her top lip was slightly larger than her bottom, and her two front teeth were just big enough to peek out so that it looked like her mouth was open for the taking. The heels she wore added a bit of height to her short five feet, three inches.

It wasn't like the girl radiated innocence. Not with smooth, bare legs traveling out beneath a flared dress, hinting at the curve of her thighs and the swell of her ass. And certainly not with a mouth that looked like it was ready to be used or filled.

Calisto's throat tightened momentarily as his thoughts flew by. He tampered down the sudden heat flaring in his groin and readjusted his seat on the chair.

Admitting he found his uncle's bride-to-be attractive was one thing. Feeding the attraction was quite another. One that would find him in a grave next to his murdered father and dead mother.

He surely didn't need that.

"A pretty face will only go so far when the attitude makes her ugly," Affonso said quietly.

Calisto openly frowned. "Is it attitude, or stubbornness and unhappiness?"

"Is there a difference?"

Not to Affonso, maybe.

Calisto thought there was.

"Besides," his uncle added, waving flippantly, "... I know exactly how to make women like that happy, Calisto. They're like all women."

"Shovel nice things at them to distract their whims with possessions," Calisto said.

"Exactly. She's difficult now, but that'll only last so long before her tune changes. Once she realizes how much she will have and what she can be given if she follows my rules and expectations. She's been a princess her whole life—time to start acting like a queen."

Not all women wanted to be queens.

Calisto didn't correct his uncle.

"Where did she go?" Calisto asked. "Aren't I

supposed to be keeping an eye on her for you?"

"To the bathroom. I think she can handle that business alone, Cal."

Whatever.

It was Affonso's problem if the girl ran.

"The dinner party is in a few hours," Calisto informed his uncle.

Part of his job was making sure Affonso knew where he had to be, while also taking care of the man's wants and needs for *la famiglia*. While in Vegas that part of his job was pushed to the side as there were no men to handle, but Calisto still picked up the slack elsewhere.

"Mmm," Affonso responded noncommittedly.

The man's attention was somewhere else entirely. Like on the swaying, tight ass of the server across the room.

Calisto resisted the urge to snap his fingers. Once Affonso caught something he liked in his sights, the man went after it without hesitation.

"Your bride-to-be will be coming back soon," Calisto said dully.

Nothing.

Not even a blink.

Affonso pursed his lips, then smirked as he caught the eye of the early-twenties waitress. The Donati charm was flicked on like a light switch. In a blink, Affonso's hardened features darkened. His posture softened enough to make him seem approachable, and he waved at the woman, asking her over.

The girl came.

Calisto wasn't surprised.

"Would you like another drink?" the girl asked.

Affonso's smirk melted into a wide, pleased smile. "No. I had a thought and I wanted to ask you about it."

Amusement danced on the woman's features when Affonso hooked a finger in her direction, silently asking her to come closer. She did, just like a little moth following the pretty lights.

"Tell me," Affonso said, "how old are you?"

"Twenty-two, sir."

"Young. College?"

"Yes."

"Working on what, exactly?"

"Business, mostly, but some arts."

Affonso laughed. "Arts will keep you amused through the boring business nonsense, at least."

"It's worked so far, sir."

"I bet," his uncle murmured. "Tell me something else."

Calisto sighed harshly.

His uncle loved this game.

"What else?" the girl asked.

"Student debt. I imagine you owe quite a bit, hmm? That's probably why you're working here. Part-time student. Full-time worker. That must be difficult."

"I'm doing okay, but it's still tight."

"Sure," Affonso said quietly. "Come here."

Hooking his finger again, the girl dropped down so that Affonso could whisper something in her ear. A disgust welled heavily in the pit of Calisto's stomach and the bitter taste of hatred rested on the back of his tongue.

The young woman's eyes widened and her teeth cut into her bottom lip.

The offer was made.

Calisto watched this scene a dozen times before.

Give me a few hours, his uncle would say. *Whatever I want, however I want it, wherever I want it. Give it, and I'll fill a blank check with whatever number fits your fancy.*

"When are you off?" Affonso asked.

The girl swallowed hard and glanced at the wall.

She was the typical victim for his uncle's amusement. A young woman, likely a little naive. Financial stability was welcome to anyone, and wanted desperately.

Self-worth or money? Calisto was never surprised at

how easily people would decide between the two.

"Ten minutes, actually," the woman said. "I have a couple of weekend classes and the restaurant works around my school, thankfully."

Affonso nodded. "Four hours. Forty-thousand. I think that's worth missing a couple of classes, don't you?"

Indecision flickered over the woman's features, but only for a quick second.

"Yes," she said.

Affonso smiled. It was nothing like his earlier grins. This one was far more predatory. "Wonderful. I have the black Benz in the parking lot with a driver. Be there in twelve minutes, no later, or I drive away."

"Yes, sir."

Calisto shook his head as the waitress spun on her heel and made a beeline for the back of the restaurant.

"Like flies and honey," Affonso said to himself.

"You know, a hired escort or a prostitute will do the exact same thing, uncle," Calisto said. "You don't have to make that girl question her choices and her self-worth for the rest of her life, just for the sake of a quick fuck in the back of a Benz while Arthur watches."

Affonso flashed his teeth in a wicked sneer as he stood from the table. "How do you know I want a quick fuck this time, Cal? Her ass caught my eye first. And I plan on filling it."

Cristo.

Calisto's expression never wavered. "And the other one? What about her?"

"Which one?"

"Emma," Calisto clarified. "The one you brought here. The one you're marrying. What am I to do with her while you're fucking some new girl in the car you drove Emma here in?"

"You have the rental Mercedes. Amuse her for the rest of the day."

Calisto's jaw tightened. "Amuse her?"

"I didn't stutter."

"And what about your absence? How do you want me to explain that away?"

Affonso shrugged. "Why bother? Don't lie to the girl. She might as well start learning now."

Nope.

Calisto still wasn't surprised.

• • •

Calisto leaned against the wall, propping his foot behind him. An unlit cigarette dangled from his lips, demanding to be lit and enjoyed. He planned on doing exactly that once he got out of the damned restaurant.

Emma had been hiding in the bathroom for quite a while. Calisto wasn't exactly sure what she was doing in there, but the last woman who left the space assured him a dark-haired, green-eyed girl was still inside.

Two more minutes passed.

No Emma.

Calisto's patience withered away. His job was to keep an eye on the woman, but it sure as fuck didn't include feeding to her emotional waves. She could handle her tantrum at another time. One where *his* time wasn't being wasted waiting on her.

Knowing there were no other women inside the bathroom—as none had gone in since the last entered and left—Calisto pushed off the wall and opened the swinging door. He didn't make it two steps inside before he turned into a statue.

Emma had perched herself up on the bathroom counter. Maybe he expected to find her crying her little eyes out and having a hissy fit of epic proportions, seeing as how her life wasn't working out the way she wanted.

Instead, he found her puffing on a cigarette, her creamy, smooth legs crossed, and her heels tapping a beat to the tiled counter. Not a lick of her makeup was smudged to say she'd been crying. Her hands remained steady as she fluffed out the waves of her hair with her fingers. And she seemed calmer than she had earlier.

Calisto pulled the cigarette from his lips with two fingers. "Christ, if you wanted a cigarette, you could have just gone outside."

Emma didn't even look up from her lap. "What, did he send you in to find me, Calisto?"

His name rolled off her tongue in the most interesting way. She'd said it with an almost disinterested flair, except for the ring of sensuality following close behind.

He'd noticed that about her, too. When she spoke, her voice held a sexual quality. She probably didn't even realize it.

If Affonso thought he was getting a virgin for a bride, he was highly fucking mistaken. Calisto could tell that Emma wasn't pure, just by the way she spoke and watched him under her dark, long lashes.

Women who were unaware of their sexuality didn't watch men like this one was watching him.

"Affonso didn't send me in for you. He's gone."

Emma arched a single brow high. "Oh?"

"*Sì.*"

"Good."

Calisto couldn't help it, he laughed. "Your resentment is showing."

"It's not a resentment. You can't force yourself to like a person. He reminds me of a pig."

More than she knew.

"Or maybe a snake," Emma added quieter.

"Both could work," Calisto said before he could stop himself.

Emma dropped her still burning cigarette down the drain of the sink. Uncrossing her legs, she pushed off the counter and dropped onto the floor with a click of her heels to the tile. Just the action alone gave a flash of more skin and black lace.

Calisto's mouth went dry and his cock perked. Squeezing his hands into tight fists, his nails bit into his skin. He reminded himself of exactly who this girl was and why his attraction was entirely inappropriate. He then reminded himself that he wouldn't like the taste of bullets when a gun was shoved down his goddamn throat.

His inner thoughts didn't help much when Emma turned to the mirror, leaned over the sink a little, and dabbed at her pink lips with her fingertips. The slight pout of her upper lip, showcasing a hint of those two white front teeth, looked downright sinful.

What man wouldn't notice that?

You're going to get yourself killed, like your father, his mind taunted.

"I like red lipstick more than this pink garbage," Emma said absentmindedly.

It didn't sound like it was meant for him.

Nonetheless, Calisto still heard it.

He thought red would look better, too.

It might make her mouth look even more fuckable. It would leave little red stains around the base of his cock when he fucked her mouth hard enough to reach her throat.

Jesus.

What in the fuck was wrong with him?

Emma grabbed her coat and clutch. "Where did Affonso go?"

Calisto hesitated briefly. Earlier, the girl seemed ready to cut tail and run. Like she was out of her fucking league and knew it all too well.

Now, he was looking at someone entirely different.

He'd done his research.

He knew a bit about her.

Calisto didn't think Affonso knew nearly enough.

"He picked up a waitress," Calisto said, settling on the truth. "She's probably in the back of his Benz right about now."

Emma sneered into the mirror. "Likely wishing she wasn't."

"You're not angry?"

She glanced over at him. "Why would I be? As long as he's fucking someone else, then he's leaving me alone."

4.

Calisto

"So you're my appointed babysitter, huh?" Emma asked from the passenger seat.

Calisto didn't answer right away. He focused on the unfamiliar highway, and the bastard trying to cut in front of him to drive a little faster.

"Don't you talk at all ... Calisto, is it?"

"Cal," he said, gruffer than he intended. "I mostly go by Cal."

From the corner of his eye, he watched her purse her lips.

"Cal isn't as attention drawing as Calisto, I guess."

"There aren't a lot of us around, if that's what you mean."

Emma smiled. "It was."

"It's a surname, mostly. Comes from my grandmother's side of the family on my mother's side. She liked the ring of it, and passed it onto me."

"Huh."

Her simple response made Calisto pause. Without realizing it, he'd easily blurted out private information about himself and his family that he rarely shared with anyone. Nearly every new person he met questioned him on his name, and he never offered clarification as to how it came about. This girl barely said a thing and he spilled every bit.

"Is your mother artsy? That kind of name makes me think she would be artsy."

Calisto's hands tightened around the wheel, his knuckles turning white from the pressure. Emma didn't miss his automatic reaction.

"Did I say something wrong?" she asked.

"Not intentionally. My mother died last year. But

yes, she liked to paint, draw, and make things. Sitting outside for hours in front of an easel was her favorite thing."

Again with the oversharing, he thought.

"I'm sorry she passed," Emma said softly.

Calisto did his best to ignore the compassion and sadness in Emma's tone. The young woman didn't know him from a goddamn hole in the ground. Her feelings couldn't be very honest or true, but rather, a useless platitude said to make herself feel better.

Just like everyone else.

"What about your father? Was he artsy, too?"

"You ask a lot of questions," Calisto said instead of answering.

His father was almost always off-limits for him. That was mostly because the people who could talk to him about his father were men who did nothing to help Richard, and the others were men who had killed him.

"Sorry for being curious," Emma said, looking away from him. "I was just trying to learn a bit about you, Cal, seeing as how you'll be spending the next month making sure I wipe the right way."

Her crude statement took him off guard. He couldn't remember a time when a well-dressed, beautiful, and by all appearances, intelligent woman had spoken so crassly in his presence. The women he had heard speak like that were of neither class nor status.

Calisto barked out a laugh, unable to hold it back. His one laugh led to another, and then another until his hands had loosened from their tight, angry grip and his shoulders were shaking. The stress at the idea of having to discuss his father drifted away almost instantly, and shit ...

How long had it been since he laughed?

Calisto didn't have an answer for that.

Sobering quickly, he sat a little stiffer in the driver's seat as he came up behind an eighteen-wheeler going ten over the limit and being what Calisto liked to call bait. He liked speed, loved a fast-moving car and having all the control of it under his hands.

"Slow down," Emma said.

"Why?" Calisto said. "I can fucking drive, thank you."

"Because police are thick around here, and hand out speeding tickets like Tic Tacs."

Calisto nodded at the eighteen-wheeler in front of them. "Bait, *ragazza*."

"What?"

"Bait. They'll catch his speed on radar, not mine. By the time they flick their lights, I'm either going past him or slowing down. Chill out."

She didn't look entirely convinced. "Do you always drive this fast?"

"Mostly."

"Why?"

"Speed is a form of freedom, maybe."

Emma snorted. "Okay, then."

"You asked, Emmy. I answered. Truthfully, for that matter. I like the way a fast car feels under my hands and feet. That kind of power is rarely controllable, but when I hold the wheel, and press the pedal down, I have all the say."

"Until the roof of your car meets the pavement."

Calisto chuckled. "Well, that's the thing, right? You don't know if that will happen. You just keep pushing the limit, thinking you're in control, and walking on thin lines. Like I said, freedom—it's a thrill like anything else. Like sex, even. Fucking hard, fucking fast, and being insane about it in a way that could get you killed. Makes the relief of it even more intense. Nobody says it has to be worth it, Emmy, it just has to feel really goddamn good."

Emma bit down on her bottom lip. Calisto barely noticed, but ignored it all the same. He didn't need that image in his fucking mind, too. The ones he already had were inappropriate enough without adding to them.

DONATI BLOODLINES: PART 1

He pushed down on the pedal, making the car lurch forward.

Emma sucked in a quiet breath. "You can't get your thrills elsewhere without playing Russian Roulette on the highway?"

"Sure I can. And quite regularly, I do."

Emma eyed him from the side. "Like how?"

She probably didn't want to know.

"Ways," he answered vaguely.

"I don't know what that's like."

Calisto drummed his fingers on the steering wheel. "You sure about that?"

"What's that supposed to mean?"

"It means I think you know more about chasing thrills than you let on. Two years ago, you skipped out of Vegas right under your father's and uncle's eye and jumped on a flight to Germany. Maximo sent his son and three enforcers to bring you back. You were expelled from two private schools for fighting before you ended up at your final boarding school where you graduated. You've been pictured in the socialite magazines coming out of clubs at all hours of the night when you're not even legal to be inside one of those joints. I would say you know something about looking for fun and trouble in whatever way you can find it. That, Emmy, is a thrill."

Emma's mouth popped open. "You ... you did a search on me?"

Calisto made a dismissive noise under his breath. "I was curious. Affonso was dead set on this marriage plan of his, and as his consigliere, I wanted to know more. I'm not judging you. I'm simply stating facts I know about you."

"Does he know?"

"Probably. It doesn't matter to him what you did here. What matters to him is what he can make you do in New York. Big difference, believe me."

"Oh, my God," she mumbled.

The look on her face was horror churned with

39

embarrassment.

Calisto found it mildly amusing. "Got nothing to say now, Emmy?"

"Stop it with that name. You don't know me, Calisto. Don't use it."

"You prefer it, don't you?"

"So?"

"So," he drawled, giving her as much attitude as she showed him, "... maybe when you're in New York, Emmy Sorrento won't exist anymore, *dolcezza*. It'll be Emma Donati all the way. Wouldn't you like for at least one person to remind you of who you are beneath Affonso Donati's name?"

Emma blinked back at him, hurt settling over her pretty features. "Why do you care?"

"Honestly, I don't. But I also don't like Affonso, and if calling you Emmy pisses him off and makes you happy at the same time, I don't see the harm. I look it at like killing two birds with one stone."

"He's your uncle, but you don't like him."

"Do you like your *zio*?" Calisto asked.

Emma stilled in the seat before saying, "Point taken."

"I thought so."

"You're awfully arrogant."

Calisto smirked, kept his eyes on the road, and his hands on the wheel. "You haven't seen anything yet."

• • •

Calisto took in the penthouse suite apartment with wall-to-wall windows overlooking the busy Vegas Strip. The major casino had one hell of a view from up this high.

"I wasn't aware that the casinos rented out their penthouses as apartments," Calisto said.

He'd heard the quiet clack of Emma's heels hitting against marble floors as she walked up behind him. He didn't turn to face her, but instead, continued his surveying of the view.

"You know Maximo owns this, don't you?" she asked.

"This casino specifically?"

"Yes, but he's got major stakes in a few others. The penthouses can be rented, like any other penthouse apartment. You have to pay a little more for it."

"But everything is right at your fingertips," he said. "Service. Laundry. *Qualunque cosa ti serva.*"

"Essentially."

"How big is this penthouse?"

"I don't know. Maybe four-thousand square feet. It's two levels."

Yes, he'd noticed that.

"Is your uncle going to let you keep it?" Calisto asked.

"Ask him. Ask Affonso. I don't know anything. I simply get told what to do, Calisto."

"I told you, it's Cal."

And he wished she would start using it more.

He liked his full name in her mouth far too much.

"Do you want to see the rest of the place?" Emma asked, ignoring his comment.

Calisto shook his head. "No. I'm sure I'll see it when you have to pack it up."

"Thanks for the reminder."

"Sorry you have to grow up, but that's life."

Emma scoffed. "No, that's the mafia life. And that has nothing to do with growing up, thank you very much. It has to do with the fact that I own a vagina instead of a cock, so that makes me even more useless to my father and uncle. Instead, they've found another way to put me to good use. By marrying me off to a man thirty years my senior."

Calisto flinched at the truth in her words. Spinning slowly, he faced her. Somehow, he managed to keep the shock off his face at the change in her attire and makeup. She hadn't said much when she mentioned wanting to stop at her casino penthouse, other than to say she needed a minute to grab some things.

Apparently, those things included a much shorter, tighter dress, a wool trench coat, fire-red lipstick, and suede boots with sky-high heels.

The innocent, young-looking woman from earlier was gone. Her Sunday dress, pink lipstick, and give-a-damn were forgotten. While her morning attire had given off a taste of her sensuality, her current wardrobe, dark makeup, and ruby smile spoke entirely of her sexuality.

This woman looked a hell of lot more like the one Calisto had done his research on.

"Fair warning," he said, "Affonso despises red lipstick."

"I know. My father made me wash it off this morning and use my mother's pink garbage."

"And the dress you were wearing?"

"Something else picked out by my father."

Calisto cleared his throat. "What are you trying to prove? I can't exactly let you go out like this."

"You don't have to do anything. All you have to say is that you let me run up to the penthouse, and I came back like this. You didn't have a choice because we were going to be late."

That was bad.

Dirty pool.

Calisto liked it.

"Do you have no interest at all in making Affonso into some kind of bearable husband for you?" he asked.

Emma didn't even blink. "Why should I? He doesn't give a damn about being a good husband to me."

He'd bested her in the car.

She had him this time, however.

"Point taken," Calisto admitted. "Don't say I didn't warn you, Emmy."

DONATI BLOODLINES: PART 1

"I won't." Emma looked over her manicured nails as she said, "You know, you didn't answer my question in the car. The one about your father."

"Because I don't know the answer."

And because he didn't want to talk about it.

"Is he in with the Donati family, too? He's Affonso's brother, right? I know better than to ask anyone about New York business. No one talks."

Calisto scoffed darkly. "In with the family? You could say that—once. Don't you have the internet? Do a web search."

Emma's brow furrowed. "I don't need a recap on the hierarchy or rules of the mob, thanks. I'm aware of how that all goes down."

"Oh, *ragazza*," Calisto murmured, shaking his head. "What you should be more concerned with is the family you're about to enter and how the man who heads it got where he is. That is the information you might want to brush up on. Unless, like your spoiled lifestyle might suggest, you prefer to bury your head in the sand."

"Hey, now, don't be an ass—"

"Don't bark at me," Calisto interrupted coolly. "I'm just giving you a heads-up. We have a couple more hours before the dinner party. Do you want to go through some of your things while we have the time?"

Emma made a face. "Nope. But the casino is open for business. That sounds like fun."

Calisto knew better. He did.

"Are you any good at poker?" he asked.

Emma smiled slyly. "I'm a Sorrento. We're all good at poker."

• • •

Emma had a damn good poker face. Calisto gave credit where it was due. He'd thought she was slick with cards, seeing as how she kicked his ass at the poker table,

43

but the fake smile she plastered on for the crowd, and the pretty, innocent girl act she put on for Affonso was something else entirely.

Then again, it was hard to seem innocent when the girl sported sky-high heels, a dress that was short enough to make a man's mouth water, and a smile that said she knew it, too.

Calisto found himself paying more attention to Emma than he knew he should be.

The dinner went by smoothly, and for the most part, quietly. After they first arrived back to the Sorrento family home for the dinner, Emma had brushed off her father's questions about her attire and her uncle's demands that she wash the red lipstick off.

Ten minutes later, Affonso had arrived.

Calisto had watched, amused to no end, as his uncle took his spot beside his soon-to-be bride with an indifferent expression, but anger burning in his eyes. Affonso certainly wasn't happy that his chosen bride-to-be had sexed up her classy attire and darkened her makeup for the dinner.

Emma was playing with fire. It was liable to get her burned. Calisto still enjoyed the show.

Sipping from a glass of cognac, Calisto moved around the edge of the living room as the main couple of the dinner party took the head of the room. Words exchanged between Maximo and Affonso.

Another show for the crowd.

Calisto was bored.

Then Emma stepped in beside Affonso when he called her name. Instantly, the false smile she had been wearing all evening for the crowd suddenly melted away when a ring was produced. Even from Calisto's spot twenty feet away, he could discern the shape and color of the jewelry.

A blue sapphire, cut princess-style, rested atop a white gold band. The piece was massive—ostentatious, even.

"… and to solidify an old friendship," he heard his uncle say.

"Friendship," Maximo echoed.

Emma allowed the ring to be slid down her finger.

But she was blank all over.

After downing the rest of his liquor, Calisto found the closest server he could to hand off the glass. Stepping out back of the large home to the enclosed porch, he lit up a cigarette and watched Maximo's men laughed in a large group while the pungent smell of weed wafted through the space.

The men didn't even notice he was there.

Calisto didn't mind.

He'd just rejoined the people mingling in the house when Affonso settled in beside his nephew.

"Making friends?" Affonso asked.

Calisto resisted the urge to scoff. "I'm not the one cementing friendships here tonight, uncle."

Affonso chuckled dryly. "True. Nonetheless, it would still benefit you to make a few connections here in Vegas, Cal."

"Why? I have no intention of doing business here. The business I handle in New York is more than enough."

"Mmm. You would make a fantastic boss, Cal. All you have to do is—"

"Be like you?" Calisto interrupted coldly. "No, thanks."

Affonso scowled. "You chose this life. There is no out. Perhaps if you would embrace your blood, legacy, and position a little more, you might find it easier to accept and move on from the past, Calisto."

Right.

That was a joke.

"I chose this life because I wasn't given a choice. Because *you* tricked me into believing one thing, when in fact, all you did for most of my life was feed me lies. Once you had me in, there was no getting out. You didn't give me a choice, uncle. And now I won't give you one."

Affonso sighed harshly. "I only wanted to give you a chance to succeed after Richard was gone."

"Gone. That's an interesting way to put it. Why don't you say it like it is, huh?"

His uncle didn't respond. That wasn't anything new.

"I'm leaving," Affonso said quietly. "There was an issue back in New York that came up. A scuffle between one of the Capo's crews and the Marcello territory line. A sit-down was requested. Immediately. I wanted to stay another day at least, but I think it might be best if I go now. I would say Emma needs a bit of a cool down period."

"Have a good flight."

"Is that all you have to say to me?"

Calisto shrugged. "You're my boss. I have to respect you. If you ask for much more, uncle, I will start taking things back."

Affonso didn't respond to that. Instead, his uncle spun on his heel and walked away. Calisto didn't bother to watch Affonso go, either.

Knowing his uncle was out of the house reminded Calisto that he still had a job to do here in Vegas.

Watching Emma until the wedding in a month.

He was starting to wonder if he should be doing that at all. His wayward thoughts earlier in the day about the confusing girl were worrisome. He didn't need the problems they could bring. Keeping a healthy distance might help to clear his thoughts, but that wasn't exactly possible when he was expected to be the person who kept the girl out of trouble.

Across the room, Calisto found Emma talking with the woman he knew to be her mother.

She still didn't look particularly happy.

He didn't think that would change for her anytime soon.

5.

The girl across the counter slid the cup of hot steeped tea over the cash and into Emma's hand. Paying for the drink and thanking the barista, Emma moved to a private corner booth in the back of the small café, and settled in with her touchscreen tablet in hand.

Maybe a bit of reading would clear her head.

The new piece of jewelry on her left ring finger caught her attention when she turned on the tablet. The large, three carat sapphire caught the reflection of the overhead lights and shimmered. The engagement ring was beautiful, to be sure, but Emma still hated it.

Hated that it was a life sentence imposed on her.

A punishment for being a girl—a Sorrento girl.

On her wrist, a thin bracelet glittered with diamonds. She didn't want to wear it, either, but apparently it wasn't her choice. Affonso had been sending gifts to Vegas for her every day since his departure the week before. A new laptop with a shiny Apple logo on the top. She also wore a necklace with a circular pendant decorated in even more diamonds. A mink fur coat, as January in New York was a great deal colder than in Nevada. Or so Affonso's note on the gift said.

Wedding plans were on.

Emma ignored every bit she could.

Her mother brought over pictures of table settings, linens, dress choices, and color swatches daily, trying to get Emma involved in the process more and more. Affonso hired event planners for the small, private affair that would be their wedding, but her mother still demanded that the church be decorated to some extent, as well as the venue for the small reception afterward.

Both of her parents, and a few select family

members—as well as her uncle's closest men—would make the trip to New York for the wedding. Invitations were being sent to other syndicates in New York and out of state, as far as Emma understood from the private conversations she had overheard.

Emma just ... didn't care.

What difference did it make?

It wasn't *her* day.

It was her father's day. Her uncle's.

Affonso's day.

At least with Affonso gone back to New York, her parents and her uncle backed off a bit. Her lipstick color wasn't criticized and the length of her dresses were overlooked.

Her babysitter, on the other hand, was never too far behind.

Keeping her head tilted down, Emma shot a glance at the presence sitting a couple of tables away from hers. Calisto tipped up a coffee, took a sip, and then grinned in that knowing way of his. The way that said he knew she was watching him.

The man had been keeping a distance lately. He rarely approached her, didn't speak unless they were in the same room and he didn't have a choice, but he was always close by somewhere.

Watching her.

Keeping tabs.

Unsettling her.

When she exited the elevator that took her from her penthouse to the casino's foyer, Calisto was waiting. The black rental he was driving stayed glued to the bumper of her car, regardless of where she drove. He followed her into restaurants, stayed outside of her friend's homes when she visited, and kept quiet the entire time.

Emma didn't know why Calisto had decided to stay further away from her while he kept an eye on her, but she was both relieved and bothered by it.

DONATI BLOODLINES: PART 1

Relieved because she needed to breathe. She wanted to feel normal for a little while longer, and the closer Calisto was, the harder it was for her to pretend like she wasn't going to be married in just three weeks.

On the other hand, it left her bothered because Emma didn't know much about Calisto at all. When they first met, he didn't seem to have a problem talking to her or sticking close. Now, he had taken on an attitude of indifference. Her father and uncle treated him with the utmost respect, handed the man a wide berth of space when he entered their homes, and never questioned his job of watching Emma.

Not that they cared.

She supposed her feelings on Calisto's distance shouldn't matter. He wasn't her friend, he was her watchdog, reporting her whereabouts and activities to her soon-to-be husband back in New York. Mistaking Calisto's charming smile and conversations from the week before as an offer of friendship might do more harm than good. The last thing Emma wanted or needed was a snake waiting to bite her when she wasn't looking.

The fact that Calisto was both Affonso's nephew and his consigliere couldn't be ignored. Loyalty to the boss was everything in Cosa Nostra. Emma wouldn't pretend like she had an ally in Calisto Donati, simply because the man had given off the impression that he wasn't all that close to his uncle.

Sighing, Emma went back to her tablet to check her emails. A few were from friends at school, wondering where she had been for the last week. Another was from the head of her study group, asking if her spot could be filled with another student, since she obviously wasn't using it. Under her father's instructions—by demand of her uncle—she had withdrawn from her three classes at college.

She hadn't exactly been serious about college before. Mostly, she had treated it like a part-time thing that gave her something to do. Now that she didn't have the choice at all regarding her schooling, she was starting to wish that she had taken more time to appreciate it.

All over again, her fuckups were staring Emma right in the face. Her gullibility mocked her without saying a single word.

George and her mother Minnie had never pushed Emma to go to college. After high school, she was given a stipend of her trust fund at the beginning of each month that was deposited straight into her bank account for whatever she wanted. The penthouse had been a gift from her father, as had her cherry-red Mustang.

Growing up like she had, spoiled and kept like a little doll, had made her think that's how she would always be. Taken care of by someone else. Wealthy without lifting a single finger. Overindulged, with material possessions to make up for the lack of emotional connection.

Emma hadn't realized how awful all that was until her mistakes were laughing at her.

She was disgusted with herself.

Maybe she did deserve what she was getting, after all.

"You look like you just swallowed a spider," came a voice at her side.

Blinking out of her daze, Emma glanced up from her tablet to see Calisto sliding in across the table. Not wanting him to know about her internal war and self-hatred, she clicked off her tablet and donned a mask of indifference.

"Zoned out. Checking emails can be a boring task."

Calisto arched a brow like he didn't believe her for a second. "I didn't know you had so much work, friends, and business to do that your emails were flooded daily."

Ouch.

Even little old Emma with her head stuck firmly in the sand could hear the jeer in Calisto's words.

"Making fun of me is a little low, isn't it?" she asked

bitingly.

"I'm not making fun of you."

"Aren't you? Listen, I realize that to you, I'm probably nothing more than a spoiled mafia princess who is finally being put to use for her family, but I'm also a person, Calisto. A real fucking person with feelings. I don't need you to point out my flaws—I am well aware of them."

Calisto leaned back in the booth, his stare never leaving hers. A million and one questions flickered through his gaze, but the man stayed quiet.

It unsettled her.

"Stop doing that," Emma snapped.

"Doing what?"

The deep tenor of his voice lifted a bit in his confusion. Emma still thought Calisto's tone was almost musical. Like just speaking was an art form for him. She didn't know anyone else in her life who could talk with emotion in their voice while their face was nothing more than a blank slate, unreadable and cold.

Emma fidgeted under the booth table. "Looking at me like that, like you're trying to pick me apart or something. Quit it, Calisto. I told you, I'm aware of my flaws. There's no need for you to go pointing them out, too. Everyone else is already getting a wonderful laugh at my expense. Can't you let me suffer in peace?"

"I'm not sure what you mean, *dolcezza*, but I was only trying to make you smile with a joke. You were over here frowning and letting your tea get cold. I thought maybe ..." Calisto trailed off, scowling. "You know what, I thought nothing. Your unhappiness isn't my concern, you're right. And if you feel like your suffering is by your own hand, then that also isn't my concern. Growing up, I was taught that those who make their beds deserve to sleep in them."

If his earlier words had hurt, those ones damn well ached. He could have slapped her and it would have felt better.

Emma's jaw fell open, and a breath caught painfully in her chest. "I didn't make this bed."

"That's not what you just told me."

She fiddled with the sleeve of her coat, feeling the rough tweed rub against the pad of her thumb. For a moment, the action soothed her for whatever reason.

"I was thinking of something before you came over," Emma admitted. "What you said struck a nerve, and I didn't take it as the joke you meant it because of that. I shouldn't have snapped at you, Calisto. I'm sorry."

He took in her words without responding. Lifting his cup of coffee, he took another sip and then set it back on the table.

"The spoiled *Mafioso principessa* nonsense that you barked at me," he said quietly. "Was that what you were thinking about?"

Emma glanced away, refusing to meet Calisto's piercing brown-black stare. She never was any good at hiding her true feelings. She didn't want him to see the anger and shame that had to be shining brightly in her eyes.

"Yes," she said.

Calisto hummed under his breath with a sound that came off as understanding and interested at the same time. Emma felt her invisible walls shudder at Calisto's vague offer of sympathy. She was again reminded of who this man was, the person he was close to, and how he could hurt her with it.

She wouldn't give him the ammo.

Not willingly.

"I was mistaken," Calisto murmured.

Emma's gaze cut back to her companion instantly. "About what?"

"The bed I thought you made. What I said, I guess."

"Actually, you were right. My unhappiness isn't your

concern. You're not required to fix how I feel or make it better. I don't want you to."

Emma figured putting that out there was better for both her and Calisto. That way, the man knew she wasn't up for playing games with him. If all he wanted to do was try and get closer to her in order to feed information to Affonso, then he had another thing coming.

"Not what I meant," Calisto said, waving a hand as if to dismiss her words. "Although, someone telling you the truth might help the way you feel, no doubt."

"How do you know anything about what I feel?"

"You wear your emotions on your sleeve when you think no one is watching. You should get better at that, *ragazza*. In front of a crowd, or even with your family, the mask you wear is perfectly in place at all times. Last week at the dinner party, no one would have guessed you were unhappy and angry about everything that was happening around you. But when you're alone …"

"It's obvious," she said.

Calisto shrugged. "You should know by now that you'll never truly be alone once you take Affonso's last name, Emmy. Someone will always be close behind. Someone else will be watching. He'll have different ways of making sure you're behaving, interacting with the right people, and keeping up the image that he wants you to maintain. Better you start acting now like you're never alone then to fuck up later and have to answer for something he considers you've done wrong."

A shiver worked its way down Emma's spine. That was the second time someone had subtly offered information to her about Affonso's actions toward women in his life.

Actions suggesting violence.

Her stomach rolled.

"Is he like that with his other women, too?" she dared to ask.

Calisto's brow furrowed. "Affonso, you mean?"

"Yes. His mistresses, too. My father mentioned something to me last week. He said Affonso had a ... taste for pain when it came to women who don't listen. You just said something similar. I wondered if that was true. Is it?"

Silence answered Emma's question.

Then, Calisto said, "I've never seen him hit a woman."

"But you don't know for sure, right?"

"I know he can be a monster." Calisto's eyes hardened, but he wasn't directing his coldness at Emma this time. "I know he's hurt women—*a* woman—someone told me that once."

"I don't understand. Who did he hurt?"

"Someone," Calisto answered vaguely, offering nothing else. "What I meant when I said that you would have to answer to him for your choices after marrying him wasn't that he would turn physical with you. I don't believe he would, with his wife. People are watching you, and him, Emmy. Affonso knows better than to hit his wife and leave a mark that might be seen. And there are other families like his in New York. Families with far more power than he has. One of those families' boss, Dante Marcello, is known to step into personal business for the sake of a woman."

Emma didn't know what to say. "Really?"

"Honor is supposed to be the most important thing a man has in Cosa Nostra. The way he treats his wife and his family falls in line with that. There are men in *la famiglia* who never forget that being honorable, that being a good *made* man, is more important that being your boss's man. Despite being a boss, Affonso is watched like anyone else. He has standards that he's expected to keep just like anyone else.

"I don't believe he would put his hands on you," Calisto continued quieter. "Your father was likely just trying to scare you into compliance by playing on a fear that every woman has buried somewhere inside of them."

DONATI BLOODLINES: PART 1

"But he doesn't actually need to hit me to hurt me," Emma replied.

Anyone with any sense knew that.

Calisto nodded. "You're right. And that's what I meant. He can remove people from your life, take away your things, shame you privately, or ignore you publically and make you seem unworthy of your position at his side. Pride is a terrible thing to have taken away. Sometimes, in this life where a woman is only valued for her last name and position, her pride might be the one thing she has. The worst kind of men know exactly how to rip it out of your heart without ever laying a finger on you."

"Are you warning me that Affonso is one of those men?"

"I'm saying that he's good at hiding the monster he doesn't want you to see."

Emma's shoulders tightened with tension. It was like a little knot in between the blades that wouldn't leave, no matter how hard she tried. With every reminder pushed at her that her time as a free woman was quickly coming to a close, the knot grew a little more.

Just like the heaviness in her stomach. Or the emptiness in her heart.

Calisto was still watching her closely, gauging her reactions and emotions. At that point, Emma didn't give a damn. She didn't want to be somebody's perfect housewife and doll to play with when it was convenient.

Why did she have to pretend like she wanted that at all?

"You did hear what I said, didn't you?" Calisto asked.

Emma swallowed her emotions down. "Yes."

"Practice makes perfect. Work on it."

"That's easy for you to say. You're not the one being forced into a future that you don't want."

Calisto's lips curved wickedly and his gaze narrowed, darkening his features. The handsome ruggedness of his face sharpened into something far sexier in a blink. Emma had to look away again, refusing to get caught up in a crush on a man she couldn't have, didn't know, and wasn't sure if she wanted to.

Releasing a short, clipped laugh, Calisto asked, "And how do you know that, Emmy?"

"I don't." She turned back to him, adding, "But I would think that you didn't wake up one day with your entire life turned on its side while every decision you ever thought you made was nothing more than a lie that taunts you. Am I right? Because that's how I feel right now, Calisto. That is the hell I'm living with. Pretending nothing is wrong might seem easy to do, but until you step into my shoes, you have no idea how hard it really is."

His jaw ticked, and his hand balled into a fist against the tabletop. Then, Calisto grabbed his cup from the table and stood from the booth quickly. His rushed movements and stiff back told Emma that she had struck a nerve.

Something …

What had she said that pissed him off so much?

"What are you doing?" Emma asked.

"Going back to my table," Calisto muttered. "Maybe you were right, Emma."

The way he used her full name instead of her nickname felt wrong. It came out of his mouth stilted and emotionless. Not like how he usually spoke.

"Right about what?"

"You. The overindulged mafia princess with her poor-little-me complex. Keep feeding that, let it fester and grow. I'm sure in five years, that'll be the one thing still going strong inside of you when everything else is used up and gone. Affonso will keep the silver spoon in your mouth, gagging you quiet. Don't worry about that."

Emma's heart clenched, but her mind screamed louder. Unlike earlier when his words had hurt her by accident, this was not the same.

Calisto meant to hurt her.

DONATI BLOODLINES: PART 1

His words had a purpose. He probably meant to distract her from his own secrets by cutting her with his words. She wouldn't let him do that. He was hiding something.

Emma wanted to know what it was.

"I upset you," Emma said softly.

Calisto froze solid as he turned to leave, and a shudder worked over his shoulders at her statement. "No, I—"

"I did. What was it?"

He glanced over his shoulder, his stare locking onto hers and holding strong. For the first time, Emma felt like she was getting a good look at this dangerous, attractive man. A familiar discontent colored his irises, barely hidden. A story was right on the tip of his tongue. Hatred twisted his features into a mask of pain, taking away his usual apathy and replacing it with a man she might be curious to know.

A man who looked *raw*.

Beaten by unseen things.

Used by unknown beings.

Sore to the touch, like unhealed wounds.

She knew those things.

All of them.

Because she had them inside, too.

"What was it?" Emma asked again.

"You assumed I didn't understand. You assumed I didn't know. Your life, your feelings, and your mistakes. You assumed. And you were wrong."

6.

Emma

The building in front of Emma gave off bad vibes. All she had to do was look at it and dread slipped into her veins, freezing her solid.

She didn't want to do this.

How many times had she told her mother no, brushed her off, or skipped out on appointments in the past three weeks?

Several.

Too many.

Emma let out a shaky breath, eyeing the lace and satin on display in the shop's window with as much disdain and hatred as she could. Her mother had Emma's size. She knew her height and measurements. Emma, quite vocally, had refused to do this very thing and had told Minnie that she would wear whatever in the hell was supplied for her to put on.

Anger surged through Emma.

Wedding dresses covered mannequins in the window. Pretty, delicate veils draped their faces. Crystal covered shoes, meant for brides wanting to be their very own Cinderella for the day, rested on raised platforms, catching the sun's rays and glittering.

"Damn you, Mom," Emma growled under her breath.

A light chuckle drew Emma's attention to the side.

Calisto leaned against a black car, a lit cigarette dangling from between his lips. Just the way the light of the sun shone down from behind him lit Calisto's tall, fit form up like a halo. When he slowly released a cloud of smoke from his lips, his features and amused smirk were shadowed by the gray plume. The man looked damn good standing there like he didn't have a single fuck to give but for the smoke on his lips.

Emma ignored the chill running down her spine.

Because it wasn't cold.

It was hot.

And something deep in her stomach pulsed, right along with the ache between her thighs.

Stop it, she told herself.

She learned Calisto could be an asshole, a mystery, and sometimes entertaining when he wanted to be. He was mostly quiet, and he watched people a lot with those piercing eyes of his. He rarely engaged others for any kind of interaction.

It only made Emma wonder about him even more. That certainly didn't help the growing interest she seemed to feel every goddamn time he was around.

And the man was always around!

The fact that she was getting married in just a couple of weeks did not deter the strange attraction building up heat and crashing through her bloodstream. It was intent on infecting her until she couldn't ignore it any more.

Probably going to get myself killed over this.

Emma ignored her inner voice.

Calisto's dark chuckles made Emma snap out of her daze. The pulse between her thighs didn't let up, because frankly, Calisto looked like sex on legs with dark-wash jeans hugging his hips, a leather jacket resting open against his taut, cut chest, and that fucking *cigarette* …

She hadn't realized she'd been staring at the man like he was some kind of God. Snapping her mouth closed, her walls slammed up high and the defenses came out.

Emma's attitude had always been her best protection, after all.

"What do you find so funny?" she asked.

Calisto quieted. "Well …"

"Well, *what?*"

"You looked fit to tear that fucking store down for

a second. Like you were thinking you could set the place on fire just with your glare alone. Who knows? Maybe you would have, if I hadn't interrupted you. Sorry to break up your hate-fest. Please, resume. It amuses me when you're annoyed at something."

Emma's hackles rattled at his teasing. "I'm not annoyed."

"I beg to differ, *dolcezza*. You're ten shades of annoyed and ready to rip someone's face off. A stubborn woman can never hide her anger, no matter how hard she tries. It's a sign of a passionate person—I didn't say there was anything wrong with it, only to work on hiding it."

"No, I'm not annoyed. I'm pissed off. If I were annoyed, I'd push on through with a fucking smile on my face. Right now, I can't even muster up something like that to get me through this."

"It's just a wedding dress," Calisto said quietly.

"Right. Just a wedding dress. It's not the end of my freedom or yet another pair of shackles for them to wrap around my leg to keep me contained."

Calisto laughed deeply. "My God, you are ..."

Emma stiffened when Calisto's gaze traveled over her body like he was taking her red dress, leather boots, and the curves of her body in for his memories. It didn't feel innocent, not with the way his throat bobbed with a swallow, his teeth bared a little, and his eyes narrowed.

"I'm what?" Emma asked, trying miserably to hide the air in her voice.

How could someone turn her on just by looking at her?

Worst fucking crush ever.

"You are one dramatic girl, Emmy," Calisto finally said with a sigh. "But dramatics won't get you out of the marriage or the dress shopping. It won't change your future or the decisions that have already been made for you. I suggest you plaster on a fuck-you smile and do what you have to do."

DONATI BLOODLINES: PART 1

Emma wanted to scream out her frustrations. "I wish it were that easy."

"Unfortunately, that's life. It's a part of growing up and being an adult. We don't get what we want just because we want it, and nobody is looking out for you right now. They're all looking out for them and what they can gain from this. The easier you let it be done, the quicker it will be over."

"And then I'll be married to a man I don't like, want, or could ever possibly love."

Briefly, Calisto frowned before his face returned to its usually passive state. "My mother once said she learned to love my father. Their engagement lasted three years before they married; however, so I suppose it isn't the same thing."

Stunned at his candor, Emma struggled for a response. "Your mother and father had an arranged marriage?"

Calisto nodded. "*Sì*. She was eighteen. He was twenty-four. Young, but they apparently got on quite well. I know in the early years my father didn't settle down with her. He ran with a lot of women for a while. Then things changed and they became closer. Best friends, my mother used to say."

"What kind of things changed?"

"My mother was in an accident that almost killed her. A motorcycle that my father had bought her. He kept promising to teach her how to ride."

"But he was too busy with other women to remember his promises."

Calisto smiled, but the sight was sad. "Something like that. Anyway, she decided to go on ahead and teach herself when my father didn't come home again one night. It ended terribly."

Emma shuddered. "I'm sorry."

"Don't be. A couple of broken bones later, and my father finally figured out what was important in his life. My mother said it made the pain worth it, just to see him come home every night to her and not run to someone else."

"And then you came along, right?"

Calisto's features darkened.

There was no hiding it.

"Shortly after the accident, my mother found out she was pregnant with me, yes."

Emma could plainly see the anger in Calisto's gaze. Once again, he was holding back information from her. Something secret, something hurtful, that he didn't want to share.

Was he ashamed of whatever it was?

"She was still young. Only twenty-four," he added.

"That would have made your father thirty, right?"

"Yes."

Emma fiddled with her fingers, mulling over what she knew. She had done a quick search on his family like he had told her to, but it hadn't brought up a lot. It seemed like a lot of info was simply speculation or precise, known facts.

Birthdays. Weddings. Official positions within the Donati Cosa Nostra ranks and who held them. Maybe Emma hadn't looked at the right stuff. Google had never been her friend.

"Didn't your dad die when he was thirty?" Emma asked, willing the nervousness out of her tone. "From some kind of motorcycle accident?"

Calisto turned to ice right before her eyes. At his sides, his fists balled and then relaxed just as quick. "Richard died at thirty, yes. He was showing my mother how to handle the machine properly, took a ride away from the house with his brother, and died when the brakes gave out. At least, that's how the story goes."

What were the odds of that? How tragic, that his father had died before he was even born. Calisto made it sound like there might be more to it, but Emma chose not to ask or press for more information.

"That's awful. I'm sorry."

"It was a long time ago, and I wasn't even born to meet him. I didn't lose out on anything in that regard."

She disagreed entirely. Not that Emma had much to talk about. Her relationship with her father had always been at arm's length, and the space between them had been filled with material things as her father's way of buying her love and loyalty. It wasn't healthy.

Emma's heart went out to Calisto for his loss of his father, but she was quickly reminded of his relationship with Affonso.

"I also noticed that your father was the older one between him and Affonso. I guess a big deal was made out of the marriage to your mother because your grandfather planned for him to take over eventually, right?"

Calisto cleared his throat, settling back into his relaxed posture with an indifferent attitude rolling off him in waves. "I see you've been doing your research."

"You told me to."

"I did. Find anything else interesting about the Donati history?"

Emma shrugged. "No. Why, should I have found something?"

Calisto didn't answer her.

"So, I guess Affonso must have been the main father figure in your life, huh?" Emma asked.

Calisto's jaw tensed. "You could say that."

"How would you say it?"

"I wouldn't say a thing at all," Calisto muttered. "Not for Affonso."

Ouch.

Calisto's tone could have frozen steel with the coldness it held.

"I had my grandfather for a few years, but he died when I was starting into my preteen years. I don't remember much about him, because he didn't have much to do with me." Then, he nodded at the dress shop.

"Hurry up. Your mother is waiting, I imagine. Grit your teeth and get it over with."

"I still don't want to."

Calisto smiled sadly. "Yeah, I know, Emmy. But hey, if you get through it without too much of a fit, I'll let you take me on another round on the casino floor tonight. Drain my pockets again. I'll sneak you a couple of drinks."

And that right there was exactly why Calisto was such a mind-fuck for Emma. She didn't understand his intentions, his motives, or why he sometimes seemed like maybe he actually gave a shit about her.

He had nothing to gain.

Neither did she.

But you have nothing to lose, her mind taunted.

"Well?" Calisto asked.

Emma grinned. "I'll take that deal."

• • •

"Oh, now that is lovely," Minnie exclaimed.

Emma cringed at the high volume of her mother's voice. She hid her reaction by turning to face the mirror and making sure her fake smile was plastered back on when she met her reflection.

"Really, Mom. You think this is lovely?" Emma asked.

She didn't even bother to hide her disdain.

The princess-style ball gown was big enough to hide four grown men under the skirt. It swept the floor like the bottom of a swinging bell when she moved even the slightest bit. A sleeveless, sweetheart cut neckline showcased her neck and collarbones. Nothing was holding the dress up but for the corset in the back nearly choking her to death.

The dress had a mixture of crystals, pearls, and other beadwork that covered the skirt and bodice. Emma couldn't look this way or that way without seeing a cascade of colors glaring off a window, mirror, or wall.

The damn thing would blind somebody.

"Well, it is a little too white," her mother muttered.

Emma glanced up at the ceiling, praying silently. *God, give me the fucking strength ...*

It didn't help.

"White, Mom? That's the problem?" Emma asked.

"You have to wear off-white. You know why. And also, ivory is a terrible color on you."

"Mom, this dress is ugly."

"It is not, Emmy!"

"It looks like something a beauty queen puked up with her last meal."

Minnie pursed her lips, clearly unhappy with Emma's reaction. "See, this is why I wanted you to come dress shopping. Your tastes are very different from mine."

Emma held back from snorting.

Different was one way to put it. Her mother believed the bigger something was, the better it would be.

No doubt, her mother had set it in her head to convince Emma on this sort of style. Honestly, the little shoe horn with the pointy handle hanging off the wall looked like a good instrument to inflict a deadly enough wound to get herself out of this hell.

Emma did smile that time.

Calisto was right.

She was a little dramatic.

Emma waved at the skirt of the dress. "Less pouf, Mom. Less beads and shiny things. I want sleeves, capped at least. Something to make me feel like my tits aren't going to pop out and give everyone a show when I bend over."

"Emma," her mother scolded. "Your mouth, my God."

"Ask the woman to find another dress. This one isn't it."

Minnie scowled. "Fine. But it does look nice."

"If I were a debutant on show, it would be perfect."

"Now you're starting to offend me, Emmy."

Her mother had been a debutant from a well-to-do political family that had a hand in a crime syndicate down south. Minnie had met Emma's father during college when George had gone down south for business under his father's request. Twenty-five years in Vegas had cured most of Minnie's southern quirks and verbal expressions, but an occasional "bless your heart" still slipped through with just the right amount of sarcasm behind it.

"Fine. I'm sorry. It's a beautiful dress," Emma said. "But not for me."

"You're not sorry," Minnie muttered, still staring longingly at the gown. "Another one, then?"

"Something different this time. Not something you want to wear, Mom."

Minnie conceded with a huff. Pushing up from the couch, her mother disappeared out of the private sitting area, likely to find the woman who owned the shop again and search for another gown. With her mother out of sight, Emma's frustrations grew all over again at the situation she was currently in.

Dress shopping.

For *her* wedding gown.

A wedding happening soon.

"Yes, George," Minnie said as she came around the corner with a phone pressed to her ear and no dress in hand. She waved at her daughter and pointed to the phone like Emma was supposed to know what in the hell was going on. With her mother and father, it could be anything. The two got off on their occasional spats. It was kind of unnerving. "I told you, I left the goddamn ticket on your—"

Minnie's words cut off as her gaze narrowed. "Don't you yell at me, George, just because you can't find the stupid ticket for your dry-cleaning. I know where you sleep, you fucking pig. Keep it up."

DONATI BLOODLINES: PART 1

"Oh, my God," Emma groaned, rubbing at her temples.

A headache began to throb there all of the sudden. This was exactly why Emma kept a distance between herself and her parents. Sometimes, their nonsense was overwhelming. How the two had stayed married for almost three decades, she didn't know.

Her mother was pushy and spoiled. Her father was a bastard with a superiority complex. Yet, the two seemingly adored one another.

"Sweet Jesus, George, you are hopeless. Utterly hopeless," Minnie said, sighing. "I will go get your suit and bring it to you. Thank you for ruining this day for me. I was so looking forward to this."

For her.

Emma didn't miss her mother's words. She wished they weren't true, but she knew they were. Her mother had pushed and wanted this dress shopping day far more than Emma. Minnie had her hand in planning the wedding from afar. Minnie was looking forward to it all.

Emma was ready to cut tail and run.

As fast as she fucking could.

If only …

"Emma, dear, we'll have to cut this short," Minnie said, drawing Emma from her thoughts.

Relief flooded Emma.

The headache ebbed away.

"No problem, Mom," Emma replied.

"Dinner tonight?"

The hopefulness on her mother's face kept Emma from refusing. Despite the strangeness around her parents and their sometimes difficult personalities, she did love her mother … and even her father.

"Sure," Emma said. "At your home or somewhere else?"

"I'll wrangle George into getting us a table at the Grand."

"Perfect."

"You know," her mother started to say, glancing around at the gowns in bags and the others hanging off the wall. "Emma, you could try a few on just by yourself. I know you're not exactly excited for—"

"Not even a little bit."

Minnie nodded. "I know. But you have a duty, as your father has explained so much that my ears hurt just hearing the damned word. Nonetheless, you could, Emmy. Try on a few alone. Maybe you'll find something in here that you like—something to make all of this worth it. Hmm?"

Emma doubted it.

She still agreed to appease her mother.

Once Minnie was gone again, it was just Emma alone in the private sitting room. She wondered where the lady that was helping her get in and out of the dresses had gone. More than anything, Emma suddenly wanted to rip the one she was currently wearing off. Just getting another glimpse at it in the mirror was enough to make her sick.

The chiffon ... silk ... crystals ...

Emma blinked.

A church, an aisle, and flower petals filled her vision. Quiet music, a waiting priest, and a man with his hand out, waiting to take hers.

A man she didn't want.

Emma didn't realize she was having a panic attack until her throat tightened to the point where she couldn't breathe. She turned away from the mirror, unable to look at the dress or herself for another second for fear of throwing up the breakfast and lunch she had eaten.

Jesus.

Where was that goddamn woman?

She needed the dress off right now.

Right the hell now.

Slipping on the too long skirt of the gown, Emma stumbled off the slightly raised platform. She managed to catch herself, but not before a sob caught in the back of her throat. Tears welled in her eyes without her permission, promising a breakdown was close by.

Damn it.

She had done so well.

She'd not cried yet.

It wouldn't do any good.

Hot tears escaped as she fumbled with the back of the corset on the dress, desperately trying to find the ties to undo them even a little bit.

Just enough to take a breath.

She only needed the *one*.

How was she supposed to get married if she couldn't even wear a wedding dress without having a panic attack?

Emma was fucked.

She knew it.

7.

Calisto

"*Zio*," Calisto greeted respectfully the moment he answered his ringing cell phone.

"Calisto," Affonso replied, sounding more chipper than usual. "You know, my boy, you could always drop the pretense when I call and address me the way we both want you to."

"As in, 'Afternoon, asshole'?"

Affonso grunted under his breath. "Hey, now."

"I'll stick with uncle," Calisto said, dismissing the entire conversation with four words.

"Such a shame. You could save me all the trouble and heartache in the world if you would simply just—"

"Are we going to do this again today?" Calisto asked. "I thought Vegas was supposed to be a break from me. Wasn't that what you said? You would be happy to put some distance between you and I for a while. You're contradicting yourself, *zio*, and we're not even in the same goddamn state as you're doing it."

"Watch it."

Two quickly spoken, angry words were enough to check Calisto's attitude. Regardless of his feelings toward his uncle, the man was still his boss. Despite the way Calisto had entered Cosa Nostra, under false pretenses and years of lies spoon-fed to him, he'd spoken an oath and he intended to keep it.

Respect.

Honor.

A boss is a boss is a *boss*.

Even if a man despises that boss.

"My apologies," Calisto said, the words practically choking him on the way out.

"Thank you." Affonso sighed heavily before saying,

"I did think a break would benefit us both, Cal. I hoped you would see how much respect and clout has been practically handed to you simply by having you grow up under my wing, carrying the Donati name, and taking a proper position in the family. Vegas isn't even New York, my boy, but look at how they treat you like a prince just waiting to take his throne. Imagine how much more you could have if you would only forget about past mistakes and move onto the future."

"Mistakes."

"Well, yes."

"*Mistakes*," Calisto repeated, spitting the word through his teeth. "Is that what you want to call what happened?"

Affonso didn't answer at first. When he did, he changed direction entirely. "This was not what I called you for today, Cal. Once again, you're getting stuck on things that used to be instead of focusing on what could be."

Calisto's irritation jumped a notch. "You brought it up first."

"And now I'm dropping it."

"I wish you would leave it that way, uncle."

Calisto knew damn well that nothing irked Affonso more than when he reminded the man of what he was to him. Not a friend, father figure, or much else. Simply his uncle.

"You could make a fantastic boss, Calisto," Affonso said, his tone gentler than ever before. "It is right there at your fingertips. You could take it without even giving me what I want, my boy. Don't you see that at all?"

"I would have taken it," Calisto replied quietly. "I would have followed your pack of lies to the very end. Whatever you wanted, I would have done for you. Not now, *zio*. *You* want me to be the boss. *You* want me to run *your* family. It's what you want *me* to do. And because it's what you want, I don't want it at all."

"I indulged you too much," Affonso muttered

heavily.

"No, you lied to me. There's a difference."

"You and I … it's a sad thing, Cal."

"So be it, *zio*."

Affonso let out a grumble. "Did she enjoy her gift today?"

Calisto fought the urge to roll his eyes. Affonso's plan of bribing Emma into compliance with gifts of all sorts was doing little but reminding the girl of someone she didn't want to be. Even Calisto, with his usual disregard for other people's feelings, could clearly see Emma's issues.

The young woman had already been spoiled by a man—her father. And that same man turned on her, feeding her to a wolf like Affonso the first chance he could. Emma was not going to allow Affonso to trick her the same way her father had once done.

"Well?" Affonso demanded.

"She got the spa documents this morning with her breakfast, as far as I know. I had the casino add it on top of her cart as it was wheeled into the penthouse."

Today's gift had featured a spa of sorts that Affonso had purchased a year or so ago. He had apparently asked for his lawyer to change the ownership documents to reflect Emma's name as the other side of a minority shareholder in the business.

Most women would probably love the idea of free spa days, owning their own business, or simply just the gift itself. Calisto didn't believe that Emma was like most women. She could probably see the gift for what it was. Another way for Affonso to keep an eye on her, to control her, and for him to take something else away, should she misbehave.

"She did get it," Calisto said again.

"That tells me nothing, Cal."

"I wasn't inside the room. Do you want me to spend evenings in her place?"

DONATI BLOODLINES: PART 1

Affonso grew deadly quiet. "You're toeing a very thin line at the moment."

"I don't have much else to tell you. She didn't mention it when we did talk earlier."

"Earlier? What were you doing with her earlier that you had time for a conversation?"

Another contradiction.

Affonso's jealousy was showing. The man despised anyone coming close to his women, in any respect. He could be violent toward men who he considered had crossed a line with one of his mistresses or ... well, his wife. But it wasn't like Calisto could find out if Emma enjoyed her latest gift—bribe—without talking to the woman.

Calisto didn't bother to point it out to his uncle. "I was having a smoke when she finally got out of her car to meet her mother. I wanted to make sure she was feeling up to the day, I guess."

"What are they doing?"

"Looking at wedding dresses."

And likely wishing for a black hole to appear so she could disappear forever, Calisto held back from adding.

Maybe Emma wasn't the only one who could drudge up the most dramatic bullshit at the drop of a hat. Calisto wondered if he should lay off the girl.

"No princess-y garbage," Affonso said suddenly.

Calisto rubbed at the spot between his eyes as an ache started to form behind his skull. "What?"

"Those big, awful dresses that takes three people to get a woman in and out of a car, never mind through a fucking door. They may look nice on a mannequin, but I can assure you they are hell in a bedroom when you just want to get the terrible thing off."

Again, what?

"Is there a point to this?" Calisto asked.

"*Sì*, make sure she doesn't pick a dress like that. If she does, I am holding you personally accountable for it. I

73

hate those. *Cose brute*."

Wonderful.

Just fucking perfect.

Hedging on the line he knew better than to cross, Calisto dared to say, "Isn't it supposed to be her choice, as it's *her* day and all that jazz?"

"Hers." Affonso scoffed. "Another pile of garbage to wade through. I'm paying for it, Cal. The wedding, the things her mother wants, and even the dress she's buying today. It's coming from my bank account. The least they can do is provide me with easier access on the wedding night."

Jesus Christ.

That was ten shades of wrong.

All *wrong*.

Emma was more than just a wedding night—more than easy access. She was young, sure, but anyone with two eyes and a half of a brain could see the woman was unhappy, worried, and anxious about what was still to come. Couldn't Affonso see that, too? Couldn't the man make the transition a little less painful by allowing Emma her own choices, or even a little more time?

People had to see she wasn't ready for this nonsense to happen.

Like her wedding night …

With *Affonso*.

Calisto didn't like how his entire body seemed to want to recoil against that realization. Like he didn't even want to think the words because that would somehow make it true. Bile filled his throat, but he swallowed his disgust and the sickness back down. What else could he do?

Emma wasn't his to protect.

Her feelings couldn't bleed into him.

It would do him no good.

"Make sure she picks something beautiful, but simple and easy to remove," Affonso said, bringing Calisto from his thoughts.

He didn't want to speak.

He didn't have another option.

"Whatever you need, *zio*."

Calisto hung up the call just as Minnie Sorrento stormed from the dress shop, sporting a scowl that could rival even the devil's. Without so much as a glance in Calisto's direction, the woman scuttled across the street and jumped into a white Lexus. Tires squealed as Minnie took off.

Maybe Emma had thrown a fit after all.

It was the very last thing he wanted to do, but Calisto stepped up on the sidewalk and made a beeline for the dress shop. He hadn't been inside one before. Not a wedding dress shop, specifically. Pulling open the door, shades of white trimmed with lace, beads, and glittering panels assaulted his eyes.

Stepping in further, Calisto noticed a mid-thirties, heavy-set woman with large-framed glasses chatting on a phone at the desk. She didn't see him as he looked the place over. Dresses hung from hangers and poles on every wall. Shoes, veils, and matching clutches had been displayed in glass cases.

Good God.

This was hell.

A crinoline, silk, and satin-walled *hell*.

Toward the back of the shop, Calisto took a hallway directing customers to dressing rooms and sitting areas. It wasn't long before he found Emma.

A dress that was big enough to be a house was the first thing to catch his eye. The second was Emma. Tears streaked down the young woman's cheeks as she stumbled over the layers and layers of crinoline. She grappled for the back of the dress, failing to grab the ties at the bottom of the tightly woven corset. She didn't notice him in the doorway of the private sitting room, but her panic was as clear as day.

What had caused her to react like this?

More tears spilled as another sob echoed. Emma tried to reach for the ties again, and managed to get one free. She still couldn't loosen the back of the dress quickly enough for her satisfaction, apparently. She grabbed at the sweetheart neckline and yanked for all she was worth. It looked like she was trying to rip the damn dress right off her body.

"Jesus Christ," Emma mumbled. "I want this *off*."

Her voice, heavy with pain and anxiety, struck Calisto in the chest like a hot knife slicing through butter. She probably didn't think anyone was watching her breakdown happen, and she likely wouldn't want him to step in and help her.

Calisto couldn't help but move forward with his hands outstretched to soothe Emma. It was like some kind of fucking cord had suddenly wrapped itself around his middle and tugged hard, making him step over the threshold, around the white leather couch, and closer to the woman with her smeared makeup, her mussed hair, and her pain shattering all over a hardwood floor.

No one should cry like she was doing. No one should hurt like that. Hell, it made him ache just to see it.

Calisto figured that Emma's reasons for her emotional collapse wasn't all that important for the moment. Getting her calm, comfortable, and breathing normally again was what needed doing before anything else could get better.

Emma bent over at the knees, still not seeing Calisto behind her, and grabbed at the sleeveless, princess-style gown to pull at the bodice again. Her hard panting, like she was gasping for a breath that just wasn't there, was accompanied by a broken sob.

His black heart, incrusted with years of layered ice, cracked.

Calisto tried to ignore it.

He wanted to …

"Now," he heard her mumble. "I want this off right *now*."

Closing the last couple of feet between him and Emma, Calisto's hands landed on her bare shoulders. He felt every muscle in her body jump under his touch, but he didn't let her go.

"Hey, it's all right, Emmy," he said softly.

Emma straightened fast before spinning around. Calisto's hands went with her, moving from her shoulders to her neck in a flash. He tried hard to ignore the softness of her peaches and cream skin under his palms, or how the heat of her body seemed to fuse straight into his bloodstream.

Wiping at her eyes, Emma mumbled, "Go away. I'm fine."

"You're not."

She was so far from fine that it wasn't even funny.

Emma's breath caught on another sob.

Calisto flinched. "Turn around. You want this awful thing off, right? That's what you said when I came in here. Let me take it off, Emmy. I'll help."

At first, it seemed like she was going to argue with him. Her green eyes welled with tears all over again, and her bottom lip quivered just enough to shake what resolve Calisto might have had left.

"It makes me feel like I can't breathe," she said.

"Turn around and I'll help, Emmy."

Calisto didn't wait for her to do as he asked. He spun her around, fisted the ties keeping the corset tight, and yanked. Over and over, he pulled the silk bands out until the bodice of the dress was falling apart and away from Emma's body.

It also did something else he hadn't thought about.

From the swell of her ass to the middle of her back, Emma's skin peeked through the breaks in the ties. Smooth, unblemished, pale skin. It didn't help that Calisto was still touching her. He could feel her shivers under his hands, and if he just moved his palms down a little lower, the dress would slide right off and leave her naked and bare.

His teeth clenched. A heat bloomed deep in his gut, shooting straight down to his cock and balls. Inside his head, he knew it was bad. To look at Emma Sorrento in a less than innocent way would surely earn him a few bullets. To act on the dark lust spinning around in his blood would be a nail in the coffin.

If he even got a funeral.

Despite what Calisto knew, it didn't stop his erection from straining against the zipper of his jeans. It didn't help the hunger, never mind the confusion.

Space, his mind said. *Take some space.*

Calisto dropped his hands and stepped back, putting a foot between him and Emma. It didn't make much of a difference to the mind his cock now seemed to have. Emma didn't care that Calisto had stepped back either, considering she was pulling the dress down and shimmying her hips to free the skirt.

"Uh, Emma … let me get out of here before you—"

Calisto's words and thought process stopped as the mountain of silk and crinoline fell to the floor. Emma stood in the middle of the pile, her shoulders heaving and her back bare, as she sucked in a deep breath.

Black lace covered her backside, drawing Calisto's gaze straight down to Emma's ass. His fingers itched to reach out and run over the swell of her ass, just to see what she would do.

Would she shiver?

Shake?

Ask for more?

Calisto swallowed hard, trying to come up with something to say. Emma wore no bra, so when she turned with her arms covering her chest, he could see the sides of her breasts peeking out to give a hint of her beauty.

DONATI BLOODLINES: PART 1

Wary eyes found him still as a stone. Emma chewed on her bottom lip and avoided his stare.

She was all skin, curves, and sin, standing there like that. A body that looked fit to be touched, tasted, and explored. He bet his hands would fit perfectly in the dip of her waist while his other disappeared down her panties. The kind of lace covering her sex and ass was just the right material to grab on, pull hard, and rip right off when he had her bent over a flat, sturdy surface.

This wasn't good at all.

"Thank you," Emma said.

Calisto nodded tightly. "No problem."

"I didn't mean to freak out like that."

How was she being normal right now?

Couldn't she see he was fucking struggling?

"You should put something on," Calisto said, hoarse and husky at the same time.

Emma didn't act like she heard him. "It just caught up to me really fast."

"Did your mother leave because you were having a fit?"

"No, my father called. I panicked after she left."

Calisto shouldn't care; he shouldn't ask. "About what?"

"Wearing a dress. Walking down an aisle. It felt real all of the sudden and then I couldn't breathe, or get the dress off. I'm sorry."

"Don't apologize."

Emma glanced down at the dress. "God, that's a lot of material for something so ugly."

Calisto somehow managed a laugh. Considering the majority of the blood in his body was still owned by his cock, it was the best he could do.

"Get dressed," he said again.

"Haven't you seen a naked woman before?"

"Yes."

Not you.

The longer you stand there, the more I want to.

"Keep your eyes up above the neckline and you'll do okay," Emma told him.

"Funny," he replied. "You're fucking hilarious."

"Calm down. I'll get dressed. My clothes are in the changing room."

She stepped out of the pile, and moved toward the changing room. Calisto tried not to watch the way Emma's hips swayed as she walked. For most women, they learned how to move just the right way to draw a man's eye.

Emma's sway wasn't learned—it was all natural.

Once she was safely hidden behind the dressing room door, Calisto took a much needed breath. He ran through the alphabet, times tables, the American anthem, his Cosa Nostra oath, and anything else he could think of to get his erection down.

Anything to get the woman out of his head.

It didn't work.

Cazzo.

"What did you come in for?" Emma asked behind the door.

"Affonso called."

Emma groaned. "Weren't his letter and gift this morning enough? He can't leave me alone for a day?"

"Sorry, Emmy. Don't kill the messenger. Didn't you like the gift?"

"No," she said sharply. "It's another attempt to buy my loyalty and good behavior."

Smart girl, he praised silently.

"He wanted me to check on your shopping," Calisto settled on saying.

Honesty was the best policy.

Emma yanked open the door and glared at him. Her dress hung off one shoulder, barely covering her breasts. She hadn't gotten the other arm in, obviously.

Calisto averted his eyes.

"Are you serious?" she asked.

"*Sì*. By the way, the one on the floor is in no way acceptable for his standards."

Emma's lips drew thin. "I should wear it even though I hate it, too, just to piss him off."

Calisto was inclined to urge her on, but he didn't. "Don't you want to pick your dress?"

"Not really."

"But it is your dress, Emmy, and despite what Affonso doesn't want you to wear ... well, you do have a choice in the matter. Some women like to keep their dresses and have them made into things for their children. Christening gowns or whatever."

Emma blinked, her features softening. "My mom did that with hers. I still have the miniature gown."

"You could do the same thing. Instead of seeing this as something awful, turn it into something to look forward to."

Because children with Affonso was sure to be wonderful. Calisto hated himself the more he spoke. He shouldn't be encouraging her to pick a wedding dress so she could marry a man he hated.

"I could," Emma mused. "But that means I expect to have his children."

"Caught onto that, did you?"

"I don't think it's really optional with him."

"Probably not," Calisto admitted.

"Is he making you ensure I pick the right dress?" she asked.

"Essentially."

"Sucks to be you."

"You don't even know how much."

Emma smirked bitterly. "I think I do."

8.

"My apologies," Calisto said, chuckling. "I can only guess how you're feeling right now, and it's probably a lot worse than me."

"Probably," Emma echoed.

She shifted on her feet, and the swell of her breast peeked out from the side. Calisto's jeans tightened all over again.

"Would you please get dressed or fix your dress?"

She quickly corrected her dress, sliding her other arm in and letting the fabric fall down her toned figure. The dress clung to her curves and the skirt swayed when she moved.

Calisto had to look away.

Naked or clothed, it didn't really matter. The woman was still gorgeous. Calisto was beginning to wish he didn't notice these kinds of things about Emma. It wasn't helping his dangerous attraction.

"Well, the good news for you is that I'm done shopping for today. No need to babysit what dress I'm picking out."

"Oh?" he asked.

Emma shrugged. "One panic attack is enough. I'm not interested in shooting for a second."

"I don't blame you."

But she would need to pick one. She was getting married, the girl would need a dress to wear for the day. Affonso wouldn't accept Emma walking down in her jeans, or God forbid, a black dress that showcased how she truly felt about the day.

Calisto's stomach turned at the thought.

"I guess our deal is off, huh?" Emma asked.

"Pardon?"

DONATI BLOODLINES: PART 1

"I had a 'fit,' as you put it. You said if I didn't, we could have some fun tonight and I could empty your pockets at the casino. I lost the bet. Hence, no fun."

Calisto frowned. "There was no bet. I was trying to get you to do what you were told. We'll still go. I might have to limit your time at the poker table, seeing as how I like my cash, but we'll go."

Emma's smile came off brilliant and bright. "Yeah?"

"Why not?"

You know why not, idiot, his mind growled.

Calisto ignored it.

He'd never pushed aside his gut feeling before. It had never failed him, not once. When something felt like it was off, then it probably was. If someone gave him a bad vibe, they were probably hiding something.

That was how he lived.

By his gut.

It kept Calisto alive.

The problem with his gut instinct was that it didn't seem to be giving him anything useable where Emma Sorrento was concerned. It felt both good and bad—a should and shouldn't kind of feeling that left him nowhere but confused.

"Okay," Emma said quietly. "I have a dinner with my mom and dad later first."

"I'll be around."

"I don't doubt it."

Despite her teasing laugh that followed, there was a sadness in her eyes that she hid well. Calisto still saw it. He knew Emma hated that he was constantly following her. To her, it probably seemed as though he was keeping tabs and reporting back to his uncle on her whereabouts and doings.

Mostly, Calisto gave Affonso the same info: nothing to see here. There wasn't anything to report. Emma was, for the most part, keeping a clean nose. She wasn't doing anything wrong, she hadn't been out living up the Vegas nightlife since the engagement, and she kept quiet. But even if she did ...

Calisto wasn't sure he would tell.

"Miss Sorrento, I'm so sorry that took so—Oh!"

Spinning on his heel, Calisto found the heavier set, dark-haired woman standing in the entrance to the private sitting room. He had noticed her earlier talking on the phone.

"Hello," the woman said, looking him up and down.

Calisto offered a smooth smile. "Hello."

"Calisto, this is Marian. She's the owner and a friend to my mother."

Glancing over his shoulder at Emma, he took note of her unhappiness.

Ah.

Well, that explained the half-hidden frown Emma was sporting.

"I didn't see Minnie leave," Marian said.

"She rushed out after my father called, needing something. I'm finishing up, anyway. Next time, okay?"

Marian scowled. "But ... well, I found a dress for you, dear."

Calisto could practically hear Emma's teeth grind behind him. "I think Emmy wants to head out and finish this up at another time."

"One more, please?" the woman asked, brushing Calisto's comment off. "I promise you'll love it. Those dresses your mother demanded were not suitable for you, Emma. It's what she wanted to see you in, not what you wanted to be seen in. This one is perfect, I know it."

Emma sighed heavily.

Calisto passed her another look. "You don't have to, if you're not in the mood. We can go. Do this another day, Emmy."

"You want her to look beautiful when she walks down the aisle to meet you, right?" the woman asked.

He damn near choked on his answer.

"I'm ... uh, not—"

"Get the dress," Emma said, interrupting Calisto's stumbling words.

"Jesus," he mumbled when the woman was gone. Turning back to Emma, he found her shaking her head and giggling. "I thought you said she was a friend of your mother's? Doesn't she know who you're marrying?"

Emma scoffed. "Arranged marriage is only acceptable in certain cultures and the mafia. Just because my mother supports my marriage to Affonso doesn't mean her arrogant, superficial friends won't stick their noses up at her. She has to save some kind of face. That doesn't include explaining that my future husband is thirty years older than me."

"Damn."

"I have to say, I really enjoyed watching my mother fumble for a response when Marian asked earlier where her invitation was."

Calisto grinned. "Lost in the mail?"

"Apparently, it's not sent out yet."

"Smooth."

Emma lifted a single shoulder like it didn't make a difference to her either way. "My mother has always been a good liar. And she knows that if she explains the wedding is happening in New York, the mouths will run that it's a connected wedding. If you know what I mean."

"A mafia wedding."

"Mmhmm. She doesn't want more people talking than what already do. That, or George doesn't want people talking and making rumors. Dad wants this all to happen as quietly as possible. Mom isn't the only one who doesn't want to hear people's opinions over the fact that he's marrying his daughter off to someone thirty years older than her."

"Doesn't she read the socialite magazines?" he asked.

"Probably. It's like an addiction. She knows better, but she runs to the store every week for the new issues."

Strange.

Calisto dropped the topic when Marian strolled back into the sitting room with a garment bag slung over her arm. It was a much smaller, thinner bag than he expected to see for a wedding gown. Pointing at Calisto with her free hand, the woman barked, "You, out."

"He stays," Emma said quickly.

Marian's mouth opened to argue, but she didn't get a chance.

"I want him to stay," she clarified.

Calisto cocked a brow at Emma. "You're sure?"

"Lots of men see their brides in dresses before the wedding. I want his opinion."

Calisto clenched his jaw in an attempt to keep quiet. He didn't want to sit through Emma putting on another dress, but he knew what she was doing. She was likely giving him the chance to see what the dress looked like and tell her if it was appropriate for Affonso's tastes and demands.

"Fine," the shop keeper muttered. "But it's her dress, mister."

"Hers," he agreed.

Calisto found the closest chair and sat down. The seat was so plush that the butternut colored leather practically swallowed his lower half. He admired the stitching design on the arm of the chair as the women chatted inside the dressing room. Safe conversation, he noticed. Marian asked about wedding details, and Emma answered vaguely.

Smart girl.

The shuffling of a garment bag echoed out to his spot, drawing his gaze up from the leather toward the closed door. He found his reflection in a mirror hanging off the door. Instead of a woman coming out in her wedding gown, he found himself. His impassive, unfeeling self—except he was neither impassive, nor unfeeling in the reflection.

A curious excitement buzzed in his gut. His gaze burned brightly with interest. He would usually sit in such a way that his side was turned to the room, keeping his posture unavailable for conversation with others. Now, he was sitting forward, ready to be involved.

This was all wrong.

How many times had he thought that very thing just today alone? Calisto could hear his mind screaming at him, warning him and taunting him all at the same time.

What are you doing here? You know better than this. Step back before you fuck this up. There's a bullet waiting for you. And a seat in hell.

He pushed his thoughts away. He indulged the bit of attraction thickening in his blood for a woman he didn't know all that well, but was still unobtainable. He forced back the little voice warning him that he was toeing a very fragile line of acceptable conduct with Emma.

Calisto had control of this shit. He knew what was right and what was wrong where his uncle's fiancée was concerned. He didn't have to give in to the lust still keeping his cock semi-hard, or focus on the image of Emma's bare back under his palms.

He wouldn't feed into this.

Whatever it was.

Right?

The high wail of a phone brought Calisto out of his head with a bang. He straightened even more in the chair and realized he'd been holding so tightly onto the arms that his fingernails had left scratches on the leather.

"Oh, damn it," Marian muttered behind the dressing room door. "I have to get that. I'm going to shoot my new girl for not coming in today. Will you be okay for a minute, dear?"

"Sure," Emma said.

Her quiet response caught Calisto's attention

instantly. Her sweet tone came off as unsure, confused, and weighed down. He didn't have the chance to think on it for long.

Marian slipped out of the dressing room, closed the door behind her, and gave Calisto a pointed look that told him to stay where he was without even saying a word. She quickly hurried from the private sitting area, mumbling on about her missing employee.

Calisto fidgeted in the chair, waiting.

Then, Emma opened the dressing room door and poked her head out. His gaze founds hers right away, and he knew that he was right. The brightness of her eyes was dulled like she had something new on her mind.

"Hey."

"Hey," he said.

Emma dropped his stare. "Could you help me really quick?"

"Sure." Calisto pushed up from the chair in a fluid motion. "What do you need?"

"Marian had most of the buttons done up in the back herself. There were just a couple left toward the top. I mean, if you wouldn't mind."

Calisto swallowed the words wanting to come out, the ones that would tell her that he minded a great deal. He still wasn't going to feed into that nonsense, after all.

"Not a problem, Emmy."

Stepping up on the raised platform, Calisto grabbed for the doorknob, and opened the door just enough to slip into the dressing room. Emma already had her back turned, but white lace surrounded his vision from all sides. Mirrors lined all four walls of the dressing room. It was impossible to ignore the beautiful, classic, A-line dress with capped sleeves she wore. From the top of the gown to the very bottom, intricate, off-white lace hugged Emma's body and curves.

Calisto forced himself to focus on his task, instead of how amazing Emma looked in the dress. He quickly found the last four pearl buttons on the back, and did them up. It was a perfect fit. Not an inch too big or too small. The pearls made a pathway from the middle of Emma's back to right above the swell of her ass. It left a peek of her shoulder blades and skin exposed.

Enough to be tasteful.

Just a promise of what was below.

It was both regal and sexy.

"You look wonderful," Calisto said, trying to tamper down the huskiness in his voice.

Get a grip, man.

Emma sucked in a hard breath, eyeing the gown in the mirror. "She was right."

Calisto found Emma's stare in the mirror, and held it. "Pardon, *dolcezza?*"

"Marian. She was right about the dress. It's perfect. It's beautiful. It's very me, I guess."

"You love it," he said, filling in her obvious blank.

Emma frowned and wet her lips as her hands rubbed together nervously. "Yes."

"So why are there tears in your eyes, Emmy?"

Shouldn't it be a good thing that she had found one thing in this awful mess of her arranged marriage that she could actually love? Even if it was something silly like a dress, couldn't she take some sense of happiness from it?

"Why does it have to be so goddamn perfect?" Emma asked, her voice barely above a breath.

Calisto didn't understand. "I—"

"Why does this have to be the dress, Cal?"

"You've lost me."

"*The* dress. The one. Every girl has her one dress. She dreams about it; dreams about finding it and wearing it as she walks down the aisle to meet her groom. It's a focal point for a bride. Why does this have to be *the* dress for me? *Why?*"

He didn't have an answer for her.

Calisto put his hands on her shoulders and turned

Emma around. Quickly and quietly, he wiped away the few tears that had escaped from the corners of her eyes. She shivered under his hands, but didn't force him away.

Instead of letting her go like he knew he should, Calisto kept holding Emma's face between his palms. He liked her heat, and the fire in her eyes that was sometimes hidden. He liked the softness of her skin, and how she seemed to lean into his touch, curious and hesitant.

It was dangerous to feed attraction.

It was stupid to indulge emotion.

Calisto was smarter than this—he *was*.

But his mother, Cam, had always taught him to treat women, no matter what kind of woman she was, with the utmost respect. She had told him never to make a woman cry, to apologize to a woman he had done wrong, and to wipe a woman's tears away—no matter if he was the cause or not.

Calisto was not a good man. He'd taken lives before it was their time, he'd skipped church more than he went, and he'd rarely felt guilty over his actions and choices. He was unapologetic. Sometimes he would lie and cheat his way through something just to say he could do it, and he liked the smell of dirty money in his hands far more than clean, hard-earned cash. He had drug dealers on speed dial, a collection of illegal guns, a rap sheet a foot long and enough familiarity with police to be on a first name basis each time he got arrested just for being him.

Good was not a word to describe Calisto Donati.

But he wouldn't let a woman cry.

Good, no.

Honorable where it counted, however … yes.

"*Shh*," Calisto soothed, sweeping his thumbs over Emma's high cheekbones again to remove the remaining tears. "Don't cry, *ragazza*. You've got far too beautiful of a face for it to be covered in your tears."

"Don't say that, Calisto."

"I prefer Cal, you know."

Emma batted his hands away, but he held strong. "Stop it, I said."

"You like the dress, don't you?"

"I said that I did."

"And you look great in it," he pressed.

"That's not the point."

Calisto frowned. "It's the dress. Yeah, I got that."

"I don't want to wear the perfect dress, the one that's perfect for me, on a day when I have to marry a man I will never love. How is that even okay?"

It wasn't.

She was right.

"I'm sorry," Calisto murmured.

His words didn't help Emma much, if her fresh round of tears was any indication. Knowing wiping them away wasn't going to help that time, Calisto pulled her into his embrace without a word and wrapped her in a tight hug so that Emma could hide her pain for as long as she needed.

In his arms, he hoped he could help her.

Somehow.

It also felt good to hold her—intimate even.

Too intimate.

"I want the dress," he heard Emma mumble.

"You can have it."

"I don't want to wear it for him. Someone else, but not him. This isn't fair."

Calisto didn't know what to say. He'd already crossed a dozen lines where this woman was concerned.

A knock on the dressing room door made Emma and Calisto break apart quickly.

"Emma?" Marian asked.

"Just a second. Calisto helped me fix the dress."

Shit.

Calisto's mind ran a million miles a minute. It only took one person's misguided and half-truths being whispered for word to spread. Just the wrong person talking would cause him and Emma a hell of a lot of trouble.

It didn't matter if nothing was going on.

"I'll be outside," Calisto said.

Outside of the damn dress shop.

Emma blinked up at him, confused. "Okay."

"Get the dress."

"But—"

"Get it. The rest doesn't matter. This is still going through, whether you want it to or not, whether you are happy or angry at the world. The least you can do for yourself is have one thing for you when they force you into it. Get the dress, Emmy."

"Okay," she whispered.

Without another word, Calisto left the dressing room. He moved past Marian without so much as looking at her.

Behind him, Calisto heard Emma call out his name.

"Yeah?"

"Is your deal still on for tonight?" she asked.

No.

No way.

Nope.

Calisto wasn't an idiot. He knew where to draw the lines.

"Yeah, Emma, we're still on."

But apparently he was saying fuck all the lines tonight.

• • •

Calisto tossed back another shot of rum, needing the burn in his throat and the distraction for his overwhelmed mind. The sounds of the club behind him were only a dull roar to his senses. He barely heard it at all.

Stupidly, Calisto had thought that coming to a club, having a few drinks, and watching women dance would be enough to clear his head before he had to meet up with Emma after she had dinner. He wasn't supposed to leave her alone at all, but he figured she was safe enough with her parents.

She didn't even know he left.

Turning slightly, Calisto rested his arm on the bar and surveyed the crowd. Beautiful, young women moved throughout the people, their hips swaying in their tight, short dresses. Skin-tight. Short as hell. All a man needed to do was pull their dresses up a bit, bend them over, and pull their panties to the side.

Easy fucking access.

Yet, none of them interested Calisto.

Not a damn drop.

He wanted a distraction. Something to take his mind off the experience he'd had earlier with Emma, or the way he was still thinking about it—her—and her naked skin under his palms.

"You're looking awfully lonely here by yourself," said a sultry voice from his side.

Calisto met a brown-eyed girl's stare, unaffected. She, like most of the other women in the joint, was dressed for the occasion and looked good. He just wasn't ... there. Not for her or any other female.

His dick had apparently settled on someone else.

Someone impossible.

"I enjoy my own company," Calisto said.

Take the hint.

The woman didn't.

"Why don't you buy me a drink?" she asked. Calisto pulled a bill from his pocket and handed it over to the woman. She looked down at the bill, her brow furrowing. "What—"

"Buy yourself a drink, sweetheart."

With that, he pushed away from the bar and strolled out into the dancing crowd. Calisto made a beeline for the front of the club, more stressed than he had been when he entered. He just wanted to get his mind off things, and somehow, he'd made it worse. He was still thinking about Emma, her body and curves, and his interest only seemed to climb higher.

Why did Emma have to catch his attention?

Why her?

Calisto walked past the bouncers and out to the street. He made his way toward the lot where he had parked his car, each step he took was a little rawer than the last.

His cock was hard.

It had been painfully fucking hard since he touched Emma.

This was ridiculous.

Calisto was ridiculous.

Once he was inside the rental Mercedes, Calisto placed his hands on the steering wheel and leaned over it, letting out a heavy breath of air. He thought about whatever he could to get his erection down. Nothing worked.

The zipper of his pants bit into his tender cock through his boxer-briefs, irritating Calisto further. Readjusting his length did nothing but make his dick jump in his own hand. More frustrated than ever, he checked the time and noted it was close to when Emma was supposed to be finishing her dinner with her parents.

He couldn't do this shit.

He needed to get that girl out of his fucking head.

Biting hard on his lower lip, Calisto hoped the pain would be enough to distract him from his thoughts of Emma for long enough to handle his little problem. He undid his pants and slipped his hands under his boxer-briefs. As long as he could get the damned hard-on to go away, he'd be fine for the evening.

Surely.

The very second his hand wrapped around his length and tugged with a firm grip, relief flooded his bloodstream. Unfortunately, his thoughts shot right back to Emma. Her pretty lips, inviting, red, and needing to be filled.

He stroked harder, faster. His cock throbbed in his hand.

Groaning, Calisto clenched his teeth, letting his thumb roll over the head of his cock with every pull. He was still focused on her.

Perfect curves, the kind a man would kill for. The kind that fit perfectly in a man's hands—his hands. Silky skin made to bite and taste, or paint with a stream of his come.

He bet she felt like fucking satin inside.

Fucking Emma would be heaven. His fingers digging into her skin, turning it red as he fisted her hair and listened to all the sounds she would make for him.

Yeah, perfect.

That one thought alone was enough to send him over the edge. Calisto came hard, his semen spilling over his shaking fingers in hot, sticky streams.

Calisto sucked in a hard breath and rested back against the seat, still holding his hard cock. At least it wasn't aching anymore.

As for him?

He was still fucked either way.

9.

Emma

"Tell me you managed to find a dress after I left," Minnie said.

A waiter set three plates on the table. Emma was grateful for the momentary distraction, as the waiter began to prepare wine glasses and sparkling water. Once the young man was gone, however, her mother's gaze turned on Emma again.

"Well, did you?" Minnie demanded.

"She's been pestering me all damn day," George muttered. "If you didn't find one, she'll blame me, Emmy."

Emma didn't pay her father's tirade any mind.

"I found one," Emma said. "I charged it to the card Affonso left."

"Did you take it to your penthouse?"

"I had it shipped to New York."

"Emma!"

Minnie's loud exclamation made George drop the fork he was holding. It landed with a clatter in his plate of tiny steak.

"Jesus, Minnie," George growled. "Lower your voice. Sometimes, it's like living with one of those goddamn Yorkie dogs with you."

"And what is that supposed to mean?" Minnie asked with narrowed eyes.

"You know what it means, woman. We're eating, not at the fucking races. There's no need for you to jump out of your skin and shriek like a banshee over the smallest things."

"Maybe you should take note of where we are and fix your language, George."

"Maybe you should—"

96

DONATI BLOODLINES: PART 1

Oh, my God.

"What's the issue with me sending the dress straight to New York, Mom?" Emma asked, wanting to diffuse the fight starting between her parents. God knew if those two got into it, they would fight the dinner away. No eating would be had. Not peacefully, anyway. "It's one less thing I need to have shipped later, or take on the plane with me when I do go. Plus, I won't have to worry as much if it does get lost on the way because they'll have more time to find it."

"Fittings, Emma," her mother said like it should have been obvious. "You can't just wear a dress right off the rack."

George pointed his fork, the one he'd picked back up, in his wife's direction. "Agreed. It's like a suit. You need to take the time to have those things fitted properly."

"I can and I will wear it right off the rack." Emma shrugged. "It fit perfectly. Even Marian said it didn't need to be fitted."

Minnie pursed her lips. "Huh."

"*Sì.*"

"I would have liked to be able to see it on you at least once," Minnie said.

"You will. At the wedding."

"As long as you don't gain any weight," her father added.

Emma didn't grace that with a response. Her appearance, weight, choices in clothing, makeup, and hair had always been something her parents monitored closely. She could only wear the best of the best, be done up in the most beautiful ways—by the most talented people—and she had to always look the part.

It could mess with a girl's head.

Emma didn't allow it to mess with hers.

"I'm sure Emma will look wonderful," Minnie said.

George scowled. "She better. She's representing the whole family by marrying into the New York bunch. This is important, Minnie."

Emma felt a lump rise in her throat. It kept her quiet, even though she wanted to shout as loudly as she could about how little she really cared for the importance of her arranged marriage. It wasn't like her parents would care. Her feelings weren't important.

That was how the mafia life worked. A woman had to be blind to the things she didn't want to see, happy about the things that made her sad, deaf to the murmurs down the hall, and oblivious all the times in between.

"She knows it's important," Minnie said quietly. "Worry not, George."

George passed Emma a silent look that somehow managed to chastise and warn her without even saying a word. "Well, I believe she does. We raised her, after all. Affonso wants a well-behaved, pretty-faced, young woman to stand at his side ..."

Well-behaved. Pretty-faced.

Emma's body went cold all over.

"... and no one can say that we didn't raise our girl to be a good mob wife," George finished. "She knows the score. Don't you, Emma?"

"Yeah, Dad. I know the score."

George smiled. "That is all that matters, sweetheart."

• • •

In her hand, Emma held the Queen of Diamonds and the King of Spades. On the table, another queen, king, and two aces had been flipped over by the dealer.

Emma tossed another two-hundred into the pool, raising the bet. The pile in the middle was now a foot wide and a couple of inches high. The other four people at the table had folded with scowls at missing a large pot.

Calisto was still in.

Emma watched him from across the table, and

ignored the other four pairs of eyes on her. She had been whooping their asses throughout the game, but this one hand had left her chips dwindled down to a few hundred and not much more.

Calisto was clearly going for broke.

Or he wanted to make her go broke.

"Bet, check, or show," Emma said, grinning. "We don't have all night here, Cal."

Chuckles passed around the felt top, leather-lined table. Emma rested back in the high-back leather chair, still uninterested in the other players.

Under his dark lashes, Calisto's eyes lifted to meet Emma's. Amusement danced in his gaze while his face remained impassive and unreadable.

Then, his hand lifted. He stroked his bottom lip with his thumb.

Emma had watched Calisto enough throughout the game to know that was one of his tells. Every poker player had them. Some didn't even know, despite trying hard to keep from showing their tells to the other players. Sunglasses were common, as were ball caps. Some women even liked to play with fresh Botox done, simply because then they couldn't show even an ounce of emotion at the table.

It brought a whole new meaning to "poker face."

Touching his lip was one of Calisto's. It usually happened when he was forced to consider his next moves, or he was weighing the cost of continuing on. Emma had seen him win with a great hand after showing that specific tell, or lose a decent pot after doing it.

"All in," Calisto murmured.

Emma's stare snapped up, finding Calisto watching her intently. His murmur had passed over the table with the slowness of a crawl to reach her spot. And when it got to her …

She shivered.

Pushing aside the inappropriate lust circling in her

gut, Emma focused on the cards in her hand again. She checked the table once more. Three-pair didn't exist in poker. A player had to choose their best pairs and then use the next highest card as a kicker.

King and queen in her hand. Two aces, a king, queen, and Three of Hearts on the table.

Pair of aces.

Pair of kings.

Queen as the kicker.

The lower number card on the table wasn't important. It wouldn't do her any good.

Her hand was good.

It was Calisto's she wondered about.

Emma decided to take the chance. She answered Calisto's raise to the bet by pushing in the rest of her own chips. The dealer waved at the last two playing from his respective spot behind the table.

"Go for it, Emmy," Calisto said, smirking in that way of his. "Let's see what you've got."

Technically, she could have made him flip over his cards first, but she didn't mind showing her hand on the table. Turning over her hand, she showcased the pairs she had and the kicker to top it off.

An older man whistled at the end.

A woman in a tight, red dress with matching hair leaned closer to Calisto with a slow smile spreading over her flawlessly done face. Emma could see the woman's arm lift slightly at her side and then lower back down. Had she touched Calisto?

The woman ... had she put her hand on his leg?

Higher, even?

Something tight and hot balled in Emma's stomach, making her angry and sick all at the same time. Leaning even closer, the woman's blood red lips moved in a whisper as she said something to Calisto. Emma barely refrained from snapping at the woman to remove her hand from wherever it was on Calisto's body, but only because she knew it wasn't her right.

Calisto wasn't hers.

Emma didn't get to claim him.

Her jealousy still seared through her heart, flaring and growing like a wild fire that had found dry land to devastate. She swallowed back the ache it caused, pretending like it wasn't there at all. Acknowledging it would only lead to bad things.

Emma found that Calisto was still watching her from the other side of the table in that silent, intense way of his. A way that said he knew exactly what was going on inside her head and the war that she was feeling in her heart.

Why did he have to do that?

The woman was still close to Calisto, leaning in with her hand under the table somewhere on his body, and talking like she was trying to gain his attention. Calisto wasn't giving the flirting woman a damn thing.

In fact, his attention was all on Emma.

Waiting ...

It unnerved her.

Then, he tossed out his cards with a two-finger wave. Two aces faced upwards, and the table erupted in noise. Four of a Kind—aces, the best Four of a Kind for a poker hand. Emma was out her chips—all of them—and Calisto had played her right off the table.

Fuck.

Calisto had played her well.

Emma stared at the cards, amused and annoyed at the same time. She ignored the cheers of the other players as they congratulated the winning hand and how well it had gone down. She was too busy gazing between the cards and Calisto's knowing grin.

A sexy grin.

Sexy as sin.

Calisto was still ignoring the other woman. The dealer moved the pile of chips toward Calisto with a hooked baton. A lovely ache settled between Emma's thighs as Calisto began to organize his chips.

Her hands were over.

She was out of chips.

Strangely, Emma didn't mind losing to Calisto Donati.

This time, anyway.

• • •

Emma leaned against the entrance wall of the casino, swallowed by the flood of patrons moving in and out. Across the golden decorated, overly ostentatious foyer of the venue, Calisto stepped up to the chip desk. He dropped a satin bag, handed out to the guests when they needed to carry a load of winnings to be verified and cashed in, on the desk. He rested against the desk, and by the looks of it, barely spoke to the woman behind the counter as the chips were taken and dumped into the electronic sorter and counter.

Like this, behind Calisto and far away where he didn't know Emma was watching, she had an entirely different view of the man.

An easy posture. A lazy smile. Drumming fingers. His left foot hooked behind his right ankle as he waited. Relaxed shoulders.

Instead of the seemingly aloof, unapproachable right-hand man to Affonso, Calisto now seemed his twenty-seven years, loosening up and having a bit of fun for an evening. Nothing more, nothing less.

Appearances certainly were deceiving.

Any woman would probably see Calisto and think he was a charming, handsome man. If the woman were lucky enough, maybe she could catch his eye. A man like Calisto, one that radiated confidence, intrigue, and sexiness all in one wave, was impossible to ignore.

He demanded attention.

DONATI BLOODLINES: PART 1

But he didn't seem like he noticed.

Calisto had changed from the jeans and leather jacket attire he'd sported earlier in the day when he had interrupted her dress shopping. Tonight, he'd opted for a flat black suit with sharp lines and perfectly tailored hems. All black, actually. Black, like the color of his dark gaze, something else about Calisto that Emma noticed drew people in closer to him. The sort of darkness that made people wonder, like little moths flying straight toward a brightly burning flame, wanting to touch the pretty colors only to be burned into nothing but ashes. From the dress shirt underneath, the tie with a straight, tight knot, to the pants and Italian leather shoes he wore, everything was black.

And the man looked good in it.

Really good.

She bet he thought dressing in dark clothing would allow him to blend in more, but she thought it made him stand out.

Calisto was trouble waiting to happen.

She could feel it in her blood.

So why couldn't she bleed the curiosity out?

Emma averted her gaze, hoping that if she quit watching Calisto—and wondering about everything little thing that surrounded him—maybe that would help.

Surprise.

It didn't.

Sighing harshly, Emma pushed off the wall. She fixed the skirt of her dress, readying to meet Calisto when he was done cashing in his chips. He hadn't seemed all too concerned earlier when she left the table. Emma figured he would only have to play a few more hands to knock out the other players in the poker game, take his winnings, and run with it.

She'd been waiting for an hour.

Briefly, the jealous flare she'd felt when watching the woman try to flirt with Calisto came back to Emma with a vengeance. Had that been what took him so long? Had he taken the woman up on some kind of offer? Was that his reason for taking an hour, instead of the maybe twenty minutes it should have been to end the game?

Why do you even care?

Emma brushed off her inner voice. Other than being mocking or confusing, her instincts weren't helping her out all that damned much lately. Especially not where Calisto Donati was concerned.

She knew right from wrong, though. That was the important part. It didn't matter what Emma felt for Calisto, it was still wrong to act on it. It wouldn't make a difference that the man could make her heart race, her lungs stop breathing, or her blood heat up with a single look ... not when acting on the attraction would only put her in a grave.

And him, too.

Emma couldn't forget that.

Running her thumb over her finger, Emma felt the band of her engagement ring press against the pad of her digit. It was a good reminder of the weight already resting on her shoulders, and how she certainly didn't need to add any more to it.

Glancing up from the floor, Emma stilled in place. Calisto had turned around, cash in hand, and was watching her from across the casino's foyer. She stopped toying with her engagement ring instantly.

How long had he been watching her?

Calisto nodded toward the elevator as he shoved the small wad of cash into the inside pocket of his jacket. Emma thought the wad looked smaller than it should have been, considering what he won in that last pile.

It didn't matter.

He'd followed through on their deal of letting her try to make him go broke at the poker table. Emma had lost.

Fun time was over.

DONATI BLOODLINES: PART 1

Back to reality again, her mind taunted. She didn't even know what her reality was now.

Calisto met Emma at the elevator with one of those easy, smooth smiles that could make a woman wet just at the sight alone. The small flash of his teeth when his grin deepened and his gaze raked over her form let Emma know that she was not immune to the man's charms.

Was he purposely doing this?

Emma shook off the oddities and pressed the button for the private elevator. While there were several elevators in the casino, this specific one took patrons straight to their very expensive, and high penthouses. Once inside, all Emma would need to do was swipe her card and the elevator would take her directly to her penthouse apartment without stopping.

"Ready to call it a night?" Calisto asked.

Emma shrugged. "I'm out of cash."

"Oh? I thought you had a trust fund to dip into when you wanted."

"Nice. Cheap shots."

Calisto smirked. "I'm joking. Don't be bitter that I beat you."

"I'm not."

"Then what's with the pout, *dolcezza?*"

The elevator door opened, allowing Emma a reprieve from answering Calisto. She stepped inside, expecting him to stay behind like he usually did. This time, Calisto stepped in with her.

"What, you need to see me walk into the apartment tonight?" she asked.

"No," he answered simply.

Emma didn't press him for more information. "That was a good hand, by the way. I don't think I've ever pulled pocket aces like that."

Calisto chuckled. "Luck and nothing more."

"It takes a bit of skill."

"Sure. A damn good poker face will get you

everywhere. Bluff it until they fold it."

"Exactly." Emma shifted in her heels, aware of how close to Calisto she was in the small elevator. The mirrored walls let her see every angle of the man without even needing to turn. She simply had to look through her lashes and admire in silence. "Took you a while."

"Business."

"Oh?"

"Mmm. No good made man wins a decent sized pot in a Don's casino without paying the man some kind of tribute for the business. I found one of Maximo's guys and paid him a reward to deliver half of my chips to the boss's offices."

Emma blinked, stunned. It wasn't the woman in red that kept Calisto away for longer, or anything like that. "Oh."

Calisto glanced down at her. "What?"

"Nothing," she said quickly.

"You're lying."

"No, I'm—"

Calisto turned quickly, his hand coming up to snag Emma's wrist tightly in his palm. Heat siphoned immediately from his skin to hers, making her feel drunk and awake all at the same time.

"Lying," he interrupted. "Did you think I was going to leave you to do whatever while I was playing poker?"

"No."

"I didn't think you'd mind if I took a bit longer. You know the place, after all. You live here. What's the issue?"

Emma's cheeks pinked and she refused to look at him again. "Nothing. Leave it alone. It's not important."

Calisto's hand tightened around her wrist before he dropped it fast. "The woman at the table, was that it? You might as well have 'pissed off woman' stamped on your forehead, Emmy. What, did you think I kept you waiting so that I could get a quickie with that woman?"

Why did he have to be so astute?

Goddamn him.

"Did she offer?" Emma asked.

She knew better.

"She offered something. I wasn't interested. Does that make you feel better?"

Yes.

"Should it?" Emma asked. "What does it matter? It doesn't. I told you to leave it alone."

Calisto didn't answer. Emma peeked up at him through the shielded veil of her sharply cut bangs. The distance on his features was something she had seen him wear all too often. The confusion setting his mouth down into a frown was new, however. As was the sadness coloring his stare.

"It's not important," Emma said weakly. "It was a stupid, errant feeling that doesn't have any say on anything."

Emma didn't believe her own lies.

She had seen the way Calisto watched her at the table. And earlier in the day at the dress shop? God, she had the pleasure of seeing him stare at her then, too. Like he was fucking starved for something beautiful, and his hands had suddenly felt it the moment they touched her skin.

He'd comforted her, but he hadn't needed to.

He'd helped her, but it wasn't his job.

And it had been there—right there in his soul-black eyes.

Desire. Hunger. *Lust.*

Calisto wanted her, too.

Emma wasn't dumb.

"Not important," she repeated.

Maybe if she said it enough, it would make it true.

"Yeah," Calisto said gruffly. "You're right."

It still hurt.

10.

Emma

"Have a good evening," Calisto said quietly when the elevator dinged.

Emma stood unmoving, even with the sight of her penthouse apartment opening up before her. She was unsteady on her feet and unsure in her heart. A part of her wanted to ask Calisto if he would come in and have a coffee with her, talk, or … something. When the man was open and not being an asshole, he was enigmatic to her, drawing Emma in like a magnet. The other part of her, the rational one, kept her quiet and demanded she get out of the elevator.

"The elevator only stays open for so long, Emmy," Calisto added.

Her nickname coming out of his mouth sounded a lot more affectionate than she was willing to admit. He spoke it soft enough to make her think that maybe he cared. Emma couldn't get mixed up in that trap.

Whatever it was.

The elevator dinged and the door started to close. She still hadn't moved. Calisto reached out and stuck his hand over the sensor. He didn't drop his arm, so the elevator door wouldn't close until he did.

"You all right?" he asked.

"Thank you for the poker game," Emma said.

Calisto offered her a smile. "Don't thank me for that. I beat you, after all."

"But you gave me the distraction I needed. Losing the money was worth it."

"Well, then I guess you're welcome."

"You didn't need to come up with me, you know."

Calisto chuckled. "You said that already. And I know that I didn't, but I'm ready to call it a night as well."

It took Emma far too long to catch onto what Calisto meant.

"You have a suite in the hotel?"

"I have to keep an eye on you, don't I?"

Emma glanced away to hide her frown. "Sure, but this elevator is used for the expensive suites, not the regular ones."

Calisto nodded toward the other side of the elevator. "Once the door closes to your penthouse, I just have to swipe my card and the other side of the elevator will open to the penthouse apartment that was rented for me to use this month. Affonso wanted me to be as close as possible to you, instead of a few floors down like I was first situated."

"Oh."

"It also makes it easier on me with the hotel security," Calisto added. "They simply call through to my room to let me know the sensors are showing activity in your apartment in the mornings. It gives me a chance to get up and downstairs to meet you. I'm usually already up, but there have been a couple mornings when I slept in."

Her heart clenched painfully. A fast rush of anger followed right behind. Emma wasn't exactly surprised that Calisto had been situated directly across from her penthouse for the duration of his stay, but the security thing was new information.

She had no privacy.

The security in her penthouse apartment was meant for break-ins or other kinds of trouble. If there was unusual activity, she would get a call to ask if she was all right or needed help.

"They've been using my security system to alert you when I start to get ready in the mornings?" Emma asked.

Calisto's expression remained a blank slate. "Yes."

"Oh, my God. That's ... fucking ridiculous. It's my private space."

"No one expects you to like it, Emmy. That's

probably why you weren't let in on the secret. Nonetheless, it's what Affonso wanted. He demanded someone have eyes on you as much as possible. I couldn't keep watch if I didn't know something as simple as when you were leaving the penthouse in the mornings."

It didn't matter how Calisto tried to spin it, Emma still didn't like it. It left a bad taste in her mouth, not to mention she felt violated in a way.

"I haven't done anything wrong," Emma said, trying to keep her tone level and hide the anger flooding her heart. "I've followed the rules, stayed quiet, and did whatever that asshole wanted. Doesn't he trust me at all?"

Calisto cleared his throat. "You're a woman, Emmy."

"What does that have to do with it?"

"Affonso doesn't trust any woman."

Well, then.

Fuck him.

"Is this what my whole life is going to be like now?" she asked.

The sharp, rugged lines of Calisto's face softened when he smiled crookedly. Despite his small grin, sympathy flashed in his midnight-gaze.

"Without a doubt. It may seem like you're alone, but you never will be. I explained this to you once. Did you think I was lying?"

"No, but ..."

"Hmm?"

"I thought he would give me a bit of leg room to breathe. If all Affonso wanted to do was put me in a locked box, he might as well have just dragged me to New York when he left instead of leaving me here."

"Leg room?" Calisto asked. "For what, to let you run?"

Emma's fingernails bit into her palm when she squeezed her fists tight. "I never suggested I might run."

"I didn't say you would, either. Affonso thinks

differently."

"I'm really just a child to him, aren't I?"

"You're something else he can control, if that's what you mean."

Emma swallowed the painful lump in her throat. "Once I'm in New York, I'll still have a babysitter."

"You already know this."

"It won't be you, though."

Calisto tilted his head to the side slightly before saying, "No, it'll be whoever Affonso decides is the best to watch you. I have a job to do back home. And it doesn't include keeping an eye on you, *ragazza*."

But did he want it to?

That was the better question.

Emma didn't ask.

Steeling her spine and refusing to give away her inner turmoil, Emma smiled. What in the hell else could she do? "Thank you again, Cal."

Calisto nodded. "No problem."

"Goodnight."

Emma stepped out of the elevator and into her penthouse. Calisto dropped the hand covering the sensor the moment she was gone.

"Goodnight, Emmy."

She didn't look back at him when the elevator door closed.

• • •

Sleep didn't find Emma. She tried everything to clear her mind enough that she could forget about the day and rest, but nothing worked. Frustrated, she tossed and turned until she was on her back, and staring blankly up at the ceiling.

Emma didn't know how long she stayed like that. An hour, maybe more. The darkness of the bedroom would usually soothe her, but tonight it almost felt like it was taunting her. Staring at the ceiling helped to slow her racing thoughts enough that she could think.

In just a few days, she would be on a plane to New York.

A married woman.

Her life irrevocably changed.

Emma had done her best to ignore what was happening around her by staying out of things and keeping quiet. She couldn't do that anymore. The changes were staring her right in the face, about to take over, whether she was ready for it or not.

Slowly, Emma's thoughts began to drift in another direction. Calisto's handsome features filled her mind. She was still angry after what she learned earlier, but only because no one had thought to tell her sooner. What made her more confused, was how she was angry with Calisto for not telling her.

Calisto owed Emma nothing.

He was nothing to her.

And yet, she was still angry with him.

Thinking about Calisto while Emma was in bed was not a good thing. It was bad enough that her strange attraction to Calisto wouldn't let up no matter how much she wished it would. Being alone with thoughts filled with only him left her with an ache between her thighs that she couldn't settle or soothe. She shouldn't let a man that she couldn't even have affect her.

Calisto wasn't hers.

Simple as that.

Annoyed and unsettled, Emma shoved the blankets away and pushed out of the bed. Her bare feet hit the cold hardwood, and a chill filled her to the brim. Padding out of the bedroom, Emma made her way to the kitchen. She made a peppermint tea, hoping it would calm her nerves and let her sleep. As the tea steeped, she went in search of something chocolatey and sweet.

Indulging a craving seemed fitting.

DONATI BLOODLINES: PART 1

Her mother would have a fit if she knew Emma kept a secret stash of sweets hidden in the pantry of her penthouse. Heaven forbid Emma eat a cookie and gain five pounds.

Pressing on the slightly indented panel on the wall, the hidden doorway swung open under Emma's hand. The pantry was a five-foot by eight-foot section of the kitchen that Emma rarely used, as she didn't need the extra storage. Usually, she went out to eat more often than she cooked for herself.

Emma flicked on the pantry light, illuminating the space. She snatched the package of cream-stuffed chocolate cookies on the top shelf and turned to leave. The gray, metal door on the other side of the pantry caught her eye, stopping her from closing the pantry door.

It was the second exit to the penthouse. Fire code demanded that every suite in the casino which used a private elevator access have a second emergency exit, in case of fire or something else. The door led to a staircase that went up to a rooftop fire exit, or down to the ground floor where the underground garage was situated. Each fire exit locked from the inside and couldn't be accessed from the outside unless the master key was used.

Emma never thought about hers. She hadn't needed to use the door before. Her heart raced again, but she didn't want to allow herself to consider what using the door might mean.

Security would know she skipped out.

Wouldn't they?

Emma shook her wayward thoughts off. They were crazy, after all. She couldn't indulge errant ideas that would probably only get her into trouble. As she flicked off the light and closed the pantry door, Emma was still watching the metal fire door.

Stop it, she told herself. *It won't work. It's pointless.*

Emma hadn't even gotten back to her tea before the penthouse phone rang. She looked to the decorative clock hanging on the kitchen wall, noting it was well after midnight. No one should be calling her at this time. She made it to the phone on the third ring.

"Hello?" Emma asked into the receiver.

"Miss Sorrento, it's Mark from security downstairs. We noticed your sensors were showing activity and wanted to make sure everything was fine."

Emma blew out a breath and pinched her nose. She should have known. It wasn't like she wandered the halls of her penthouse every night, but that didn't help her agitation.

"Didn't you notice the sensors started to show movement from my bedroom?" Emma asked.

"Well, yes, but—"

"You must have known I entered the apartment earlier, went directly from my bathroom to the bedroom, and never opened the elevator to let anyone in," Emma interrupted.

Her anger bubbled up even faster than before. She knew it wasn't the security's fault. They were just following orders. She was still pissed off like nothing else.

"Yes, we did notice that no one had entered," the man said quietly.

"Then you had to know it was just me walking around in my own goddamn apartment."

"Yes, miss, we did."

"And yet you still called me," Emma muttered.

Mark spluttered for a response before lamely saying, "I apologize."

Emma gritted her teeth, again reminding herself that it wasn't this man's fault. Her anger didn't necessarily need to be directed at him. "Please let Calisto Donati know that I'm just wandering my halls and not trying to sneak out. I know you either have to call him, or already did. No need to make the man jump out of bed and get dressed for nothing."

"I'll do that right now," Mark said on the other end

of the call.

"Thank you."

Emma hung up the phone, leaned against the wall, and willed her annoyance to go away. When that didn't work, Emma grabbed the phone and pressed three digits. The call rang through to security, and the same man who had called earlier picked up.

"Miss Sorrento, hello. I apologize again for earlier. What can I do for you?"

"Put me through to Calisto Donati's penthouse suite."

"Uh … well, we don't really do that, Miss."

Emma scoffed. "I'm not sure that should make a difference to me, considering you give him a call every time I move from one room to another. You already told me you would call him. He must be awake. Unless he's got a visitor and I'm interrupting him, I want you to put my call through to his suite. *Now.*"

"Yes, miss. Hold for a moment."

A click resounded in Emma's ear a second before the call began to ring again. On the fourth ring, Calisto picked up.

"Donati speaking," he said.

Emma ignored the way Calisto's timber deepened even more over the phone. She hated how her body wanted to react to this man like he might be able to satisfy her if she just gave into the urges thrumming through her blood.

"Calisto, it's Emma. I just wanted to let you know I was wandering my place and decided to grab a snack because I couldn't sleep. I'm sorry if the security woke you up over nothing."

Calisto laughed. "It's fine, Emmy. I wasn't sleeping, anyway."

Damn.

Emma had asked the security if Calisto had a guest and the man didn't answer. Was that why Calisto wasn't sleeping? A ball of jealousy burst in Emma's gut. She refused to pay it any mind.

"I didn't mean to interrupt."

"You're not," Calisto replied quickly. "I couldn't sleep, either. After watching the shadows on the wall, I jumped into a cold shower to see if that would help."

A cold shower?

Weren't those only good for when a person needed to wake up or if a man needed to get his ... Emma shook her head, wanting to get as far away from those thoughts as possible.

Emma cleared her throat. "Oh. Well, I just wanted to let you know."

"No problem," Calisto replied easily.

"I'll let you get back to whatever. Good night, Calisto."

"Wait a second."

Emma held the phone tighter. She wanted to end the call instead of talking more. Adding to the little issue that she was attracted to Calisto, and curious about him, was not a good idea.

"Yeah?" she asked.

"Since we're both up with nothing to do, and I have a movie starting, do you want to come over and watch it? It's action, not some chick flick."

Yes.

Emma clamped her mouth shut to keep from shouting the word.

"It's just a movie," Calisto added when Emma stayed quiet. "You won't get in too much trouble for a movie, I promise. Let's just say the security of this hotel are a bit more partial to me than my uncle. I'm the one paying them the most for information, if you get my drift."

"Just a movie?"

"Sure. Car bombs, a bit of blood, and lots of guns. Unless that's not your thing and you prefer a sappy romance. If that's the case, I rescind my invitation."

"I like action movies," she said quietly.

"Do you have popcorn?"

"Who doesn't?"

"Bring it," Calisto said. "Press five-oh-four into the elevator. I'll let you in."

Before Emma could respond, Calisto hung up. Emma stared at the phone in her hand for longer than she wanted to admit. Putting the phone back on the hook, she wasn't sure what to do. A single night of innocent movie watching wasn't wrong. She wasn't doing anything bad.

Calisto offered, not her.

Emma grabbed her cookies, a bag of popcorn out of the cupboard, and her peppermint tea. Once she was inside the elevator, she pushed the numbers Calisto had told her, and waited. The elevator didn't move, confirming what Emma already knew. Calisto's penthouse was in fact situated directly across from hers.

The elevator door opened to a suite that matched Emma's in layout, but not in design. The earthy colors on the walls and the leather benches in the short entry hallway gave off a warm feeling while hers was white, bright, and sterile looking.

"Down here," Calisto yelled.

Emma followed his voice. Each step she took helped to take away what hesitance remained. It wasn't that she didn't want to spend time with Calisto.

She did.

That was the problem.

Spending time with him might feed her interest. It could lead her into something she couldn't handle. It might make something come of nothing, and then where would she be?

Fucked.

That's where.

Emma kept walking until she was in a black and white designed kitchen with stainless steel appliances. Calisto stood leaning against the island with a phone pressed to his ear, a coffee in his one hand, and nothing but sleep pants hanging low on his hips.

Her gaze couldn't be stopped as she took inventory of a bare-footed, naked-chested Calisto Donati. A light dusting of dark hair was sprinkled across his muscular chest. His railroad path of abs led straight down to the hard cut V of his groin. The sleep pants Calisto wore hugged his hips, but still rested low enough to showcase the trail of dark hair that traveled from below his navel and disappeared below cotton. Not only was the man tall, dark, and handsome, but he had a body that looked as if it had been chiselled from stone.

Emma's mouth went dry.

Jesus.

This was a bad idea.

"Yes, obviously I know she's left the penthouse. She's in my fucking suite," Calisto barked into the phone. "Seems you're really dropping the ball tonight if you can't even figure out the girl is just walking from one room to the next."

Calisto hung up the phone and put it on the counter. Then, he flashed Emma a sinful smile that was enough to make her gut clench and her cheeks get hot.

Bad all over.

"Ready for a movie?" he asked.

Emma was going to ask him if he would put some clothes on. She knew it was the right thing to do. Hugging her peppermint tea close to her chest, and grabbing the cookies and popcorn tighter, she decided not to say a thing. As long as she didn't act on her thoughts, she was doing nothing wrong.

"Yeah, sure."

11.

Calisto

"That's not even possible," Emma said, laughing. "The least they could do is make it believable."

A small sports car on the movie swerved in and out under an eighteen-wheeler as the hero of the flick attempted to retrieve his kidnapped girlfriend whilst in the middle of a high-speed chase. Calisto chuckled at the absurdity of it all. Emma had a point. The scene wasn't exactly realistic, considering the hero was also shooting a gun out of the driver's window while he did the dangerous maneuvers. Earlier in the movie, the man didn't even know how to handle a weapon.

"It's the action and drama of it all," he explained.

"Still a little over the top."

Calisto conceded to her point. "Fine, but you're ruining the movie for me, so be quiet."

Emma winked, grabbed a handful of popcorn, and pretended like Calisto hadn't said a thing. She had set herself up on the other end of the couch, as far away from him as she could get. She had taken the blanket from the back of the couch, used it to cover up with, and tucked her legs up close to her chest. She had been acting strange since she first came in, not saying much and staying a few feet away from him at all times. She wouldn't meet his gaze when she did talk. It wasn't like the Emma he knew.

Calisto couldn't help but wonder if there was something wrong with Emma. The tension in her voice when she had called him earlier prompted Calisto to ask her over for the movie, and nothing else. No, absolutely *nothing* else.

Definitely not the dream starring Emma on her knees, the one that woke him up with his cock aching, hot, and hard in his palm. He'd woken, stroking himself in his sleep over the cotton pants he wore.

Again.

Because it wasn't the first fucking time.

The visual of Emma below him with her pink lips open and her eyes on him, ready to beg, had been downright sinful. Calisto had quickly gotten into a cold shower, needing to relieve the tension and cool the fuck down.

He'd just jumped out of the shower when security called the first time to say there was movement throughout Emma's penthouse. The fucking fools from security knew that no one had entered Emma's place, so they had no business calling her just to "check up," as they said. Calisto was sure that was ninety percent of her somber, strange mood. No one wanted to be reminded they were constantly being watched.

"You all right?" Calisto asked.

Emma didn't look away from the television. "Yeah. Why?"

"You're quiet."

"It might surprise you to learn this, since you don't actually know me and all, but I'm not a very loud person, Calisto. I like being by myself more than I enjoy company, and I prefer the quietness of night to the loudness of the daytime. Just because you found a few pictures of me online enjoying the nightlife doesn't mean I'm not more comfortable by myself. I can enjoy both things for different reasons. Appearances are deceiving. Don't judge a book by its cover and all that."

"Huh." Calisto grinned. "Imagine that."

Emma glanced over at him, her green eyes lighting up with mirth. "What's so funny?"

"I like being alone and I prefer the dark, too."

"Oh."

"Yeah."

They had more in common than Calisto first thought. They were simple things, to be sure, but those were the best kinds of interests to share with someone else. Someone who a person could be alone in a room with and not need to fill the silence. Someone who understood that sometimes a person just needed space to think.

Those kinds of people were rare.

"Thank you," Emma said softly.

Calisto watched the television, but kept one eye on Emma. "What for, *dolcezza?*"

A tiny, but still sad, smile curved Emma's lips. "For inviting me over. I was going to ask you in for coffee earlier, but it didn't seem appropriate."

"I would have come in, had you asked me."

Emma sighed. "Exactly."

Calisto didn't have the first clue what she meant. He chose not to press her for an explanation. Emma turned back to the movie without another word. She sunk lower under the blanket like she needed it for some kind of protection or something.

He had news for her.

Calisto would have to be a fool not to see how beautiful and vibrant Emma Sorrento was, but he wasn't a stupid man. Emma was spoken for—not yet fully claimed, but taken all the same. She was off-limits in a major way. Calisto wasn't dumb enough to get caught into that game.

His cock thought differently.

His brain, however, was on point.

Emma was a no-go zone.

Men who thought with their cocks got exactly what they deserved. Calisto wouldn't be one of them.

"We might as well make nice," Calisto said after a moment.

He could practically feel Emma's gaze burning into him. Sure enough, when he glanced to the side, he found her watching him under her thick lashes. The devil on his shoulder urged him to snag the blanket and pull it off so he could see the tank top and cotton shorts she wore, but Calisto beat that bastard down.

"And why is that?" Emma asked.

"In a week, we'll be family. Better to make nice with family than to avoid them. It makes for awkward dinners and holidays if you don't care for anyone."

Emma's teeth caught her bottom lip. Calisto eyed the plump, wet flesh. The tip of his index finger itched with the urge to reach up and free Emma's lip from her abuse. Somehow, he decided against it.

Too intimate.

Not appropriate.

He shouldn't care at all, let alone be thinking of things like that.

Thankfully, Emma released her lip from the bite. "I thought you don't like Affonso."

Calisto shrugged. "I don't. Not in a friendly or familial sort of way. I admire him as a boss, of course, but little else. The one reason he gets my respect at all in that regard is because of my raising. I was taught to honor and protect Cosa Nostra, no matter what. I chose this life, and so I live with what it means."

"But you don't want to."

"I beg your pardon?"

Emma cocked a brow like she was taking him in for a second time. "Your words imply that on a personal level, you have little to no respect or admiration for your uncle. On a professional level, you give him what he deserves because of his title and nothing more. To me, that says you don't actually want to do any of it, but you do it because you have to."

Smart girl.

Calisto went for a deflection. "Didn't your father ever teach you to stay out of the affairs of men?"

"Sure, but that doesn't mean I always listen. Plus, I came from George Sorrento. He had to know I was going to be a little bit like him in some way. Where do you think my curiosity comes from?"

"Curiosity kills."

"That line is old, Calisto. Get a new one."

Calisto laughed loudly, unable to hold it in. "Nice."

Emma smiled sweetly, but it managed to look entirely evil at the same time. "I try."

"Fine, I'll give you that. You're mostly right. I respect my uncle in business and *famiglia* only because I have to, not because I want to or think he actually deserves it."

"Would you tell me something else?"

"That depends on what you ask, Emma."

Emma tightened the blanket around her frame again.

"You do know that I won't rip the blanket off and defile you, right?" Calisto asked. "I have a bit of control left in me, despite the rumors."

"What rumors are those?"

"There's a few."

"Indulge me," Emma said.

Indulging her was the entire issue wrapped up with a sexy little bow. The more Calisto fed into conversation that opened his personal life up to Emma, the more she would know about him, and the closer they might feel.

Those were dangerous waters.

Calisto maintained a healthy distance from everyone in his life—from his family, to those he considered friends, to even his doctor, for Christ's sake. Keeping people at arm's length allowed him objectivity to their lives. He didn't get attached. There were very little, if any, emotions involved. That way, he wouldn't have to fight with moral dilemmas or personal bias, should something happen. And keeping people away allowed Calisto the peace of mind that no one could hurt him.

Affonso did that—made Calisto like that.

It was easier.

Deflect her, his mind demanded.

"I thought you had a question to ask," Calisto said.

Emma nodded. "I do. I'll get to it in a second.

Indulge me on the rumors about you first, Cal. I bet they're far more interesting."

Calisto ran his fingers through his hair, trying to soothe some of the tension creeping over his shoulders. "People like to talk when they don't know much about a person."

"Like they're trying to fill in the blanks."

"Just like that," he confirmed.

"And what do people say about you?"

"Nothing unusual. I'm good-looking, so I must have a handful of women on the side. Normal nonsense."

Emma picked at her fingernails. "Do you date a lot?"

"No."

"Let me rephrase. Do you have a lot of women you run around with?"

"I don't fuck anything with a pussy," Calisto said, knowing damn well how crude he sounded. "I'm not a saint, and I certainly like a good lay when I find a woman worthy enough to make the effort, but I don't make a game out of it. I don't have a list of names I like to add to."

"But people talk about you like it is a game for you."

Calisto hummed noncommittedly. "You could say that. They see me out with a woman, dancing with someone at a club, or—heaven forbid—I bring someone to dinner, and suddenly the rumors flare to life all over again. I don't have the time or give a damn enough to correct people. If they want to talk about me, they can go to it. I have better things to amuse myself with."

Emma frowned. "You're twenty-seven."

"What does that have to do with anything?"

"You're saying that you have had no serious relationships at all with any women?"

Calisto blew out a heavy breath. "You're awfully nosy for a quiet girl, Emmy."

"The word you used was 'curious,' actually."

"Same difference." Calisto reached for his beer on the end-table and took a drink. Then he put it back and said, "I've had five relationships over the last decade. None that were anything important or would go anywhere. Mostly the relationships came about in my younger twenties, and then I decided that it wasn't the right time to look for something like a wife."

"Why not?"

"Because I was being pressured by someone else's wants, not my own."

Emma leaned forward, letting the blanket pool to her waist. "So ... you've never been in love?"

Calisto barked out a laugh. "I'm not even sure that exists. But no. I was close to marrying someone once, but it went nowhere fast."

"Do tell."

"This is starting to feel like a therapy session."

"We're getting to know each other, Calisto. Nothing more."

"Right," he muttered heavily. "Last year, a few months before my mother died, I was introduced to the niece of a boss from a fellow family in New York. She was nice enough—pretty, knew how to behave, and she was exactly what Affonso thought would be good for me where a wife was concerned. That's probably why he brought her to my attention. I didn't really love her, I probably never would have, but I trusted her enough to think she would be an appropriate partner for what I needed. I wasn't even attracted to her, really, but I didn't need any of that to have a wife. I simply needed an Italian woman in good standing with *la famiglia* and the church."

Emma chewed on her inner cheek before asking, "So what happened?"

"My mother died. I learned some things. I decided to take a different path from that point forward. One that didn't include a woman that my uncle had handpicked for me, never mind one that couldn't even get my blood hot enough to want to fuck her. I think she was okay with it all, but then again, I never gave her a ring, a promise, or anything else. We just were."

"And then you weren't."

Calisto lifted a single shoulder in response because honestly, he didn't give a damn. "Anyway, she was the only person that I considered marrying. We had never even had sex, I wouldn't really call it a relationship, and my affection for her was limited to what she could provide me with in the future."

"I don't understand."

"A boss needs a wife. She would have given me the right standing for my family and Cosa Nostra when Affonso was ready to step down. But as I said, things happened and I decided to change direction accordingly. The marriage wouldn't have been about what I wanted, but rather, what someone else wanted for me."

"Someone like Affonso," Emma said quietly.

It wasn't even a question.

Calisto swallowed audibly. He could have lied, but he chose not to for reasons he couldn't explain. "Yeah, for someone like Affonso."

"So, that's what he meant."

"Hmm?"

"Affonso," Emma said. "He told me that if you would just do what he wanted, then he wouldn't need me at all. The boss, right? That's what he meant, wasn't it? If you would just give him the guarantee that you would take the seat, he wouldn't need to worry about his legacy carrying on in the mafia because someone from his family would take over."

"You answered your own question, Emma."

"In more ways than you know," she mumbled.

"What does that mean?"

Emma's lips pursed before she said, "My other question that I didn't ask. I was going to ask what it was that Affonso wanted you to do that you wouldn't do for him. I can safely say I know the answer to that now."

Calisto smirked. "Yeah, that's what I won't do for him."

"Why not? It's a family thing, isn't it? Maximo's father was the boss before him. Affonso's father had been the boss, and it was your father afterward. Don't you want to carry on that legacy?"

"No," Calisto said honestly.

"Why—"

"You're making a lot of noise and making me miss the movie, Emma."

Her mouth snapped shut with an audible crack. Calisto could practically feel her glare burning into him, but he pretended like he didn't notice a thing was different. As quickly as their conversation had started, it was over. Calisto needed it to be this way.

He had to stop her before she got too far; before she dug too deep. Those scars needed to stay covered.

"Can I ask one more thing?" Emma asked in a whisper.

Calisto sighed. "Shoot."

"Why won't you give Affonso what he wants?"

"Isn't it obvious?"

"No."

Calisto glanced to the side, meeting Emma's gaze head-on and unabashed. "Because it's what the bastard wants, Emmy. I've already given him far more than he deserves. I won't give him any more."

Emma settled back into the couch without saying another thing. Calisto was grateful that she had dropped the subject and seemed content to finish out the movie. A few minutes passed them by in silence. Calisto rotated between his beer and the bag of popcorn between him and Emma.

Then, quieter than her earlier whisper, Emma said, "I don't know what it is about you, but you make me curious, Calisto. I'm not actually like this all the time."

Funny.

She made him curious, too.

• • •

Calisto woke to bright light, his back aching, and the shriek of the suite's phone ringing in the background. Groaning, he shielded his eyes from the sunlight streaming in through the windows. On the end-table, he counted the six bottles of beer he'd downed during the two movies he'd watched with Emma before he realized she had fallen asleep on the other end of the couch.

Her cute little snores had been enough for him not to wake her. He must have fallen asleep, too, considering the television was flashing a blue screen to show the movie was over. Glancing to the side, Calisto found the couch empty and the blanket that Emma had been using was tossed over the arm.

"Shit," he muttered.

Pushing up from the couch, Calisto went in search of the goddamn ringing phone. He checked his watch as he strolled into the kitchen with bleary eyes. Six in the morning.

Jesus.

In the last three weeks that Calisto had been watching Emma, he hadn't known her to wake up earlier than eight. Maybe he should have woken her up the night before and gotten her back to her penthouse and into her bed.

Calisto found the cordless phone under a dish towel on the kitchen island. That confused him more than anything. He was ninety-nine percent sure that he had brought the phone into the living room the night before after talking to security, getting the popcorn set up, and turning the movie on. It shouldn't have been in the kitchen, and it definitely shouldn't have been covered by a dish towel.

He didn't get a chance to answer the call before the ringing stopped. Calisto cursed under his breath again, noting it had been security calling. Quickly, Calisto hit the three digits for the fools downstairs and waited for someone to pick up.

"Good morning, Mr. Donati."

"Morning," Calisto grumbled.

It wasn't a good morning. He was still tired, he probably shouldn't have chugged six beers in a matter of a couple of hours, and his back still hurt from sleeping in an upright position on an uncomfortable couch.

Fuck the good morning.

"Someone called two seconds ago," Calisto said. "What did they want?"

"Actually, we've called three times. Someone was just getting ready to come up and wake you."

Calisto blinked and then rubbed at his eyes. "Sleeping off a rough night. Sorry about that. Is she up and around?"

"That's part of the reason we were calling. We noticed about a half hour ago that your sensors were activating from room to room before Miss Sorrento entered the elevator and went into her own suite. Approximately ten minutes later, the emergency door exit in her pantry was activated. We assumed you were awake as well because of the sensors in your suite, sir."

It took Calisto far too long to realize what the man was saying.

"Wait one goddamn second," Calisto muttered. "Are you telling me that you didn't begin calling me the moment she stepped into the elevator and then entered her penthouse, like you're supposed to?"

"Well, sir ... You see, after last night, the morning shift was left a note that we weren't to bother you with seemingly unnecessary calls. And again, we assumed you were also awake and knew that she was, too."

"It's morning! She entered her place alone! Yes, that is a necessary call." Calisto's agitation bubbled just below the surface. He was two seconds away from telling the fool right where he could shove his fucking note. "The exit door, you said?"

"Um, yes, sir. About ten minutes ago. We started calling you the moment it was opened."

Calisto didn't berate the man on that issue. It was his own damn fault for drinking before sleeping.

"Thank you," Calisto said.

He hung up the phone, tossed it to the kitchen table, and made a beeline for the only bedroom in the suite. The moved phone and dish towel suddenly made sense to Calisto as he searched for his suddenly missing car keys. His suit jacket was hanging off the chair where he left it, along with his dress pants. The keys should have been in the inside pocket, but they weren't.

Cristo.

Affonso would have a fit.

Calisto would be responsible.

Emma must have moved the phone. She likely tried to muffle the sound with a towel so that when it rang, it wouldn't be loud enough to wake Calisto. She probably took his keys as well.

Sneaky.

Damn, he had to admit it was a good play.

Emmy, you crazy girl ... What are you doing?

12.

Calisto

Balancing the phone on his shoulder, Calisto hastily buttoned up his suit jacket. "Allow me entrance into Emma Sorrento's penthouse, now."

"Yes, sir," said the security.

Calisto stepped into the opened elevator, pressed Emma's room number, and waited for the fools downstairs to approve his request for entry. Finally, the doors on the other side of the elevator opened after his side closed.

"Thank you," Calisto said into the phone. "And one more thing."

"What's that, sir?"

"Should Affonso Donati or Miss Sorrento's family call today wanting updates on her arrivals and departures, please make sure to keep this little incident under wraps. There's no need to go worrying them over nothing. I will handle it."

"Absolutely, sir."

"Good."

Calisto hung up the phone and stepped into Emma's quiet penthouse. His reasons for wanting to keep Emma's disappearing act a secret was obvious—she probably panicked and ran when she thought there was an opening, and Calisto was not going to be the fool who put his head on the block for her foolishness.

He got the girl, as far as that went. He didn't blame her for wanting to get away, or wanting to be free of what her future held, but he couldn't help her there.

Letting her run meant sacrificing his life.

Calisto wasn't quite ready to die yet.

He had to give Emma credit where it was due. This escape plan of hers had to have been a spur of the moment thing, considering she couldn't have known he would invite her over the night before. For a quick getaway, she had done okay so far.

Running was one thing.

Hiding was quite another.

Calisto put his cell phone inside his pocket as he strolled into the main area of Emma's penthouse. The clean, bright atmosphere of the place was magnified in the morning light. White marble floors and eggshell-toned walls lit up under the sunlight filtering in through the large floor-to-ceiling windows.

"Emma, Emma, Emma," Calisto murmured under his breath as he took a look around. "Tell me where you've gone, sweet girl, and make this easier on both of us."

He made a beeline for the bedroom that he knew belonged to Emma. After having spent the better part of the past few weeks packing things in her apartment with the help of a moving company, Calisto felt comfortable enough to know which rooms had been designated for what purpose.

In the bedroom, he found a mess. Clothes, what little Emma had kept for the duration of her stay in Vegas, had been tossed on the floor and discarded. The closet door was opened far enough for Calisto to see that Emma had taken one of the four designer suitcases out and left the other three behind. She'd taken the smallest one.

Just enough to pack a couple of things, he realized.

That explained the mess.

Even the small jewelry box on top of the dresser looked like someone had been rifling through it.

In the attached bathroom, the countertop looked like it had exploded products over the top. Calisto recognized a few obvious things that were missing from the mess. A toothbrush, hairbrush, and a small toiletry kit that Emma had asked him to tell the movers to leave alone so she could keep using it.

The scattered products didn't bother Calisto as

much as the writing on the bathroom mirror did. In red lipstick, Emma had written one word with hard strokes.

Sorry.

Calisto rubbed at his forehead, sighing. "*Cristo.* You're going to make me do this, huh, Emma?"

Irritation churned in Calisto's gut. He hated to admit it, but he was bothered by the fact that Emma had tricked him like she had. After the night before, he thought that maybe the two could be friends, and he would be able to ignore the strange attraction. At least to the point where he could be appropriate and respectful to his uncle's soon-to-be bride.

Emma played him.

Hard.

It pissed Calisto off like nothing else.

On the other hand, he also couldn't deny the concern bubbling up right behind the anger. Emma had little to carry her. No money without approval and no vehicle that wasn't able to be traced. She had only enough clothes to use for a few days, and frankly, Calisto didn't believe the girl had enough street smarts to stay low and out of sight for the amount of time she would need to get away safely.

It was bad, all the way around the board.

The cell phone in his pocket rang, bringing Calisto out of his warring thoughts. Hitting the answer button, he put the phone to his ear and said, "Donati speaking."

"Mr. Donati," the familiar voice of the security guy said, "we've got two visuals on Miss Sorrento before she was able to leave the building. We thought you might want to know what route she took to leave the casino."

"She took the exit. That's what you said."

"Yes, sir, but she had several levels down below that she could have entered from. The exits for the penthouses can only be unlocked from inside the rooms, and not from the stairwells, like the hallways below."

"You're wasting my time with nonsense. Hurry the

fuck up."

"Sorry," the guy muttered. "We first got sight of her coming out of the exit inside the underground parking garage on the third level."

Calisto's fist tightened around the phone. "Is that so?"

"Yes, sir."

"And the second visual?"

He really didn't need the guy to say it. Calisto knew what was parked on the third level of the underground parking garage.

"The parking garage camera caught her unlocking the black Mercedes parked in your parking spot, sir," the guy said quieter.

Calisto clenched his teeth hard enough to make his jaw ache.

Goddammit.

Clearly, the girl wasn't playing around. She's stolen his keys, likely thinking that she would leave him without means to chase after her. It was one hell of a risk, though, as most rental cars had GPS in them to track the vehicles. The Mercedes did have GPS in it, but it would take Calisto half of the fucking day just to get the information on locations from the company.

Not to mention, if he did call for the GPS locations, the car would be reported as stolen by the rental company. Calisto couldn't risk the chance of police becoming involved. There would be no hiding what Emma had done.

It would be better for everyone involved, Emma included, if Calisto could manage to get her back quietly, safely, and without issues. Even better if no one knew it had happened at all.

"No other visuals caught on camera?" Calisto asked.

"Just the final one of the Mercedes pulling out of the parking garage and leaving the property. She took an exit that was unmonitored by security."

Smart girl.

"Thanks for the update. Remember what I said about those calls."

"Our lips are sealed, sir."

"Wonderful," Calisto said.

"Is there anything else we can help with?"

"Actually, yes. I know the casino's hotel has vehicles on standby for the wealthier guests to use, should something come up and their rentals are unavailable. What do you have on hand at the moment that is dark-colored and can make zero to sixty in less than three seconds?"

"Um …"

"That is not an answer. If money is an issue, you can charge it to my card."

"No, that's not the problem. I would have to check. We had a couple come in this morning after checkout time."

"It'll take me fifteen minutes to get down to the garage, right?" Calisto asked.

"About that, yes."

"Have a car waiting when I get down there. Make me wait for one, and you'll be explaining to a guest why the closest dark-colored, fast car was stolen for a joy ride. Understood?"

The man on the other end cleared his throat uncomfortably. "Yes, sir."

"Great. Fifteen minutes."

He ended the call, feeling more frustrated than before. Stepping out of the bathroom and back into the bedroom, the upended jewelry box caught Calisto's attention once more. He made his way over to the dresser and riffled through the bits of jewelry to see what was there.

The engagement ring that Affonso had given Emma rested on the top of the pile. So did the bracelet and pendant necklace. Calisto took inventory of the room and the belongings scattered about once more. This time, he looked at it with new eyes.

Almost everything Emma left behind was from Affonso. The clothes, fur coat, and new shoes. Her jewelry, the new laptop on the bed, and the paperwork for the spa were tossed onto the corner chair.

When they had packed up the place with the moving company, Emma hadn't left very much except for a few outfits and things she wanted to physically take to New York herself. Calisto was only now seeing the items as Emma must have when she decided to run.

These things weren't hers.

She didn't want them.

Emma didn't want Affonso.

An ache pulsed in Calisto's chest. It felt like someone had taken a knife, plunged it into his heart, and then twisted with all their might.

The girl just wanted to be free.

Calisto had to bring her back.

Jesus.

Why did this have to be so damned difficult?

Calisto knew the answer to his question. It wasn't just his odd desire for Emma that kept poking at his nerves every time she was close by, it was also his interest in who she was beyond the engagement ring, the last name, and her pretty little mask. He'd never been very interested in a woman before. The one to finally perk his interest just happened to be off-limits in a big way.

He wanted to let her run.

He *did*.

But he couldn't.

"I gave you a head start," he said to the empty room. "But that's just about all I can do, Emma."

• • •

Calisto pushed open the third floor emergency exit and entered the parking garage. Fifty feet away, a shiny, black Porsche was parked in the spot that should have belonged to his rented Mercedes. A young man leaned against the back of the Porsche with a set of keys dangling from his hand.

"Mr. Donati?" the man asked.

"That's me," Calisto replied. "And this car will certainly fit my purposes. Well done to the bastard that managed to get this for me."

The young man smiled and held out the keys. "Here you are, sir. The tank is full."

Calisto took the keys. "Thank you."

It took Calisto all of two minutes to get the engine roaring, bake the tires pulling out of the garage, and make his way toward the exit that Emma had taken to leave. He was just pulling up to the exit that would take him to the Strip when something out of the corner of his eye made him hit the brakes.

Calisto pulled over to the side, made sure to give anyone behind him lots of room to pass, and stepped out of the Porsche. He moved around the front of the car, stepped up onto the sidewalk, and found the item that had made him stop.

A black iPhone had been tossed to the manicured grass.

Calisto knew that phone.

It was Emma's.

He plucked the device up, noting how it didn't have even a scratch on it. It turned on perfectly fine. Unfortunately, the locked screen wanted a four-digit passcode to enter the phone. He shoved it into his pocket anyway.

As Calisto got back into the Porsche, he wondered why Emma had tossed the iPhone. She would need a way to contact someone if she needed help to move from one spot to another. It was her main connection to people.

Affonso had a new phone waiting for her in New York, but this one was untouched by the man's usual methods of tracking.

Unless, of course, Emma knew something that Calisto didn't where the phone was concerned. It was a good possibility that if it came from Emma's father or uncle, it might have a tracking chip or GPS app to map her whereabouts.

Pulling out onto the Strip, Calisto hit the gas hard. "Think, man. Where would she go first?"

Calisto dug for his phone and balanced it against the steering wheel with one hand while he drove with the other. He unlocked the device and scrolled through to his email. Opening the file he had pinned at the top so that he wouldn't lose it, Calisto kept one eye on the road and the other on the pages of information he had collected about Emma before he made the trip to Vegas.

School information.

Hangouts.

Interests.

Friends.

That's what Calisto wanted. He needed to know her friends, where they lived, and which one was the closest to their current position. Emma only had so many options to help her get out of Vegas, or stay quiet long enough to take the heat off her. Without cash to help her travel, or falsified documents that would keep her from being tracked by her family, she would be left with whoever would lend a hand to help her.

Trying to go through the list of names and information attached to Emma's list of few friends was difficult while Calisto attempted to navigate the unfamiliar roads. Despite being in Vegas for nearly a month, he still wasn't entirely comfortable driving in the city.

Calisto was glad he had saved the information about Emma. After learning more about the young woman his uncle intended to marry, Calisto considered tossing away the information as it was practically useless to him.

Apparently it wasn't.

DONATI BLOODLINES: PART 1

The phone vibrated and rang in Calisto's hand, nearly making him ram into the trunk of the vehicle ahead of him. The white Mustang in front of his Porsche laid on the horn and the driver gave him the middle finger.

Calisto stuck his own right back up for the asshole to see.

Fuck him.

Cursing under his breath at the phone number flashing on the screen of his phone, Calisto steeled his nerves for a chat that was sure to be *fun*, if he couldn't manage to lie his ass off.

"Hello, *zio*," Calisto said when he answered.

He put the call on speaker and tossed it to the cup holder. He couldn't afford to get pulled over by the police because he had a damned phone in his hand.

"Cal," Affonso greeted. "How's my favorite nephew this morning?"

"I'm your only nephew. What do you want?"

"Is the attitude really necessary?"

Yes.

"I'm driving, Affonso," Calisto said, not bothering to hide the tiredness in his tone. "I don't really have time to make small—"

"You always have time for your boss."

Calisto checked his attitude. "Yeah, I guess so."

"It's ten in the morning in Vegas. What are you doing driving?"

Somehow, a lie found its way out without hesitation. "Emma is meeting up with a girlfriend for brunch. I'm following behind."

"Brunch," Affonso scoffed. "Lazy woman's breakfast. Can you at least make sure she doesn't drink?"

"She's not legal."

"Were you legal when you first began drinking?"

"Point taken," Calisto muttered. "I'll keep an eye on her, like I have been doing."

"Perfect. You're missed back here, you know."

Calisto swallowed back the immediate retort he wanted to let out. The one that would tell his uncle no, he wasn't missed, he was simply not under Affonso's thumb. "Is that so?"

"Ray is picking up your slack," Affonso explained.

Ray Missotti, Affonso's underboss, was the other great pain in Calisto's life. If his uncle wasn't on his ass, then Ray was doing it for Affonso.

"I'll be home in, what, three days? Tell him to take a fucking pill. It's not like the man ever lifts a finger. It's a good lesson for him."

Affonso chuckled. "I already did tell him all of that. Nonetheless, that's my point. He hates running around for me and keeping an eye on things like you do. And besides, you do a better job of it."

"Three days," Calisto repeated.

It wasn't just a reminder for his uncle, but also for him. He had three damned days to find Emma, get her back with no one any wiser to her getaway, and catch the plane for New York.

A part of him wanted to let her run.

The other part knew better.

"Hard to believe that I'll be a married man once again in just a week," Affonso said more to himself than to Calisto. "You know, the offer is still there, Cal."

"What offer, *zio*?"

"The option to take over the family. My marriage doesn't make a difference to that. You can still—"

"I don't want to talk about this again," Calisto interrupted dully.

"I want my *famiglia* to keep my family name, Cal. We have been the Donati Cosa Nostra for five decades."

"Then make sure your next wife pops out a boy for you."

Calisto wished he could take the words back the very second they left his lips, but he couldn't. Strangely, the odd pain from earlier pierced his chest again at the idea of Emma birthing Affonso's children.

What in the hell was wrong with him?

"That's my plan," Affonso said, unaware of Calisto's inner battle. "And I'll have to stay alive long enough to put my boy on the right path."

Calisto chewed on his inner cheek before saying, "I'd look after him."

It was the truth.

Despite how much Calisto hated Affonso, he would take care of the man's children. For many reasons, but mostly because Calisto had been taught by his mother that no matter what, family came first. More importantly, it was Calisto's job to take care of those in his family who couldn't watch after themselves.

That's what a good man did.

Always.

Affonso was the only one Calisto didn't give that gift to.

"I know you would, my boy," Affonso said heavily. "You're good in that way."

Calisto smirked, tasting a bitterness on his tongue. "Yeah, I am."

"Give my hello to Emma. Make sure she keeps her nose clean. Not long now, and you can drop the babysitting act, Cal."

"Will do."

"*Ciao*, my boy."

Calisto didn't say goodbye before hanging up the call. Rubbing at the ache beginning to throb at the base of his skull, Calisto caught sight of a flashing neon sign.

Pawns. Electronics. Gold. And More.

He smirked again, and cut in front of the car trying to pass him to make the turnoff for the business with the flashy sign.

Chances were, that place took hot items. Almost all pawn shops did. Sometimes they would report it to police, but most times they didn't. Nonetheless, if the place would take electronics, someone in that shop knew how to unlock an iPhone without losing the information on it.

Hopefully.

Maybe there was a last call that Emma had made. Someone with info about where she had gone. Even better if whoever it was happened to also be in the list of names inside Calisto's files on the girl.

Calisto was willing to take the risk.

What else did he have to lose?

13.

Emma

"Poppy, you there?" Emma asked into the payphone.

"Emma?"

"Yeah. I told you that I would call you back."

"I know, but I just had—never mind, it doesn't matter. I thought you said you were getting rid of your cell phone, remember?"

Emma's brow furrowed. "I did. I tossed it right after we talked."

"Then why do I have a text from your phone from five minutes ago?"

Dammit.

Her phone required a locked passcode to get inside. The only way someone could send a text from it was if they had broken the lock or entered the correct passcode. Emma was positive that she had thrown her phone in a spot where Calisto wouldn't find it if he came after her.

She'd hoped ...

"You there?" Poppy asked.

"Yeah."

"Did you hear what I said about the text? Why is it there?"

"I don't know," Emma said quietly. "Did you respond?"

"Not yet."

Emma's anxiety climbed higher. "Don't. Okay?"

"Yeah, sure."

Outside the coffee shop, Emma took note of the lowering sun. A pink and orange sky highlighted the horizon, reminding her that it was getting late and she needed to find a place to sleep for the night. She had taken the few hundred dollars that was stored in the bottom of her jewelry box, and the two-hundred in twenties that she found in the glove compartment of Calisto's Mercedes, but it wasn't nearly enough.

Emma hadn't thought taking off would be easy, but she stupidly figured she would be able to at least get out of Las Vegas before nighttime came. She hadn't factored in where she would go, how she would get there after she left Calisto's car in a random parking lot, or what to do after.

She didn't have enough money. She had no way to get anywhere without spending what money she had. Her plans were failing. Fucking miserably.

She felt like an idiot.

Emma had seen the cordless phone unattended on Calisto's lap, thought security might screw up who was who in the apartment, thought about the exit door, and taken a chance. She hadn't stopped to consider all that would be involved in taking off without money on hand, or any real plans to go by.

Her lingering guilt about tricking Calisto, and leaving him on the hook to explain her sudden disappearing act, wouldn't let up. It was eating away at her, but Emma forced it to the back of her mind. She didn't have a choice but to leave.

She couldn't go to New York willingly.

No way.

"Where are you right now?" Poppy asked.

"Downtown."

It was the most Emma would give her friend. Poppy Johansen came from a well-to-do Vegas family that had a hand in a few casinos. Emma met her old friend during one of the many charity events her family attended.

"A good spot or a bad spot?"

"Kind of in between," Emma replied.

"Will you tell me what's going on now?" Poppy asked.

"Better you don't know. I just want to know if you can point me in the direction of someone who could help me, Poppy. That's all. I need a safe way out of Vegas without someone knowing it's me. Did you get any more info on that guy you mentioned this morning when I called?"

Poppy made a sad sound. "Are you running, Emmy?"

Emma sighed. "It doesn't matter."

"It does to me. What happened?"

"Things," Emma said vaguely.

"Is this about what your uncle does … the mafia and all that stuff?"

Emma didn't want her friend involved in those affairs. She didn't even want Poppy to think about it. It certainly wouldn't lead to anything good.

"Poppy, stop asking me questions. I need help without a fucking inquisition. Okay?"

"Yeah, okay, I get it."

"The guy—Mika, you said. Right?" Emma asked.

"I mean, that's what we've always called him, but he doesn't give out his last name."

That didn't sound good.

"You don't know his last name?"

"Well, when someone wanted a little something-something, they gave Mika a call and he would show up with whatever they wanted."

"Like drugs?" Emma asked.

"Yeah."

It wasn't uncommon. Rich kids didn't dabble in drugs the same way other people did. Their dealers weren't shady people on a street corner, or a guy leaning out of a low-riding car. Their dealers were typically on speed-dial, showed up in a suit, and didn't look out of place in a crowd of wealthy brats.

That hadn't been Emma's scene. She knew that sometimes Poppy indulged in substances. It wasn't for Emma to judge.

"But I don't think you want to go to him, Emmy,"

Poppy said after a moment.

"Why not?"

If the guy could get her out of town, Emma didn't give a fuck how he did it.

"I made some calls and asked around. Mika isn't in the business of dealing like he used to be. He's working with other people—bad people. Or so the word is, anyway. I can't confirm any of it since I haven't talked to Mika in a year."

"But if you could get a hold of him, would he do you a favor?"

Poppy blew out a quiet breath. "I used to date the guy. We ended it on okay terms. I think he would, but it doesn't sound good. What people were saying about him, I mean."

"Like what?"

"Not a lot. But when dealing goes from a good, solid source of income to something that's only whispered about, it can't be all that safe or great, Emmy. From the sounds of it, he stopped catering to the users and might be working with skin instead. That's not the kind of shit you want to be mixed up in, all right?"

Skin ...

The term didn't register to Emma.

"Yeah, but—"

"And he might come with a price," Poppy interrupted softer.

"I get it. You're worried. I just need some help. Will you help me or not?"

Poppy was quiet for a long time. Long enough that Emma thought her friend might have hung up the phone on her.

"Will you tell me what happened?" Poppy asked.

"I'll tell you that I'm running," Emma said instead.

"I'll give Mika a call. He had a private number for me to use that wasn't the same as his number for clients. Maybe he still has it. If not, then I'll make some more calls."

"Thanks."

"Call me in the morning. It's getting late. Try to get a decent hotel room for the night, eat something, and think this all over. I don't want you getting mixed up in bad stuff, Emmy," Poppy finished, sounding sadder than ever.

"Don't worry about me. I can handle myself. And hey, if your ex can get me out of the state without trouble, then I'm willing to turn cheek to whatever business he's got going on."

She'd spent her whole life turning her cheek, after all.

What difference did it make?

"Just be careful," Poppy said. "There was a reason why I broke it off with Mika."

"Why was that?"

"Because I was starting to think I didn't even know who he was."

Emma sucked in a slow breath.

She would take the risk.

"I'll call you in the morning, Poppy."

"Be safe, Emmy."

Emma hung up the phone, and took a moment to gather her thoughts. She might not have had a very good plan before, but she was going to start by putting together a better one now.

One step a time.

She decided to start by refilling her coffee, grabbing some soup and sweets from the café to eat, and then finding a decent hotel room that wouldn't cost her a lot to sleep in for the night. Grabbing the waiting bag down at her feet, Emma made her way to the register. She ordered the coffee and food, and then paid and waited for her order.

"There's a quiet, clean motel two blocks away," the cashier said.

Emma glanced up from the floor. "Pardon?"

The cashier nodded at the small suitcase in Emma's hand. "I'm guessing you're probably looking for a room, unless you've already got one. Sometimes we see a lot of last minute tourists come in and they don't have anything booked. Like I said, there's a decent place two blocks away. Tracy's Motel. It's not very big, but you won't have to worry about strange people or bad business."

Emma didn't realize that she looked like a tourist, but with the small luggage, it shouldn't have been a surprise that the cashier assumed she was one. It didn't matter. Emma now had an idea of where to go for a place to hide out for the evening.

The woman pushed the coffee and bag of food across the counter. Emma took it.

"Coffee is fresh, as I just made a new pot. You might want to warm up the soup when you get to the hotel, though."

"Thanks," Emma said.

"No problem. Have a good stay. Try not to sleep too much of it away. Vegas is the city that never sleeps, you know."

Emma laughed.

Yeah, she knew.

"Sleeping is the last thing on my mind."

That was truer than the cashier could possibly know.

Twenty minutes and a two-block walk later, Emma found the motel that the cashier had mentioned. The parking lot had a decent amount of vehicles, and the place seemed quiet enough for being in a poorer part of the city. At the front desk, Emma paid for a room, allowed the woman to photocopy her ID in case damages incurred during her stay, and left with a new key ring in her hand.

Emma walked up the stairs outside to the second level of the motel and found her room four doors down from the left. Once she had the door unlocked and was inside, Emma finally took a real breath.

She hadn't felt like she could breathe in hours. Not since she snatched Calisto's keys, made a rash decision with nothing but blind faith in her pocket, and ran.

Tossing her small luggage into the corner, Emma found a chair by the window and sat down. Her feet ached. She was pretty sure that she hadn't ever walked as much as she did today. Her first sip of coffee was heavenly.

Emma fingered the curtain covering the window, and pulled it slightly to the side so that she could look outside. Nothing seemed out of the ordinary. Emma still let the curtain fall back in place just in case someone—no matter how unlikely it was—might recognize her. She knew she was safe for the moment. Oddly, it didn't help the nerves crawling beneath her surface.

She had felt better when she knew Calisto was watching her back, as crazy as that was.

Had she made the right choice?

Could she do this?

Would it work?

Emma hoped so.

• • •

Hugging her middle, Emma stepped up to a bouncer guarding the door. She stood on the front steps of a club that she would never be caught dead inside. This kind of club was not the sort that her father or uncle would approve of.

A sign flashed overhead, showcasing a girl grinding mostly naked against a pole.

Emma remembered her conversation with Poppy earlier in the day, and what her friend had said about the strip joint.

Mika will be in the back. Let the guy inside know your name is Emma, and that you're there to see Mika. Make sure you mention that you're a friend of a friend, and bring up my name to Mika when you see him.

Poppy had also mentioned that Emma would know who Mika was on sight, and again repeated her worries that this might not be safe.

Emma didn't have a choice.

She was out of options.

Another night in the motel would cost her eighty dollars. She'd already paid for last night, and because she needed a place to leave her bags, she booked the room for another night. With food, plus the burner phone that Emma picked up after she grabbed breakfast, her cash was dwindling fast.

She wondered if her parents knew yet that she had skipped out. Or even Affonso.

Emma couldn't go back now.

She had to see this through.

"You gonna stand there all day looking up at the fuckin' sky like it's gonna fall in on you or what?" the bouncer asked, crossing his meaty arms and snapping the gum in his mouth. "Show me your ID or get the fuck off the step."

Emma blinked, stunned at the man's crudeness. "I'm here to see Mika."

"Is that so? What for?"

"A friend of a friend sent me. Business, you know."

Emma didn't have a fucking clue what business that was exactly, but apparently that's what she was supposed to say.

The bouncer snapped his gum again. His bald head and thick neck, mixed in with his barrel-shaped chest and trunk-like limbs, certainly made Emma want to take a step back from the man. Nothing about him screamed "nice" or "safe."

She supposed he was good for his job.

"What friend?" the guy asked.

"That's not for you to know, it's for me to tell

Mika," Emma said quickly.

The bouncer chuckled. "Good one, little girl."

Little girl?

Emma bristled, but managed to keep quiet.

"You look familiar," the man stated, checking her out from the shoes she wore to the jacket she was hugging. "Like I've seen you somewhere before."

How many socialite magazines did the guy read? That was the only place she might have graced this man's presence before.

She didn't say a thing.

"Mika, you said?"

"Yes," Emma replied.

"I'll give you a warnin' before you go on in there lookin' for Mika," the bouncer said.

Emma glanced up, meeting the man's gaze. "What's that?"

"Don't go in there lookin' for him at all. Mika don't mix business with pretty, clean things like you."

"Clean things?"

The bouncer reached out and snagged Emma's arm in his palm before she could react. He yanked the sleeve of her jacket up to her elbow and waved a finger over her unblemished skin.

"You've got no track marks in your arm and your teeth are good. You don't use, which means you don't need the kind of business Mika's got working in there for the girls needin' a fix. Do you get what I'm sayin', girl?"

No.

Emma was beginning to feel like she was far more sheltered in her life than she had previously thought. She had clearly stepped out of her element in a big way. This was not her side of the tracks, and the chill running up her spine reminded her of that fact as she stared down at her unmarked skin.

She didn't use drugs, but sometimes she had fun. She liked to frequent clubs, and her family had long since been considered one of the elite families in Nevada because of their wealth and status. She had seen people pop pills with their glasses of morning wine and hadn't blinked a lash.

What this bouncer was suggesting, however, made her skin crawl.

"I don't have much of a choice," Emma said honestly.

The bouncer smiled grimly, let go of her arm, and then opened the door to a dark hallway. "Well then, I guess all I can say is good luck. And don't you say I didn't warn you."

Emma quickly fixed the arm of her coat as she stepped inside the business.

"Keep going straight until you see the girls on the pole," the bouncer said from behind her. "You'll know Mika when you see him."

Just like Poppy had told her.

"Thank you," Emma replied.

The bouncer laughed dryly. "Don't thank me, girl."

Emma continued down the hall, ignoring the creepy vibe settling deep in her stomach. The closer she came to the end of the corridor, the more music and lights she could see. She barely reached the end before a stage was practically right at the outside of the door and a girl's ass was upside down, in the smallest G-string, and pointed in Emma's direction.

"Holy shit," Emma muttered.

She quickly side-stepped the stage and moved toward the bar where a few patrons of the joint sat on dingy, red-covered stools. She pretended like their stares didn't bother her as she walked in front of them and moved past another stage.

Obviously they weren't used to seeing fully-clothed women in the place.

Taking the floor in, Emma quickly found who she was looking for. Poppy and the bouncer had been right.

DONATI BLOODLINES: PART 1

Mika was obvious. He sat in a roped off area with a bottle of Patrón on the table, a game of cards in play with another man at the table, and four more men dressed in black guarding the section.

Mika, dressed in a black suit, looked completely out of place in the dive. His well-dressed appearance and lit cigar spoke of wealth, but the strip joint was seedy as fuck.

Hell, even Emma could see that.

What had she gotten herself mixed up in now?

Do it or go back, her mind taunted.

Emma took another step forward. Then she took another, and another. Finally, she was close enough to Mika and his men that one of the bodyguards put an arm out to stop her from going further.

"I'm here to see Mika," Emma told the man quietly.

Mika didn't even glance up from his card game. He didn't say a word.

"You're here to see nobody," the bodyguard told her.

Emma didn't budge. She directed her statement over the shoulder of the bulldog of a man. "Poppy says hi, Mika."

Mika smiled slowly as his dark gaze lifted to look Emma over. "Emma, is it?"

"Emma," she confirmed.

"Come have a drink, Emma."

It didn't actually sound like an offer. In fact, it sounded like Mika wasn't going to give her a choice at all.

Emma swallowed hard, feeling something terrible well in her gut. Instincts didn't lie, and something was telling her that she had made the wrong choice in coming here. She didn't know what it was, but as she looked around at the dazed girls dancing on the stage, the men surrounding Mika, and the predatory smile Mika leveled on her, Emma just ... *knew*.

This was bad.

"A drink," Mika repeated firmly.

The bodyguard stepped aside.

Emma felt a hand press on her lower back and push her forward.

Shit.

"I hear you need some help disappearing for a little while," Mika said when Emma was sat down in a chair at the table.

"Poppy said you could help to get me out of state."

Mika chuckled. "Oh, I can help with that."

Suddenly, a clear glass with red liquid was put in front of Emma. She eyed it, wondering what in the hell it was.

"Just a Sourpuss and 7 Up mix," Mika said. "Nothing to hurt you with. We'll talk first, and then I'll let you know where we go from there."

Emma nodded. "Okay."

"Drink, girl."

She picked up the glass and took a sip. It was sour, but it wasn't bad. Mika waved at the glass as if to tell her to take another drink. Emma did, but she was still trying to figure out a way to get the hell out of there without pissing someone off or offending them.

Mika and his guest resumed their card game without a word to Emma. She sipped on her drink, still gauging the high-looking dancers and the patrons to the venue.

"What does a girl like you need to disappear for, anyway?" Mika asked out of the blue.

Emma glanced up, but her vision swam. Her mouth felt dry, too.

"I ... I, uh," Emma tried to say, fumbling for her words.

Her arms were too heavy.

Mika smiled. "Nathan?"

Nathan?

Emma felt a hand land on her shoulder, keeping her upright. She stared up, only to find the bodyguard who had let her pass was standing over her, holding her shoulder.

"You should be careful who you trust," Mika told her quietly. "Poppy, especially. She's sweet as sin, but the girl is black in her fucking soul. It's why I love her. Her daddy would be so proud, I'm sure. Good man he is, donating to the poor and helping the women's shelters. I bet he'd die to know his little girl was helping to traffic skin like a pro. She's a damn good fisher, though. I bet you'll fetch one hell of a price tomorrow, Emma. I don't know who you are, but if you want to disappear, there's no better way than the underground auctions. You wanted to disappear, after all."

What?

Oh, God.

Poppy had warned her.

But she lied, too.

The betrayal made Emma's stomach twist.

Skin ...

Emma had heard of those things before—auctions. She was pretty damn sure of what Mika was talking about. Girls went missing, sold to whomever had the deepest pockets, and were never heard from again.

She thought it was rumors.

It made her blood run cold.

"Take a few deep breaths, or you'll end up puking all over yourself when you're out of it," Mika warned.

Before Emma blacked out, she thought of one person who might be able to help her. The one person she had tricked to get away, stolen his things, and probably pissed him off.

Calisto.

14.

Calisto

Time was running out.

Calisto glared at the digital clock on the dashboard, wishing he could make it fucking disappear. He had thirty-six hours to find Emma, get her back to the penthouse, and then put her on a plane to New York.

Thirty-six hours was not enough time.

He waited out a red light. How long was the damn thing going to stay red for? It seemed like everything was taking too long, when Calisto needed it to go a hell of a lot faster.

It took the pawn shop almost eight hours the day before to unlock Emma's iPhone without losing crucial information on the device. Calisto shoved the money across the counter when the guy said it was done, and ran out of the shop, already looking through the last calls that had been made.

Poppy Johansen.

Calisto had recognized the name the very moment it popped up on Emma's contacts. Poppy came from a Nevada socialite family, and toted a father worth a couple of hundred million, thanks to his casino bids. What the girl could do for Emma in a situation like this, Calisto didn't know.

He intended on finding out.

After trying to reach Poppy using Emma's and then his own phone, Calisto had decided to give up that route. Clearly, the girl wasn't answering. Emma had probably told her not to, which was a smart move.

For now …

But time had run out.

For him.

For Poppy.

DONATI BLOODLINES: PART 1

And for Emma.

Calisto had a little information on Poppy Johansen and he intended on using it. The address to her nice little penthouse had been in the pack of research Calisto collected on a few of Emma's close friends. If the woman wouldn't answer phone calls or text messages, then he would go to her.

Directly.

The ringing of his cell phone brought Calisto from his infuriated thoughts. He grabbed the device and hit the speakerphone to answer

"Yeah, Donati speaking," he said.

"Cal, I looked into that girl you asked about. Poppy Johansen, right?"

Calisto's irritation ebbed away slowly. "Great. Give me something to work with where she's concerned. I need her to talk."

"It might have helped me to get this done sooner if I knew what I was looking for," Norris said.

Norris happened to have a mighty set of skills where computers, hacking, and tracing was concerned. The guy mostly worked off the grid, and Calisto had only needed the man's help a couple of times in his life when he needed to locate someone.

Thankfully, Norris didn't work for Affonso.

Or any Cosa Nostra.

"That's not important, just give me what you have right now. Her family is fucking nose up, right? There's got to be some kind of skeletons in their closet for me to pick at when I see her. I don't like strong-arming females into compliance. Mental nonsense works far better."

"Yeah, yeah. Shut up for a second. This is bad shit, Cal. Poppy, I mean. The stuff I found might not be the kind of thing you want to go wading into at all. Even for your kind of business, this is pretty stomach churning crap."

"You're not making any sense."

"Where are you?" Norris asked.

"Driving at the moment."

"Pull over. This is important, Cal."

Calisto did as his old friend asked. It wasn't often than Norris got serious enough to demand anything from Calisto during a conversation.

Once the car was parked alongside of the highway, Calisto said, "All right, let me have whatever it is."

"From what I gathered, Poppy isn't living off her father's dime anymore. She hasn't been for a long while. In fact, the girl hasn't been seen out with her family in a public setting in almost a year. Seems a while back, there was an issue with a man that Poppy had been running around with on the social scene."

"What kind of a problem?"

"What do you think?" Norris asked back.

"Poppy's family is big-time, right? They probably didn't approve of the guy."

"Hit the nail on the head, Cal. Here's the thing— Mika Orlov is the guy. A little checking on him told me that he came from an immigrant mother straight out of the slums of Russia's poorest. He grew up shit poor in the States, and his mother made ends meet in such a way that gave her a rap sheet three feet long."

"What kind of charges?"

"Drugs. Possession. Solicitation. Same old thing. Over and over, man."

"How's a street kid like Mika get mixed up with a socialite like Poppy?" Calisto asked.

"My guess is they met on her turf, probably after he'd gotten off the streets by making a living in the only way his mother ever taught him how to. This all brings me back around to the father issue with Poppy again—he didn't approve of this Mika. He made no secret about it. Tabloids ran with it for a while, guessing, speculating, and all that garbage."

"Let me guess, her father likely cut her off from the

money and family side of things?"

"Seems like it," Norris confirmed.

"So what am I missing here?"

"Poppy seemed like a dead end on her side of things, except she's still been seen out and about with this Mika character on occasion."

"How deep?" Calisto asked.

"Underground, man. This is the part where you don't want to get mixed up in."

Calisto didn't have a choice.

"Try me."

"Seems Mika moved on from his socialite drug dealing scene to the sale of skin."

Jesus H. Christ.

Calisto's chest tightened with anxiety, but he refused to let it show in his voice when he said, "How did he come about joining that?"

"Seems he's got some ties to a Bratva organization in Russia that transports girls back and forth across the country. That could be how his dealing worked, too, honestly. It's hard to find info on Bratva organizations because they're so fucking secretive and down-low about everything, especially when they're headed in another country."

"His mother came from Russia," Calisto noted.

"He was born in the States a few months after her arrival. She would have been barely pregnant when she immigrated, but he was conceived over there."

"His father could have been in the organization."

"Likely. Old school Bratva men are known to shun their children, usually the boys, until they become a certain age. Then they come out of the woodwork, promising to bring them into the folds."

"That might have seemed like a dream to a kid like Mika who struggled his whole life," Calisto said quietly.

"This is all speculation, man. Keep that in mind."

"But the skin trade isn't speculation."

"No, he's definitely got his hand in that. I checked in with a contact of mine on the official side of things—"

Calisto made a noise under his breath, disgusted. "Fuck, you know I don't like when you do that."

"I wanted to get this info right for you the first time."

"Fine. What did your guy say?"

"They've got a taskforce trying to pin down the ring of men running part of the skin trade in Vegas. All they can say is there's some kind of auction thing, from what they understand, that goes on every few months. It's not the only thing Mika has his hand in."

"What else?"

"He also fishes in females that would be easy to victimize. The ones no one would notice missing. You know the stories of people who hook up with prostitutes by way of craigslist or whatever?"

"Yeah," Calisto said. "What about it?"

"Well, it's like that. He grabs a girl, pumps her full of drugs, keeps her needing the fix, and makes her work in hotels. According to my guy, these girls never stay in one place for very long. They're known to take them from state to state weekly to keep on the move and out of the eyes of officials. It's one of the reasons why they're difficult to catch and why set organizations like the Sorrentos don't make a fuss because they're not really fucking with their business."

Calisto's stomach churned.

This was bad.

His best hope was that Emma hadn't gotten herself somehow mixed up in this crew of people, but that was highly unlikely, given her last calls had been to Poppy. Emma needed help, and she went to someone she thought she could trust for it.

"There's something else," Norris said.

"What is it?"

"Those auctions—they're not for the hotel girls.

DONATI BLOODLINES: PART 1

They're for the kind of girls that a man might want to use again and again. Clean, sober, pretty, healthy girls. My guy said men are known to fly in from all over the world for a chance at these auctions, and then they fly out with a slave who now has no name, no past, and no definable future."

Oh, God.

Calisto let out a slow breath. "And?"

He could hear the unfinished words. There had to be more Norris wasn't saying.

"My guy believes there's an auction happening soon. They believe them to happen in the early hours of the morning at an unknown location. Vegas is the perfect place for one because people fly in and out from all over the world all the fucking time. Calisto, I don't know what's going on with you right now, but this is dangerous shit and you have to be careful, man."

"Did your guy say anything about Mika having a hand in the auctions, or just the hotel girls?" Calisto asked, ignoring Norris's final warning.

Norris sighed. "He doesn't believe him to be directly involved with the auctions. But he said from what they do know, if Mika could get his hands on a good enough girl to sell to someone higher in his organization who does have a hand in the auctions, it would be yet another in for him. Mika is clearly an upstart—they like to keep going up."

"What about someone like a *principessa della mafia*?" Calisto asked softly.

Norris was silent for a long time.

"Jesus."

"Is that a yes?"

"Yeah, that's a yes, Cal. She would be priceless, just based on her last name alone."

Calisto swallowed the lump in his throat. He checked the time again, noting the lost minutes since he'd answered Norris's call. "Do you have an address for this Mika?"

"No. Seems he's all over the place, but he favors a few businesses in particular."

"What about Poppy? Is her address the same one I have in my documents?"

"No on that, too. Her old penthouse was sold by her father six months ago. She moved into a smaller apartment."

"I want the address, now," Calisto said.

"Sure, let me bring it up again."

He would start there.

With *Poppy*.

May God save her fucking soul when Calisto came knocking.

"One more thing," Norris said.

"Shoot."

"If you do somehow manage to get in on the auctions, make sure to bring money, Cal. A lot of it."

Calisto was suddenly grateful that Vegas didn't run on everyone else's time.

• • •

With a steady hand, Calisto lifted his cigarette for a drag. He inhaled the smoke, let it burn in his lungs, and then exhaled a steady steam to the alleyway. The sound of bells jingling as the door to a small bakery was opened rang in the darkness. Calisto pushed off the wall, and kept his cigarette in his mouth all the while.

He'd went to Poppy's place, only to find she wasn't there. A quick check with her neighbor, a charming smile and a smooth word, and the older woman let him know that she heard Poppy talking on the phone before leaving the building.

Apparently, Poppy's neighbor was nosy.

That was good for Calisto.

The old neighbor let Calisto know that Poppy had a taste for coffee and bread from a shop down the street, and that's where she told her caller she was going. The woman even let Calisto know the name of the small bakery.

Norris had emailed Calisto a picture of Poppy, one that had been distributed in one of Vegas's socialite magazines. He knew which woman he was looking for.

The waiting game was still a killer.

Stepping closer to the mouth of the alley, Calisto took another drag from his cigarette and leaned his shoulder to the brick wall. The bright lights of Vegas were everywhere. A person couldn't even see the fucking stars from down below because the lights outshined them.

It was a shame.

Calisto missed New York.

He still hated his uncle. But he missed home.

It was easier for Calisto to think about the little things that were bothering him than to let his insides be eaten away with all the worries he had about Emma. Maybe over the last three weeks, he had allowed himself to get too close to the girl, even if it was at a distance.

He'd worried about what would happen after she married Affonso. He didn't like that she wouldn't be happy. It made him sick to think about Emma being in his uncle's bed night after night.

Calisto shouldn't have concerned himself with those things at all.

So yeah, he stared at the fucking sky and let himself be annoyed by the lack of stars.

It was easier.

A redhead strolled past the alleyway, drawing in Calisto's attention. He was thankful for the distraction. Poppy Johansen could dress herself up or down however she wanted; she could hang out in the worst neighborhoods, or go to the elite parties on the weekends.

What the girl couldn't hide, was her flaming red hair.

Stepping out of the alley without making a sound,

Calisto followed behind the woman. He kept his head down, smoked his cigarette, and kept one eye on the unknowing woman ahead of him. It wasn't long before a block had passed and they were closing in on the building where Poppy lived.

She still hadn't noticed Calisto when she rounded the front of the building and unlocked the main doors to get inside. Calisto had waited earlier for someone to leave when he had entered, but being as close as he was to Poppy, this time he only had to grab the door before it closed.

That was the first time she took notice of him.

Poppy gave Calisto a strange look, smiled slightly, and then headed for the elevators. Calisto followed without a word.

Standing in front of the elevators, Calisto took note of the messenger bag Poppy had slung over her arm. She likely had a gun in there, or maybe a knife, considering her choice in company for men. He wanted to make sure he wasn't on the receiving end of any weapon she might have.

Poppy reached out and pressed the button for the elevator. The right one opened almost immediately. She stepped in, shooting Calisto a glance over her shoulder, and he walked in right behind.

"Are you new to the building?" Poppy asked as she hit the third floor button.

"No," Calisto said. "Visiting someone."

"Which floor?"

"Fourth."

Poppy hit the floor number, and the doors closed. Calisto took note of how she held her bag a little tighter as the elevator began to lift.

At the third floor, the elevator came to a smooth stop before the doors opened to allow Poppy out. Calisto gave her a smile as she stepped off the elevator, and started to walk down the hall. Just as the doors began to close, he stuck his hand out and stopped them, forcing the elevator to open and let him out, too.

Poppy's place was only a couple of doors down from the elevator. Calisto had taken note of that earlier. As he stepped out into the hallway, Poppy was just unlocking her door.

With her head down, she didn't even see him coming.

Calisto grabbed her bag off her shoulder as the barrel of his newly acquired gun met the back of her neck. The girl froze like a statue, and her keys fell on the floor.

"You should answer your phone when someone calls," Calisto said. "Since you wouldn't answer mine, I decided to come over for a little visit. It's Poppy, right?"

Poppy nodded. "Yes."

"Is there a gun in your bag, Poppy?"

"Yes."

"Anything else?"

"No," she said.

Calisto didn't believe her, but since he had the bag in his hand, he figured he was okay. "Open the door and step inside. Turn on the light. Keep quiet, or I'll blow your spinal cord out through your throat when I pull the fucking trigger. Is that understood?"

"Yeah."

Poppy did as she was told. Once they were inside the apartment, Calisto tossed the bag ten feet into the space and far away from his current captive.

"Emma called you. Where is she?"

"I don't—"

Calisto spun Poppy around fast, shoved her into the closet wall, grabbed her throat in his free hand, and pointed his gun right between her wide eyes. "Lying won't make this easier or faster, Miss Johansen. I simply want to know where Emma Sorrento is."

Poppy's gaze darted back and forth as her mouth opened and closed. Calisto knew that look. It was the look of someone trying to search for a lie.

He cocked the hammer back.

Poppy whimpered.

"His name is Mika, right?" Calisto's smile was deadly.

Poppy sucked in a ragged breath. "What?"

"I hear you like to sleep with monsters, sweetheart." Calisto dragged the barrel of his gun from Poppy's forehead, over her nose, and down to her trembling lips. "The kind of monsters that take girls just like you, shoot them up with drugs, and shove them into a room for the taking. And do you know what the monster you sleep with does with those girls he takes? He sells them, Poppy. He lets other men go in and beat them, use them, and rape them however they want for the right price. Don't tell me that you don't know the kind of monster you're sleeping with."

"And if I do?"

Calisto's smile melted into a smirk. "Let me introduce you to a whole new kind of monster. And the best part about me is that I'm not the monster fucking you, sweetheart. Did you fish her into his hands? Is that what happened? Are you trying to get your boy a little higher in his game so that you can live off the wealth of a man other than your daddy?"

Poppy sneered. "Go to hell."

"I already live there."

She blinked, stunned.

Calisto didn't give a fuck. "Make this easy, tell me where I can find either Emma, or Mika."

"I don't—"

He grabbed her cheeks, spread her mouth wide, and shoved his gun so far down her throat that she gagged on the barrel. Poppy's eyes filled with tears, and slivers spilled over her cheeks.

"Tell me," Calisto urged quieter, "and I'll seriously consider letting you live tonight. You're nothing more than a stupid, spoiled little rich girl who is so far out of her fucking league that you can't even afford the tickets to the show you're trying to see, sweetheart. I'll let you live tonight if you tell me where to find your little boyfriend. And you know what you'll get to do then?"

Poppy swallowed around the barrel, unable to speak.

"Then, tomorrow, when you wake up and see the news of your boyfriend's death plastered across the television, you'll be able to go back to your father on your hands and knees like the worthless bitch you are, and beg him to let you back in to your family. Doesn't that sound wonderful? I bet it's much better than your father having to come here and identify what is left of your face after I pull the trigger."

More tears spilled.

Calisto kept smiling.

Poppy mumbled something around the barrel of the gun. Calisto pulled the weapon out just enough to let her speak. She instantly blurted out the name of what sounded like a strip club.

"Where is that located?" Calisto asked.

"About twenty minutes from here," Poppy cried, her sobs following right behind.

She said a street and number. Calisto filed the info away in his mind for later.

"Thank you," he said, stepping back from Poppy.

The girl fell on the floor, holding her face and throat in her hands. She didn't notice Calisto reaching behind his back to grab the silencer. She cried below him as he spun the silencer into the tip of his barrel.

"I lied," Calisto said.

Poppy glanced up, her brown gaze zoning in on the gun pointing at her face.

"My apologies to your father," he added.

Calisto pulled the trigger.

15.

Calisto

Calisto checked out the small caliber handgun that he had taken from Poppy Johansen's messenger bag before he'd left the apartment. He looked the clip over, made sure the ammo inside was in decent condition, and then slid the gun into the back of his pants.

There was nothing wrong with a backup.

Across the street from his parked car, Calisto took note of the strip club that was still lit up for business. There weren't a lot of cars in the parking lot. In fact, there hadn't been very many people coming or going from the business. Checking the clock, he noted it was after one in the morning. That could explain the dwindling patrons to the club, but the more likely reason was because only certain people used the place—the kind of people that normal, everyday people wouldn't be comfortable being around.

He'd been watching the hours crawl by, and counting down the time that he was losing with every passing second.

"Antsy" was not a good enough word for what Calisto was feeling. Twice, he'd taken routine calls from his uncle over the day, and twice he'd managed to lie his way through the details of Emma's whereabouts and whatever else Affonso wanted to know.

Calisto couldn't keep that up forever.

Say in thirty hours when the girl needed to be on a plane to New York.

Second-guessing oneself was the best way to fuck up a situation. Calisto refused to even consider whether or not he was out of his league with what he was about to do. He couldn't afford the doubt. It wasn't such a surprise to Calisto that the Russians had their hand in a skin trade right under the nose of the Sorrento Cosa Nostra. It wasn't all that uncommon for many organizations, both little and small, to be working around one another. Families and syndicates weren't likely to step in on another family's business unless it was causing them some kind of problem. Maximo probably knew that the Russians were running a scheme, but unless it was affecting the businesses he had a hand in, the man wouldn't bother to put a stop to it.

Besides that, Russians and Italians never worked well together in business. The organizations were run in entirely different ways with bosses that had completely opposite morals when it came to life and the mafia. The two syndicates wouldn't put their hands in a pot together, unless it was absolutely necessary.

It didn't make Maximo a bad boss for letting the Russians run their trade. Just like it didn't make the Russians weak because they allowed the Italians the majority control over the drug and gun trade in Vegas.

That's just how things worked.

Turf wars were only good for one thing: spilling blood.

Nobody wanted that.

Grabbing the black bag in the passenger seat, Calisto stepped out of the Porsche and locked it up tight. He kept a firm hold on the bag, and felt the cold metal of the gun at his back.

The bouncer at the front door looked like he had taken one too many shots of steroids. The budging veins under the guy's skin-tight black shirt were as thick as ropes. Calisto tried to pass the guy, only to find a trunk-like arm blocking his way.

"Wait," the bouncer said. "What's in the bag?"

"Money," Calisto replied honestly.

The bouncer cocked a brow. "How much?"

"A lot."

"Why?"

"Because I intend to spend it," Calisto said, smirking.

The bouncer eyed him speculatively, but quickly seemed to take notice of Calisto's expensive suit, Italian leather shoes, and the gold ring on his pinky finger. Calisto rarely, if ever, took the ring off. With a ruby set atop the gold band, it always drew attention.

It had been his father's.

Calisto probably didn't look like the strip club's usual patrons.

But he had money.

No one refused money.

"Open it for me," the bouncer said.

Sighing, Calisto unzipped the bag. He only opened it enough to flash the cash, cell phone, and a few other knickknacks that he'd tossed in to make it look like he carried a regular bag.

"Go ahead. No touching."

"Don't plan on it," Calisto muttered under his breath as he passed the bouncer by.

Calisto strolled down the dark corridor of the entrance to the strip club, still silently counting the time he was losing with every step.

He only had one shot.

Just one to get this right.

• • •

Calisto leaned back in the worn leather seat, rested his arms over the sides, and pretended to give a fuck about the woman shaking her ass five feet away. Up on the stage, the dancer bent over and used her hands to support her weight by holding onto the metal pole. Her G-string hid nothing, and she had long since taken her top off.

She didn't hold even an ounce of Calisto's interest, but he tossed another fifty-dollar bill to the stage for her efforts.

DONATI BLOODLINES: PART 1

And for the men watching him from across the club.

Behind a roped off section, a man sat watching Calisto shower stripper after stripper with cash. A bottle of Patrón sat on the table in front of the man, half empty. A deck of playing cards rested neatly beside the bottle. His guards rarely moved from their spots, unless the man asked for something. Usually with a snap of his fingers.

Calisto would bet every dollar in his bank that the man was Mika Orlov. He'd heard a few people refer to the guy as their boss, but not much else. What was more important, was that Calisto had gained Mika's attention with his show of money and his disinterest in the strippers.

He wanted the man to question.

He wanted Mika wondering.

This was good.

Calisto waved two fingers at the girl on the stage, catching her attention. Somehow, the dazed woman managed to stay upright without swaying more than she already was in her six-inch heels. The high look in her eyes, mixed with the shitty makeup job on the creases of her arms—an attempt to hide traces of track marks—were seriously worrisome.

No wonder the club didn't do decent business.

This was fucking shameful.

"Another," Calisto said quietly.

The woman's brow furrowed. "But—"

"Take your money, sweetheart, and find me another girl to dance."

Scowling, the dancer did as she was told. Not two minutes after she had left the stage, another high, young female clamored up the steps to earn her cash like the three women before her. Calisto kept his gaze trained on anything but the stripper. Her swaying and grinding did little to wake his dead desire, and he didn't want to seem interested at all.

Calisto being interested wouldn't make Mika seek

him out.

Flashing more cash, tossing fifties and hundreds to the woman on stage, and keeping the aloof demeanor up was Calisto's main game plan. Mika, the quick, business-savvy man that he was, would surely notice the patron in his club that was spending a lot of money, but wasn't finding exactly what he wanted in the stripper's offerings.

A rich man.

Money to spend.

Bored out of his mind.

Mika, the upstart that he was, wouldn't pass up a possibility when he had the means and motive to get Calisto something far better.

• • •

A tap on Calisto's shoulder stopped him from grabbing another fifty from his bag. Subtly glancing to his side, Calisto found one of Mika's guards waiting with his arms at his back.

"Evening," Calisto said. "Am I doing something wrong?"

"No. My boss, Mika, noticed that you're spending a lot of money on women that don't seem to interest you in here tonight. He was curious if maybe you would like to have a chat about possibly correcting that issue and working something else out."

Calisto tipped his chin down, hiding his grin. "And what would that be?"

"If the dancing isn't sufficing, he is more than willing to offer you something more private in the back. For the right price."

"Of course," Calisto murmured. "Money is the kicker, isn't it? How much is he willing to make me spend for a ten-minute session with one of these junkies? I'm not interested in that, sorry."

"Yes, well ..."

DONATI BLOODLINES: PART 1

"I had a rough day. Spending money and watching females take off their clothes usually fixes that for me, but not tonight. I stopped at this club because I thought it would give me a bit of privacy. Unfortunately, these girls aren't anything like what I expected."

The bodyguard cleared his throat. "My apologies."

"I'll speak with your boss if he has something better to show me, other than these ... women," Calisto finished with an indifferent wave to the girl on stage.

"Wonderful. Come with—"

"No, I like where I'm sitting. Ask him over here."

With a quick nod, the man left Calisto alone. Out of the corner of his eye, Calisto watched as the guard approached Mika beyond the roped off section, bent down to relay the message, and then waited for his boss's response.

Mika scowled in Calisto's direction.

Calisto only smirked at the girl on stage and tossed another bill up for her to have. Five long minutes later, a form sat down in the leather chair directly beside Calisto's seat.

"I hear my girls are not up to your standards," the man said.

For a Russian man, his accent was quite American.

Calisto chuckled dryly and nodded at the girl on stage. "Look at her, is she up to your standards?"

"I look at her every night she works."

"Maybe so, but if given the chance, would you fuck her?"

Mika raised a brow. "I have."

"Before she started using, I suspect."

"You would be correct, Mr. ...?"

"You can call me Cal," he told Mika.

Mika smiled a charming sight. To anyone else, it would have come off as friendly and approachable. Calisto knew better—he worked with men just like Mika on a daily basis. Smiles were simply another way to mask one's intentions.

"Cal, then," Mika said after a moment. "I did notice you weren't drinking."

"One pleasure at a time."

"Ah."

"Your man said you may have something more to my tastes," Calisto prodded.

"For the right price, Cal, I can have anything you want in a matter of hours."

Calisto tampered his urge to grin. This was exactly what he wanted.

"Be specific with your tastes, and I will see what I can do," Mika added.

"Young, but legal," Calisto replied. "Sober. Clean. And preferably someone with a bit more class than these ladies have. I don't mind a dancer, but frankly, you couldn't pay me enough money to get my dick wet with someone that might leave something behind. You get what I'm saying?"

"Perfectly."

Calisto checked his watch. "Aren't you the least bit worried that I'm a cop?"

Mika laughed darkly. "No. If you were, you would have taken my man up on the offer of having one of the girls in the back. Any felony is a good felony, as a cop would say."

"True."

"Where are you from, Cal?"

"New York," he answered. "I had some business to do in Vegas. I'll be leaving in a day and a half."

"Hmm."

"What?"

"Just thinking," Mika murmured.

Calisto didn't indulge the man further. "Can you find me something more suitable, or not?"

"I can. How much money are you willing to spend, Cal?"

"As much as I need to. I like being able to come back to something, if it's good enough. Do you know what I mean?"

Mika smiled. "Perfectly. I may be able to help."

"Do tell."

As Mika began to chat about a private event that he had been invited to for the evening—one that would offer a variety of skin to shop from—happening in just a couple of short hours, Calisto kept his mind on the time.

Time both he and Emma didn't have.

• • •

"I take it that's your car," Mika said, nodding in the direction of the black Porsche across the road.

"Yes, my rental."

"You could follow behind if you wanted."

"Driving with you will be fine," Calisto assured, lying through his teeth.

Mika climbed inside a black SUV with windows tinted all the way around. It was impossible to see inside the vehicle. After the driver—Nathan, Mika had said earlier—got behind the wheel, Calisto jumped in the back, too.

"I have another friend going to the event tonight, and he is curious to meet you," Mika said as the SUV pulled out of the lot.

Calisto didn't plan on meeting anyone else. As it was, enough people had seen his face in all of this. Those people, like Mika and his driver, needed to be handled.

"Is that so?" he asked.

"We'll meet him at the venue. Usually I wouldn't go, but tonight I have an invitation, as I've provided something invaluable for them. I should warn you, though, that my friend is distrustful of people he doesn't know."

"This place—didn't you say everyone is anonymous in one way or another?"

"Yes," Mika said, looking down at his phone. "But everyone is apparently vouched for by someone else. Newcomers are rare."

Mika knew even less about the auctions than Norris had when Calisto talked to him. It was very likely that Mika's catch with Emma had set the man up to be invited to the showing of women.

"We'll say you're an old friend of mine," Mika said after a moment.

"Do you think he'll believe it?"

"No, but he wants to make money."

Calisto laughed under his breath. "I do have that."

"You do. So, follow along and everything should be fine."

Keeping his bag at his side, and the guns he had hidden, Calisto wondered just how much money he was going to need. Mika and his men were incredibly incompetent for a bunch of Russian gangsters. They trusted Calisto's well-dressed,-well-spoken person without question and didn't bother to check his things. To the men's credit, Calisto hadn't given them much of a reason to check him, either.

Calisto had managed to pull a good three hundred thousand from the bank earlier. The manager had nearly vomited when Calisto walked in not twenty minutes before the place was to close, demanding his personal account be emptied.

We don't usually have that much cash in the vault, the man had said.

Bullshit.

Calisto knew better.

This was fucking Vegas.

They had the cash.

Calisto likely needed more than what he did have. His offshore accounts, the one he used to hide and then pillow illegal funds into his legal accounts, toted just over ten million between his dealings and his inheritance from his father's and mother's deaths.

He could use that, if needed.

From the side, Calisto kept an eye on Mika. He didn't trust the man, but he had to keep him alive long enough for him to at least get him to the venue. By the way the event had been described by the Russian, as long as you showed up, you were let in. No one who hadn't been vouched for would be given the address to where the auction was being held.

Calisto wasn't all that surprised that Mika had quickly, and quite easily, taken to him without much question or concern. An enigmatic, rich stranger, willing to toss out money on a woman who could satisfy him was exactly the kind of client that Mika needed to get higher in the trafficking business.

Sometimes, being an upstart made you desperate to just go up.

Calisto's willingness to follow along with Mika, find some skin to buy for the evening, and part ways, lulled the Russian into a false sense of security. Cops wouldn't go this far, surely. A cop would have drunk at the club to fit in, he would have followed Mika's man to sit down at another table, and he probably would not have gotten in Mika's car.

Sure, it made Calisto uncomfortable. He wasn't in his own territory. He still didn't have time to doubt himself. This was far too important.

"Have you ever participated in an auction before?" Mika asked out of the blue.

Calisto shrugged, but answered honestly. "Yes."

"When?"

When my uncle took an operation down because they wouldn't pay him for being on his territory, Calisto thought.

"In my younger twenties. I didn't get much out of it."

Mika laughed. "I think you'll have a better experience tonight."

"I certainly hope so."

More than Mika knew.

Mika lifted his phone and showed off a message that looked like a bunch of numbers and gibberish. "This is our invitation to the event. We show it at the door, and we're permitted entrance. Nothing more."

Good to know.

"So, I don't really need you, huh?" Calisto asked. "Your driver must know where the place is."

Mika's head snapped up. "What did you just—"

Calisto pulled the gun from his back, the one he had taken from Poppy's place. The weapon met Mika's forehead with a crack as Calisto pulled the other gun he'd been hiding from the bag holding the money. He pointed the second gun at the driver.

"I don't really need you," Calisto repeated.

Mika's hands twitched like he was going to reach for something.

"Drive," Calisto barked at the driver. "Move your hands a single fucking inch from the steering wheel and I will put a bullet in the back of your head."

"Do what he says," Mika said quietly.

"Your desire to climb higher in your business makes you an easy target, Mika. Tell your girl Poppy that I said hi."

Mika opened his mouth to speak. Calisto pulled the trigger. Blood sprayed the passenger window as the man's body jerked to the side.

Calisto didn't take his eyes off the driver.

"Nathan, is it?" Calisto asked.

"Y-yes."

"Did someone named Emma come into the club tonight, looking for your dead boss, here?"

Nathan nodded.

Calisto kept his gun aimed at Nathan, but leaned over to grab the phone from Mika's dead hands. He only needed the message on the phone. That's what the fool said.

"Keep driving."

"Okay," Nathan mumbled.

Fucking sickening.

Calisto was pretty sure these fools had never come face to face with anyone worth being frightened over. They probably thought they were top dogs in their worlds, when in fact, they were at the very bottom of the food chain.

That was their problem.

He had a hell of a lot to lose.

"Drive faster," Calisto ordered.

The car sped up.

• • •

Calisto walked through the dimly lit hallways of an unmarked building that, from the outside, had looked like nothing more than a warehouse. In front of him, another man walked alongside another man who had greeted him outside of the building not ten minutes earlier. Calisto simply had to flash the message from Mika's phone in front of their faces to be allowed inside. The men had asked him a few questions, of course, and checked him over to search for any weapons. Calisto expected it and answered with a cool smile and his usual vagueness. He'd left the guns in the SUV, knowing he would probably be checked.

His voucher to the event was Mika.

But his money got him through the door.

Kostya was the man's name. He was far more Russian than Mika had been.

Thanks to the dark-tinted windows of the SUV, no one noticed a thing when Calisto put a bullet in the back of the driver's head. Once Nathan brought Calisto to where he needed to be, he took care of that little issue.

There was only one thing left.

Emma.

"You have accounts to use tonight, yes?" the man asked, turning to look at Calisto.

"Offshore."

"Those work fine. Almost there."

Calisto followed behind in silence, unsure of what he was walking into. At the end of the long hallway, a woman waited with a wicker basket in her hands. He was more shocked to see a female at an event like this than he was over the intricately designed masks in the basket.

"Please, take one," she said.

Calisto grabbed the one that was passed back to him. It was black, would cover half of his face, leaving only his mouth and jaw exposed, and had a satiny feel.

Once the other two men had donned their masks, the woman pushed open the door behind her.

Calisto didn't know what he expected to see. Cement floors, maybe. Dingy walls. Cages for the victims caught up in all of this. Well-dressed men with their faces covered to hide their identities as women were paraded in front of them for surveying like cattle.

The only thing Calisto had right was the well-dressed men.

The room opened up to what could only be described as professionally decorated gallery with earth-toned walls, stylish furniture, and artwork on the walls. Men and women, impeccably dressed, milled around with their faces hidden by similar masks to the one Calisto had put on his own face.

Some of the walls had been draped with red curtains, but none of them had windows to look outside. Doors opened at the other end of the very large room, and people traveled in and out without question. Servers walked between the people, refilling glasses of whatever liquor was being imbibed. Laughter flowed freely.

What in the fuck was this?

It was like a goddamn cocktail party.

Calisto swallowed back the heaviness pooling in his gut. "Shall we?"

The man who had been mostly quiet nodded at his friend. "My boss will direct you through the process, as I don't have the cash to participate fully tonight."

Great ...

"Come," Kostya demanded. "We will get account set up for you, comrade."

"Then what?" Calisto asked.

"Then we look at stock behind the curtains before auction."

Stock.

Like cattle.

Calisto felt cold all over.

He let his mask hide it.

Somehow.

16.

Emma

Something shoved Emma from behind, nearly causing her to stumble in the heels she had been forced to put on earlier. White heels, she remembered. Just like the white-lace pantie and bra set—brand new with tags still attached—and the white chemise that a pretty, older woman had yanked over her head.

Emma had still been drowsy then. She remembered arms putting her in the back of a car, someone removing her clothes and cleaning the vomit from her hair, and then readying her like she was a little doll about to be displayed.

Her skin had been shaven. Lotion was applied. Her face was washed, her hair brushed, and her nails clipped.

The drug that Mika had given her knocked Emma out in a big way. She had barely been able to move for hours. Her words wouldn't come out right, and her mind wouldn't slow enough for her to think, fight back, or do much of anything.

She was useless.

"Keep your head up," a voice said from behind Emma. "Stand still, be quiet, and everything will be just fine, pretty girl."

Emma blinked under the weight of the white sash that covered her eyes. She recognized the voice making demands behind her as the woman who had cared for her earlier when she was brought in blindfolded and unmoving.

Once the woman had been satisfied with Emma's appearance, she had tied a clean, white sash around her head and sat her in a chair.

How long had she waited until someone came?

Long enough.

Emma's faculties slowly returned, along with her

awareness. She had known all along that something was terribly wrong, but it was only when she could think clearly once more that she understood just how much trouble she was really in.

"You're young, fit, and clean," the woman said, her hand pushing against Emma's back to move her along. "You will fetch a good buyer, and a damn good price tonight, if you just do what you're told. Believe me when I say that you want someone from tonight to purchase you instead of being overlooked. Those who don't make the auction are discarded. We can't afford the trouble of keeping you, after all."

Emma shivered.

She refused to speak.

"The lights will feel hot," the woman said. "Do not remove the blindfold or you'll find your hands bloody and red after being beaten with a whip."

Lights?

What?

"Ready, here we go."

Emma felt her body be propelled forward with one hard shove. Her heels clattered on the floor—a sound that reminded her of heels clicking down on hardwood. She didn't have a damned clue what the woman was talking about, because a cold chill raced over Emma's skin the moment she stopped moving. Goosebumps bloomed across her arms and legs. She could feel the urge to tremble start in her shoulders.

And then she heard the click.

Beneath the thick sash covering her eyes, Emma could tell the lights had been turned on. Several lights, probably. Her body heated instantly.

The clapping and muffled murmurs followed right after.

She almost spun on her heel.

Almost.

Emma stopped herself from moving, remembering

the woman's words. She didn't want to find out what being discarded meant. She also didn't want to be sold off to the highest bidder in whatever this awful charade was.

Her fingers itched with the desire to rip the blindfold off. She wanted to see who was talking, who was clapping, and who was watching. Was it a few people? A lot?

Embarrassment and fear swirled in Emma's midsection. She could feel that the chemise she wore only fell to her pubic bone. The panties that the woman had put on Emma earlier had been nothing more than frilly, flimsy fabric.

Somehow … somehow she just knew.

Her body was being *appraised*.

Looked at. Admired. Judged.

Priced.

She clenched her fists hard at her sides, letting the bite of her fingernails keep her from crying. The tears still welled in her eyes, but she clenched her lids shut beneath the sash and refused to let the wetness escape. She allowed one, soft and shaky breath to release from her chest.

Control, her mind chanted. *Keep control*.

How was she going to get out of this?

What had she done?

The panic bubbled up faster than Emma expected it to. Every muscle in her body seemed to protest at the same goddamn time, right along with her suddenly screaming nerves. She was two seconds away from a breakdown.

She couldn't do this.

She didn't want this.

What was *this*?

A voice, clearer than the murmurs, echoed from up above.

Emma froze solid.

"Number three-two-seven-four. Caucasian. Twenty years old. Clean body, clean blood."

DONATI BLOODLINES: PART 1

A sickness rolled in Emma's stomach.

This was what she was reduced to? A number, specifications, and the best price she could fetch?

"Not pure, based on information provided," the voice continued. "Extra examination wasn't necessary to confirm."

What?

How did that person know she wasn't a virgin?

Emma quickly remembered Poppy, and how her friend had sold her out to the lowest of the low. The betrayal still stung harshly on the back of Emma's tongue, but she ignored it for the moment. She had more important things to worry about.

Like getting away.

Somehow …

"Special circumstances for three-two-seven-four includes a demand from the seller that it be removed from the state as soon as possible," the voice said from up above somewhere. "The file information will be shared with those who show interest in bidding on the piece, including the full details. I can assure you that the piece's paperwork and heritage is impeccable. It is best placed in a permanent place or a collection."

A … *collection*?

Oh, God.

Emma couldn't breathe.

She thought about all the stupid shit she had done to get herself in this position, and the man she had fooled to do it.

No one would help her.

No one would save her.

Emma was grabbed by her arm and pulled backwards without a word. She heard the click again before the lights flashed off and the wave of heat was gone.

"Well done," the older woman whispered in Emma's ear.

Somewhere behind her, the clapping started again.

• • •

Emma blinked rapidly when the blindfold was suddenly pulled from her eyes without warning. The brightness of the space around her made it hard to focus when she had been staring into darkness for longer than she cared to think about.

A man moved in front of her quickly, and put his hands on her shoulders, pushing her down. He wore a black mask, keeping most of his face hidden.

"Hey—"

"I'm sure Dory told you to keep quiet," the man said. "So do so and sit down."

Emma did as she was told, not liking the way the man's eyes flashed with the promise of violence. She had a feeling that physically fighting back against these people would do her no good. They trafficked humans, obviously. What else were they capable of?

Killing her wouldn't make waves to them.

It would be nothing.

"Five parties have shown interest in you tonight. All are considerably wealthy, and have the means to make you disappear, Emma."

"You know my name?"

"Of course, I do. The seller who brought you in had quite an extensive bit of information to go through about just who you are and where you came from. Unbelievable that you managed to wind up in our hands. Usually, we wouldn't work with someone like you—as you're too high-risk—but we didn't have much of a choice tonight. Better this than killing you, hmm?"

Emma choked on air. "Is that what you think?"

"Somehow, my dear, you found your way here. We're simply going to use it to our benefit."

Emma briefly wondered how much damage she

would be able to do to this man's face with her fingernails before someone would come into the stark white room and stop her. The thought didn't last long.

"Cross your legs, head high, and smile if it pleases you," the man said.

"Fuck you," Emma uttered under her breath.

He laughed in response.

"Oh, you silly girl. Some of these clients love defiance. Keep showing that off for them, they're watching, after all."

Emma glanced around quickly, taking in the space. For the most part, Emma was forced to keep her blindfold on at all times. This was one of the very few times where it had been taken off since she arrived.

The room was circular in nature. A single door was off to her right, while the high vaulted ceiling had specialty lighting directed down on the chair she sat in. The floor was a brushed, black marble. Shiny enough to showcase her terrified, confused reflection staring back at her. White walls with what looked like indented panels of mirrors surrounded her from every direction.

Watching her ...

She stared into one of the mirrors. Wetness filled her gaze, but she blinked it away.

"Yes, exactly," the man said, nodding at one of the mirrors. "One-sided glass. As I said, keep the defiance up. I know personally that a few of the clients interested in you love the challenge of breaking a new slave's will. Believe it or not, but that actually makes the bids fly."

There it was.

The first time the word had been said.

Slave.

Emma was frozen to the chair as more lights turned on. With a single pat on her head, the man made a beeline for the only door that would lead out of the room. Not a second later, the voice from earlier was back, echoing up above.

"Cost per bid is five thousand. Bidding starts at one hundred thousand. Increments of ten thousand per bid. Transactions are instant. Begin."

Immediately, red lights flashed above the mirrors. One after another … after another.

Emma tried to keep up; she tried to count them. There were too many. She found herself clenching her fists tight again, just to keep calm, and biting the inside of her cheek to stay quiet.

Fuck these people.

Fuck their money.

She still wouldn't cry.

• • •

"Stand."

It was the only thing Emma heard before the sound of a door opening somewhere behind her echoed in the darkness. She had been blindfolded when the red lights stopped blinking, directed out of the circular room, and put in another where she was made to sit again and wait.

At some point, Emma had gone numb.

Maybe it was when the man speaking into the speaker had announced the bids had crossed the million-dollar threshold. Maybe it was when he said it crossed the two million mark.

Emma didn't know.

But she couldn't feel the tips of her fingers, anymore. Her mouth was flooded with the metallic taste of blood, as she couldn't stop biting her cheeks and tongue long enough for the bleeding to quit. Her fingernails had cut into her palms.

She still couldn't feel a thing.

She still couldn't breathe.

Emma's eyes stung from holding back tears and her throat was raw from keeping the panic at bay. Someone had purchased her like a piece of meat at the market less than thirty minutes before. She was someone's something, now.

Well done, the old woman had said afterward.

Like she should be proud.

Like it was *good*.

Who were these people?

Uncertain of her fate, Emma stood like she had been told. Being blindfolded left her shaky and unsure of her position in the room as squeaks and soft murmurs echoed around her. She couldn't discern enough about the voices, but something was familiar.

Cologne.

Woodsy, deep, and warm.

A man.

Emma knew that smell. She was sure she did.

"Tradition for the new clients," a man said, the one from earlier who had taunted her about the bidding war. "Other bidders almost enjoy seeing a taste of what they lost out on. She didn't quite break the record, but she came pretty damn close at the two-point-two mark. Another two hundred, and she would have.

"Congratulations. Remember the remarks in her information, she needs to be out of the state by morning."

Emma shuddered, and finally, her body began to feel again. Pain constricted her chest, squeezing tight and making her ache. Her palms stung and her eyes watered. Nausea caused her to sway on the spot. A hand grazing her shoulder with the softest touch grounded her to the floor instantly.

Not a second later, a door closed.

The scent of the man surrounded Emma, making her feel strangely comforted and maybe even safe. She wasn't sure why, but his gentle touch on her skin and the smell of his cologne was familiar enough to lull her out of her panic.

"Tradition, he said."

Emma stilled.

No way.

It wasn't possible.

"Control your face, Emmy," came the dark, calm murmur along the shell of her ear. "You wear those emotions on your sleeve, remember?"

Calisto.

Emma's heart might as well have jumped from her chest. More than anything, she wanted to reach out to find Calisto, grab him tight, and not let go until she was far away from this place and these horrible people.

She tampered the need down.

Calisto's next words helped a little. "People are watching, so be mindful and follow directions. Seems this room looks a lot like the last room you were in with mirrors for windows."

Tradition.

What did that mean?

What did the people want to see?

"Okay," Emma breathed, barely letting her lips move at all.

"You scared the hell out of me."

"Sorry."

"I'm sure you are, now. Had you not gotten mixed up in this mess, I doubt you would be saying the same thing."

Emma didn't know about that. She'd made a rash decision, hoping to get out of a marriage, and look at how she ended up.

Not much better.

She felt the softness of Calisto's suit jacket as he moved around her slowly. The tip of his finger stayed pressed on her skin and dragged over her shoulder, across her collarbones, and up her neck to her chin.

At her mouth, he swept the pad of his finger over her parted lips.

"I never told you this, but I like your mouth the best," Calisto murmured.

DONATI BLOODLINES: PART 1

Emma shivered, unable to stop the reaction. It was entirely inappropriate, and not the right time, but her body heated at the sound of sex in his tone.

"I like your mouth the best because your top lip is just a little too big for your bottom lip, and your teeth peek out, even when you're not smiling. It makes your mouth look ready and open to be filled by something—a cock, preferably."

She sucked in a sharp breath when his finger ghosted back down her neck, between the valley of her breasts, covered by the white chemise, and stopped below her bellybutton.

"I've been told they can't hear what we say in here, but for safety's sake, I will keep my voice down until they're satisfied." Calisto sighed deeply and she felt his finger skim under the hem of the chemise. He continued his slow trek around her still body, lifting the bottom of the chemise and letting it fall across her skin as he went. Oddly, her skin was sensitive enough for the soft fabric to feel like it was caressing her. "I was pissed off at you for running—for fucking this up for me. My life for yours, Emma. That's what would have happened if I had to go back to New York without you. So yeah, I was pissed."

"And then?"

Her question came out breathy.

She didn't understand why.

Pressing her legs together in an attempt to soothe the ache between her thighs, Emma tried to figure out a way to calm down. She shouldn't be turned on right now. Not knowing what she did and being where she was.

"And then I was scared," Calisto admitted so quietly she strained to hear. "But there was a reason Affonso decided to let me watch you, and my ability to find people—should the need arise—was at the top of his list. Seems it came in handy, after all."

She felt three of his fingers ghost along the swell of her ass.

Emma's entire body lit up under the touch.

She wanted to see him; see his eyes, his face, and what he was doing. She didn't like the darkness, or the fear still edging around her senses.

"What are you doing?" she asked.

"Touching you. They want to see something, Emmy," Calisto told her. "Something to make their loss of cash in the bidding war worth their time and effort. I don't want them to see a fucking thing—I don't even want Affonso to see a goddamn single inch of you, but I don't have a choice. You don't know this, but I'm a monster."

"You're not."

"I am, but I'm not so much of a monster that I would force you into doing something that you don't want. I won't take anything from you, but I have to make it believable. I'll keep the blindfold on. All you have to do is feel, *dolcezza*."

Emma wondered what he meant, but not for long.

"Wider," Calisto demanded. "Open up for me. Show me what I bought."

His palm snapped against her thigh. The sting heated up her skin, shocked her still, and made her pussy clench all at the same time.

What was wrong with her?

"Emma," he said lower, "do not make me take it from you, please."

She widened her legs, still shaky and confused. "I want to leave."

Calisto was there.

He found her; saved her.

Somehow.

Why couldn't they leave now?

"I know," Calisto said, offering nothing more. "Do you know how much you went for in there?"

"Two million."

"Two-point-two."

He practically growled the number.

DONATI BLOODLINES: PART 1

Emma swallowed hard. "Oh."

"Straight out of my offshore bank account, Emmy," Calisto said.

His hand landed on her ass with a hard snap. Emma jumped in the heels she wore, shocked at the pain that seemed to travel straight from her backside to her sex. She shouldn't like this, not at all, but she did.

And she couldn't deny that she liked Calisto.

Then, his palm slid down her ass, kneaded the flesh with enough force for it to hurt, and traveled lower, between her spread legs. His hand cupped her sex through the lace panties, and Emma held her breath.

"You can't even begin to understand the shit I had to go through today to find you. You *scared* me."

How many times had he said that?

She didn't have to know what he'd done for her.

His voice said it all.

"Thank you," Emma whispered.

Calisto let out a quiet hum before his fingers rapped along the seam of her panties. She felt the light touch everywhere.

Fucking everywhere.

"You're wet," he said softly.

Emma dropped her head, feeling both ashamed and turned on.

"And hot," he added deeper.

"I—"

Calisto stopped her next words by grabbing under her throat. Emma felt him tilt her head up like he was putting her face on display as his chest molded to her back. His fingers between her thighs began to stroke without warning, sweeping back and forth overtop the lace panties, harder with each swipe.

Emma gasped in a gulp of air, shuddering when Calisto's fingers rolled against her clit again and again. It felt so fucking good, and terribly bad at the same time. She wanted more, but she knew people were watching, and she didn't want that at all.

Still, she rolled her hips into his hand.

Like a little whore.

She wanted more.

"Fuck, feel you, *ragazza*," Calisto said in her ear. "You want this, huh? And I don't even have my fingers buried inside you, yet."

Jesus.

His lips brushed her skin, tantalizing and wicked.

Promising.

"Please," Emma managed to say.

She wasn't sure what she was asking for. More of his fingers, more of his touch. More of his words, more of his breath against her skin. Maybe for him to stop, to get her out of there, to make the watching eyes go away.

"I have thought about touching you since I saw you sitting on that sink in the restaurant that day," Calisto told her, his tone husky. "You jumped down, your dress rode up, and I wondered ... And your mouth, of course. I've thought about that. I dreamed about you being on your knees, sucking me so deep into your throat that your eyes watered and you still wanted more. I've thought about a lot, Emmy."

Emma whined, unable to do much else.

"Let me do what they want," Calisto said. "Let me do what I fucking want right now, because I won't get another chance."

He wouldn't, she realized.

He saved her.

Calisto saved her, but he had to take her back. New York was calling her name. An arranged marriage was waiting for her in just a few days. He saved her, just to give her away.

Emma stopped thinking.

She felt instead.

Three of Calisto's fingers slipped under the lace panties, swept along her hot, sensitive slit, and then plunged inside with a hard, deep thrust. Emma practically fell into his hand, lost in the sensation of his digits filling her, stretching her open, and fucking her hard.

Over and over.

Her wetness smeared to her inner thighs. She heard the sounds of his fingers thrusting in, pulling out, and taking her again. She could smell her sex in the air.

The chill was gone.

She was hot all over.

"Just like I thought," Calisto said against her neck. "You feel like fucking heaven."

Emma opened her mouth to say something—anything—but nothing came out.

Calisto's hand on her neck trailed higher until two of his fingers were pressing between her lips. She sucked his digits in as his fingers fucked her even harder.

She was going to come.

On a bidding block.

With a blindfold on.

In front of God knew who.

But Calisto wanted it, he had said so. Emma gave it to him.

17.

Emma

Calisto's fingers pulled from Emma's mouth. The wet digits dragged down over her lips and chin to her neck, where he grabbed tight. She swallowed against the hold, feeling her throat constrict from the firmness in his grip.

The sensations traveling through her nervous system was wicked and sinful, intent on driving her fucking mad. Calisto didn't let up in the hard thrusts of his fingers. When he started curling them on every drive, seeking and searching, Emma started trembling.

Panting.

Needing

Wanting.

Her fingers twisted into the sides of her chemise, fisted tight, and she bit down on her tongue to try and keep her sounds quiet.

It didn't work.

"Stop fighting it," Calisto said darkly.

Emma wanted to fight it; she wanted to push aside the desire to come, the want for her release. Not here. Not with people watching. As much as she loved it, as much as her body betrayed her, it scared her, too.

But she still came.

Hard, fast, squirming in Calisto's arms, and crying out.

Emma managed to keep the scream of his name from coming out with the rest of her wailing, but barely. It stuck in her throat, trying to claw its way out as bliss and shame warred through the rest of her body.

"There it is," she heard Calisto whisper in her ear.

Emma shuddered all over.

Something hard and long pressed to Emma's lower

back. The closer Calisto pulled her into his chest, the harder it seemed to feel.

His cock.

He was hard for her, for *this*.

Emma liked that too much.

His fingers withdrew from her tender pussy, smearing wetness from her slit and back over her ass before she felt his hand come to a stop at the small of her back. It was just the lightest press of his palm on her skin, but it comforted Emma in a way she hadn't expected.

"Almost done," he said softly.

Emma didn't understand what else there was to do. Her mind wouldn't slow enough to let her think, and already, she wanted more. She shouldn't want anything from Calisto at all.

Calisto's hand slid around her hip, down to her thigh, and then he grabbed a handful of the chemise. Still unable to see because of the blindfold, Emma went off the feeling of Calisto's touch to know what he was doing or what he might want from her.

He lifted the chemise, she felt his lips curve into a smirk at her neck, and his fingers drive down her stomach and under the panties again.

Emma jerked with a whimper the second his fingers came in contact with her hot, sensitive clit. Then, his hand was gone from her panties and she only had a second to think before the blindfold was taken off her face, allowing her to see.

Calisto spun Emma fast on the spot, nearly making her stumble in the white heels she wore. She barely had time to take in the room around them, but it looked similar to the one she had been in for the bidding with glass mirrors, white walls, a lot of lights, and a high ceiling.

Wide-eyed, Emma stared up at Calisto. He wore a black mask that covered half of his face, but it was him. He was fucking unmistakable to her. Especially his soul-black eyes.

What now?

Calisto's eyes had turned from their usual hardness, to a softer glimmer as he looked her over. His hand came up to graze her cheek with a light caress. It was brief, barely there, and then it was gone.

But she had felt it.

The coldness was back. His soft touch turned into a stinging burn when he fisted her hair and yanked downward. Sucking in a hiss of air, Emma dropped to her knees instinctively. It put her eye-level with his groin. She could plainly see the length of his rock-hard erection straining against the zipper of his dress pants. Strangely, her fingers twitched with the desire to reach out and feel his cock.

Emma had to get away from that thought, and fast.

She wondered where his suit jacket had gone to, as he only wore a dark-red, silk shirt with the sleeves rolled up to his elbows. Emma's stare drifted down the length of Calisto's arms, following the roped lines of his forearms and the definition of his muscles. At his hands, her lips fell slack at the thought of him fucking her pussy deep while he stuffed her mouth full with his other fingers.

Needing something else to focus on instead of the way her pussy throbbed and her arousal soaked her panties, Emma focused on the ruby ring Calisto wore on his pinky. The golden band glinted under the bright lights. It was the first time she had ever noticed the piece. It fit his hand perfectly without seeming out of place.

Where had he gotten it from?

"I should make you service me while you're down there," Calisto said.

Emma blinked, her head snapping up fast. "W-what?"

He wouldn't.

Would he?

"Unfortunately, I don't have the urge to watch you swallow a load of my come just yet," he added with a smirk.

Jesus.

Just yet, he said.

Emma didn't miss how he phrased that at all.

"Now be a good girl, and keep quiet," Calisto said.

Before she could even agree, Calisto grabbed for what looked like a white, material bag hanging out of his pocket. He let go of her hair a second before the hood was shoved down over her head.

Emma's immediate reaction was to scream, but it only came out as a yelp. Panicked, she threw her hands out to find something and keep her steady, but she only came up with air. She could breathe through the soft mesh of the hood covering her head, but she couldn't see.

"Get up," she heard Calisto say.

Emma didn't move fast enough, because the hood suddenly tightened around her throat, cutting off her air.

"Up, I said."

She scrambled to her feet, dazed and unsure. Why did he do that? What was his fucking game now?

"Well done," a new voice said. "She's quite a prize. I'm sure you'll have all the fun in the world training her properly."

"That is my hope," Calisto intoned dully. "Where is my jacket?"

"Right here."

Emma jumped when something covered her shoulders. She suspected it was Calisto's jacket. A hand landed to Emma's lower back and pushed gently, moving her forward. The touch was familiar enough for her to recognize it as Calisto, so she followed his unspoken directions.

Almost done, he had said before.

She was almost out of there.

"Keep her covered, and you will keep her confused enough to frighten her," the man said.

"Compliant is better," Calisto murmured.

"That, too."

Emma continued walking, wondering where in the hell they were going to. Soft murmurs echoed all around—from a dozen different people. High tenors, like those of women, and deeper ones, like those of men.

She could also hear sobbing.

Gentle, breathless sobs.

Emma's heart ached.

It was the first time since she had been brought in the place—whatever in the hell it was—that she realized that it was a very good possibility there were other women being auctioned off besides her.

Of course, there were others.

Her stomach rolled.

She had help.

They didn't.

How awful did it make her that all she wanted to do was just leave?

"Everything is settled, then?" Calisto asked from behind Emma.

"The payment has been received. You are free to go. Your car …?"

"Parked along the back of the warehouse."

"Good, good," the man said. "We have control over the area during auctions, so you are safe to take her out in the open. If you're concerned about her fighting, we have—"

"I'm not concerned," Calisto interjected quickly. "I do need to get going, however."

"We hope to see you again."

"Maybe."

Emma shivered at Calisto's agreement. Would he seriously come back to do this again? To buy a slave?

She didn't get to think on it for long. She was pushed along again, and the murmurs drifted away the longer she walked until it was just the sounds of footsteps surrounding her.

Only two sets.

Hers.

Calisto's.

Emma started to breathe again.

"Like hell," she heard Calisto mutter. "Come back. Right. Christ."

His hand moved from her lower back to her wrist. He held her with a gentle grasp, not too tight or too loose. It was just enough to keep her grounded, to make her feel …

Safe.

"You okay, Emmy?" he asked.

Emma shook her head under the bag.

No, she was not okay.

She was simply holding it together.

Calisto sighed.

"I'm sorry, *ragazza*."

"I ran away," she whispered. "It was my fault."

"It was not."

"Wasn't it?"

She felt Calisto's fingers sweep over her skin with tender swipes, almost like he was reassuring her that everything would be fine.

"It's almost over," he finally said.

Emma disagreed.

Feeling him touch her, hearing the concern echo in his voice, and then feeling the light press of his lips to the side of her head … Her heart was hurting for a whole new reason. The very same reason why her mind was confused, why her body hummed with satisfaction and pain, and why her tears finally began to fall.

No, she disagreed entirely.

Her hell had just begun.

• • •

"Wait a second," Calisto said. "Just be still. I have

to move something."

Emma tried to pull the hood off her head, only to have her arm yanked back down.

"No."

Anxiety thrummed deep in Emma's blood.

"I want to see," she said. "I feel like I can't fucking breathe under here."

"You can. They're made for this. I need you to keep it on for a while longer. At least for one drive until I can switch vehicles."

Emma frowned. "Calisto—"

"Emma, my God. For once, can you fucking listen to me? Just this once. It is for your own good."

She didn't respond.

Her irritation bubbled.

Emma heard the sound of a car unlocking and a door being opened. Calisto grunted something under his breath, followed by a cuss. Then, he was back at her side, and holding her wrist again.

She wanted his hand lower.

In hers.

Fingers tightened around hers, woven with hers.

Emma shook that stupid thought away, because that's exactly what it was. Fucking stupid.

"I'll help you up into the SUV, but you need to sit still, don't touch anything, and keep the damn hood on. Please don't argue, Emma. Just listen."

"Fine," she muttered.

Emma followed Calisto's directions, stepped where he told her to, and then stayed still as she was lifted up and set back down. The plush softness of the leather seat beneath her said they were in a fancier vehicle.

"Sorry about the Mercedes," Emma mumbled.

Calisto laughed, but even the sound was tired. "Where is it?"

Emma rattled off the name of the convenience store parking lot where she had left the Mercedes. "I also left the keys on the driver's side wheel, under the side where it wouldn't be seen."

"That makes things easier."

"Does it?"

"*Sì.*"

"My things are at a hotel. I had it booked for one more night."

"We can pick them up," Calisto said.

A door slammed right after he finished. Emma sighed and fidgeted on the spot until another door was opened, and the vehicle shifted enough to say that Calisto had jumped in the driver's seat.

"Can I take the hood off now?"

"No," he said, offering no other explanation.

Emma bristled. "But—"

"I have to make a call. Be quiet."

As the SUV started to move, Emma tried to stay still in the seat while she listened to Calisto make his call.

"Donati calling," Calisto said. Silence followed before he said, "Do you have a spare set for the Porsche? Great. You can pick it up."

He talked about the Porsche, gave an address, and told whoever was on the other end of the call to pick it up as soon as possible and try not to be noticed too much. Once he ended the call, Calisto didn't say a word.

Emma fiddled with the seam of the hood around her neck. It felt a little too tight for her liking, and she tugged on it a bit to loosen it.

"Stop fucking with that," Calisto barked.

"It's tight."

"It's supposed to be."

Emma blew out a frustrated breath. "I don't like this."

"It's the hood, Emmy, or a view of the two bodies in the back seat. Take your fucking pick."

She turned into stone.

"What did you just say?"

Calisto laughed bitterly. "Fuck, did you seriously think that I somehow managed to find out where you went, get to you, and whatever else I had to do without a few casualties along the way?"

Emma's tongue felt too thick to speak.

"No," Calisto said harshly. "I left a trail of dead bodies all over Vegas between yesterday and today. You are far luckier than I can explain, Emma."

He'd killed for her.

And saved her.

All she did was scare him.

Finally, Emma found her voice.

"Stupid, you mean."

"Desperate," Calisto murmured.

Emma jerked in the seat when she felt his fingers come in contact with her cheek overtop of the hood.

"I think you were desperate," Calisto repeated softly.

"I just …" Emma didn't know what to say.

"You tried, look at it that way."

"And failed," she said.

"But you did try."

"It wasn't worth it, Calisto."

Calisto chuckled. "Depends on how you look at it."

"I can't see much right now."

His fingers stroked her cheek again.

"I can, Emma."

• • •

Emma blinked rapidly and sucked in a huge gulp of air when the hood was finally pulled from her head. It took her a second to focus in on her surroundings, and realize that she was sitting in a familiar car.

Calisto's rental Mercedes.

Glancing to the side, she found Calisto watching her from outside of the car with wary eyes. He leaned in the door a bit, keeping one hand on the car and the other on her jittery leg.

"Hey," he said.

Emma wet her dry lips. "Hey."

"You picked a good spot to drop this car."

"Why is that?"

"It's one of the only places that doesn't seem to be open twenty-four, seven, and there's an alleyway I can use."

"For what?" she asked.

Calisto smirked. "I have an SUV to burn."

Oh.

Emma shot a look over Calisto's broad shoulder, noticing a dark SUV parked in the alleyway he mentioned.

"No cameras, I checked," Calisto said. "Easiest way to clean up a mess is to burn it. Or that's what Affonso always told me when I was younger."

She recoiled at the very mention of her future husband. Calisto didn't miss the actions.

"Sorry," he said quickly.

"It doesn't matter."

"Liar. It does."

Calisto didn't say another thing. Instead, he closed the door on Emma and she watched him move to the back of the Mercedes and pop the trunk. Calisto pulled a small, red can from the back before walking over to the SUV and disappearing into the dark alleyway. Not ten seconds later, he was back in view.

Without the gas can.

Pulling something shiny from his pocket, Calisto glanced down at his hands. A light bloomed, telling Emma he held a lighter. When he tossed it, the car lit up instantly.

Emma looked away. She didn't speak again until they were driving far away from the closed convenience store and the burning SUV.

Calisto slowed the car down and stopped for a red light. He watched the cars speed through their green light, his hands tightening around the wheel enough for his knuckles to turn white under the pressure.

"Thank you, Calisto."

"Don't thank me, Emmy."

"But you saved me."

"Yeah, but what difference does it make, huh?"

Emma's heart clenched. "It makes a huge difference to me."

Calisto shrugged. "I still have to give you away now. The only difference this time is that I know the monster I'll be giving you to."

"It's okay."

She lied.

It wouldn't be okay at all.

"It won't be," Calisto said.

She watched him through hazy, water-filled eyes. She didn't understand him for a minute, but she wanted to more than anything.

Emma wanted to know Calisto.

Anything he might give.

She was too late.

Her wants no longer mattered.

"Why did you do that to me in that place?" Emma dared to ask.

"I didn't have a choice. They have rules they follow—things they do. I couldn't break them, being the newcomer to the group. It might have made me seem suspicious."

"Liar."

Calisto's jaw clenched. "Don't, Emmy. Just forget about it. I'll get you back to your penthouse, you have a few hours to spare before you have to meet up for one final dinner with your parents, and then another night to sleep before New York."

"Liar," she repeated, refusing to acknowledge what he said.

"Emma—"

DONATI BLOODLINES: PART 1

"You did it because you wanted to. You wondered what I felt like. You thought about doing that to me. That's what you said."

Calisto hit the gas as soon as the light turned green, sending Emma flying back in her seat. "You're goddamn right, Emmy."

She took a burning breath.

It felt fucking good.

"Would you do it again if I asked you to?"

"*Emma.*"

"Well, would you?"

His hands tightened on the wheel again, and his gaze burned brightly with things she hadn't seen from him before: need, lust, and want. Calisto still didn't answer.

Emma didn't really need him to.

18.

Calisto

"You should get dressed."

Emma didn't give any indication that she had heard Calisto speak from the other side of the large living room. She stayed sitting in a large chaise, twisting her fingers together over and over, while looking out the wall-to-wall windows of her penthouse.

She hadn't spoken for hours.

She didn't move.

Calisto wasn't sure what to do, but he knew that he couldn't keep worrying over Emma Sorrento. The more he thought about her, and the more he concerned himself with her emotional state, the worse he knew it would get for him.

He had first felt it at the auction. It hit him when he entered the "showing rooms," as the people had called it. He saw her behind the glass where she was standing straight, blindfolded, and swathed in white. She was compliant in the showcase, but her defiance had come through in the clench of her fist and tight set of her lips.

He'd seen it.

And felt it.

The *affection*.

It burrowed deep in Calisto's chest like a thousand little pins sticking into his lungs, determined to hurt him. He'd stayed back, watched her through the glass to keep his interest from being too obvious, but it'd taken every ounce of willpower he had left to do so.

Because he couldn't disregard her.

Something he wanted had been just out of reach. Something he worried about was in danger. Something he cared for was hurting.

Someone, not something.

DONATI BLOODLINES: PART 1

Emma.

Calisto leaned in the entryway between the kitchen and living room. Crossing his arms over his chest, he ignored the ache settling in his bones. It was goddamn hard to do.

It started in his fingers, the digits he'd used to explore, to touch, and to learn Emma, and then quickly traveled up his arm and into his chest. He tried—God, he was fucking trying—to forget her needy little sounds and the way her mouth felt, wrapped around his fingers while he fucked her with his other hand.

This was not good.

This was terrible.

She was just a woman. That's what Calisto wanted to tell himself; that's what he wanted to believe. Emma was nothing more than a woman. There were other women for him to want. To obsess over.

It couldn't be Emma Sorrento.

Not for Calisto.

She was taken.

She was claimed.

She was not his.

In a few days, Calisto would hand her off, and that would be that. He wondered why it wouldn't be that easy to let her go.

What good had saving her done?

He had simply taken her from one monster to give her to another.

Calisto drew in a slow breath, and exhaled through his nose. It was yet another attempt to cool his urges down, forget about his needs, and focus on getting the job done.

Except she wasn't just a job.

Emma wasn't a thing. She was a person. Calisto didn't know how to not see her as a woman so that he could just do what needed to be done. She was struggling with what she had done, what happened, and what was yet to come. He could see the weight on her shoulders, pushing her deeper into her seat with every passing second.

"How long do I have?" Emma asked quietly.

Her voice, raspy and tired, surprised Calisto. She hadn't spoken in so long that he wasn't sure she would speak to him again at all.

"Before what?" he asked.

"The dinner with my parents, Cal."

Calisto tossed a look at the clock on the far wall. "An hour and a half, *mia dolcezza.*"

Emma's shoulders stiffened at his casual use of a pet name. My sweetheart, he called her. Calisto wasn't sure why it had bothered her. It wasn't the first time he'd used it on her when they conversed.

But it is the first time you called her yours, he thought.

Calisto grinded his teeth in an effort to shut out his inner voice. The damn thing hadn't been helping him much lately, so he wasn't about to start listening to it now.

"I have a little bit of time before I need to get ready," Emma said.

"I thought maybe you would want to get over there early and spend some extra time with your mother and father, or even your uncle, before tonight's flight."

Emma shook her head subtly. "No. I'll see them enough in New York before the wedding."

"They're your parents, Emma."

"They're just people who brought me here. DNA doesn't mean love, Calisto."

She was right.

Calisto was living proof of that.

Sighing, he ducked his head when she turned to look at him. "Are you just going to keep sitting there doing nothing?"

"Maybe," Emma murmured. "Can I ask you something?"

"Sure."

"How many others did you see in there last night?"

Calisto stilled on the spot, taking in her question. "What do you mean?"

"Girls. At the auction. How many?"

"A lot."

Emma's stony features cracked when she openly frowned. "How many is a lot?"

"About ten."

Maybe ten wasn't such a high number, but for the price those girls cost the men who bought them, ten was enough to make a killing.

Quite literally.

It disgusted Calisto, but he saved the one he could. There was nothing more he could do.

"Who were they? The girls, I mean," she said.

Calisto thought about the term he had heard used at the auction. "Valuable collectables."

Emma flinched. "Oh, my God."

"Slaves, Emma. They'll have no past, no future, and no real present because they'll no longer exist as regular people. But girls like you, girls like the ones they had gathered for last night, are considered collectables to those people. Whoever they are. It's a very private event, and the only reason I was able to get in like I did was because of the methods I used to do so and the money I was able to show for the effort."

"So they have more than one."

"Likely," he confirmed softly.

"Aren't you worried that they'll come after you because you didn't hide me like they said?" Emma asked.

"You mean getting you out of state?"

"Yeah."

Calisto shrugged. "No. In a few days, Emma Sorrento will no longer exist as she is. She will be—"

"Emma Donati," she interrupted calmly.

Calisto clenched his fists at his sides, letting the bite of his fingernails soothe the rush of possessiveness that filled him at hearing her name when it was changed. He liked it—but he hated who it would be changing for.

"Yes," he managed to say. "And who you become matters very little to them as long as you're someone else. Their concern was only with making you disappear before your family realized who had taken you. You were worth a lot for them on the auction block, but the longer they kept you, the greater the risk of outside influence or retribution. Simple as that."

Emma wet her lips and stared down at her lap. "It has a nice ring to it, doesn't it?"

"Pardon?"

"Emma Donati. It has a nice ring."

Calisto swallowed hard. "It does."

"It's too bad, really."

"What is, *bella*?"

"My name. I like it, but I hate the man giving it to me."

Calisto had to agree, but he chose not to voice it.

Emma smiled crookedly, and glanced up at Calisto again as she added, "Well, I guess that depends on how we look at which man. I only hate the one, after all."

"The man you're marrying?"

"Yes. But I don't hate the one giving me to him."

Oh.

Well, then.

Damn.

"You should get dressed," Calisto said lamely. "Your engagement ring and other jewelry is where you left it."

Emma stared at him, unmoving and seemingly unashamed at her boldness. The fire in her eyes had replaced the blankness from before. She was still wearing that white ensemble from the auction, but only because she had refused to do anything when they returned.

She looked almost innocent, but her sensuality was hard to forget.

Sinful, still.

Calisto was all too aware of her sins.

His, too.

"What?" he asked, annoyed at her staring.

"I might ask you to do it again."

Calisto shut his eyes for a brief second, wanting to wave those words away. Was she testing him? He didn't want to play those games.

"I might," Emma repeated. "And I bet you won't say no."

Opening his eyes again, Calisto found Emma's piercing, knowing stare still leveled on him. He had known even before opening them that she was still watching him. It was like he could feel it.

Feel her.

On him. Over him.

All through him.

"You won't say no," she told him again, confident and sure.

He would try to refuse her.

And *fail*.

· · ·

"Heavenly Father, thank you for this meal and for our health, family, and our many blessings."

The beginning of Minnie Sorrento's prayer drew Calisto out of his thoughts and back to the dinner at hand. Checking out the other people sitting at the long table, he noticed that everyone had their heads down, eyes closed, and their hands connected with the person beside them if they were close enough.

Calisto sat beside Emma, but her hand stayed firmly seated on the table and far away from his. He wasn't complaining.

"Thank you, Minnie," Maximo said from the head of the table. "Let's eat."

Food was served. Dishes filled. Mouths were fed.

Calisto listened in on the conversations that filled the dining room, but didn't bother to join in unless he was directly asked a question. At his side, Emma stayed quiet with her head drawn down as she pushed pieces of chicken pesto around on her plate.

It took Calisto another two minutes to realize he was doing the same damn thing.

"How do they not know what I did?" she asked quietly.

The loud conversations, continuous laughter, and the wine being shared between the people at the table allowed Calisto and Emma a mostly private conversation. He wasn't concerned about being overheard, what with the volume of the noise.

"Because I knew what would happen if they did," Calisto said.

Emma shot him a look that asked a million questions. "Should I thank you?"

"You already did."

"For saving me, not for protecting me."

There was a difference. She had made a distinction that he hadn't quite realized before.

"Don't bother," Calisto said with a smile.

"But—"

"Emma," George said from the other side of the table. "Do us a favor and play something?"

Calisto didn't miss the frown that Emma quickly hid with a bite of food.

"Oh, yes," Maximo said. "The piano was just tuned last week, too."

"I haven't played in years," Emma finally replied. "I'll be rusty, and it'll sound awful."

Calisto hadn't known Emma could play the piano, but he wasn't too surprised at the news. Most wealthy families had their daughters in a multitude of extra-curricular activities to fill their time and spend their money on. High-society liked for their girls to be cultured, polite, and well-trained in all things.

Emma didn't look particularly pleased at being asked to play the piano.

"I doubt that," Calisto told her. "I'm sure it'll sound wonderful."

Emma stared at him, not saying a thing.

No one else seemed to notice his comment. He was grateful. It was a little too comforting for a man that these people knew to be cold in his demeanor and aloof all the other times in between.

"Play, Emma, please," Minnie said.

Emma sighed. "Ma, I'm not really in the mood."

Before someone could pressure Emma again, Calisto stood from his chair and tossed his napkin down. "I will."

Emma's head snapped up, her eyes finding his and searching. "You play the piano?"

"Quite well," he admitted, offering no other explanation. Turning to the man at the head of the table, Calisto waved his hand in the direction of the baby grand in the corner. "May I, Maximo?"

Maximo nodded. "Absolutely."

Calisto strolled across the dining room, ignoring the curious gazes of the guests. Taking a seat on the white leather bench, he flipped open the top of the casing covering the ivory keys. A pain settled in his chest, stabbing and heavy, but he tampered it down.

Clenching his fists, Calisto felt his knuckles crack. A bit of the lingering tension drifted away when he placed his hands on the correct position to start, and felt the ivory kiss his fingertips. The memory was right there, teasing him and hurting him at the same time.

When he began to play, he could see her again.

A younger her.

A younger him.

He played the song she taught him first.

"It's a beautiful sound, isn't it, baby?" Camilla asked.

Calisto pressed the four keys in time, like his mother had shown him. The sound flowed from the piano. "Sì, Mamma."

"And now," his mother said, taking his hands in hers, "... we go like this."

His mother pressed his fingers down on another four keys.

More sound.

More music.

A rhythm, she called it.

"Can you try those now, baby?" Camilla asked. "Do you think you can remember the first four notes and these, too?"

Calisto nodded. "Sì."

"Show me."

He did as his mother asked, hitting the first four notes using only two tiny fingers, and then following with the second set of four notes.

It was starting to make a song.

Calisto liked the sound.

"Who made this?" he asked.

"Hmm?"

"The song, Mamma. You says people write them. Who made this?"

Camilla ducked her head when her son turned for an answer. "Um, this is just something I learned a while ago."

"But someone made it."

"Composed, baby. But, yes, someone wrote this. They made it."

"Who?" he asked again.

"Your father," Camilla said quickly. "Can you show me the notes again?"

Your father.

Calisto, in all his five year old glory, knew better than to keep asking after hearing those two words. His father made his mother cry. That's all he understood. Whenever his father was mentioned, his mother became sad.

He hated seeing his mamma sad.

DONATI BLOODLINES: PART 1

Turning back to the piano, Calisto pressed onto the keys again with two fingers, playing the notes faster the second time around. He didn't miss a single one.

"Well done," Camilla said. "You're a natural, Cal."

"He's very talented, but it'll do him no good to have delicate hands, Cam."

Camilla stiffened at the new presence. Calisto straightened on the bench at the sound of his uncle's voice. He spun so fast on his seat that he nearly toppled over the large books his mother had used to sit him on to make him higher.

"Zio!" Calisto shouted.

Affonso stood in the entryway of the music room with a wide smile. "Calisto, my boy. Come here and stop playing around. We're busy men, we have things to do."

Calisto felt his mother's arms tighten around his middle for a brief second. It was almost like she didn't want to let him go. Then, just as quickly, she kissed the top of his head.

"We'll practice more later," she told Calisto.

Calisto was already jumping off the bench, out of his mother's arms, and toward his uncle. Affonso was waiting with a hand open and outstretched. Calisto took it, feeling the golden ruby ring on his uncle's pinky finger when he grabbed tightly to the digit.

"Cam?" Affonso called.

Calisto's mother didn't turn around after she closed the piano up. "Yeah?"

"Do you want to—"

"No," his mother interrupted before Affonso could even get the question out.

Calisto was too interested in finding out what his uncle was going to do with him today to think about why his mother seemed sad again.

"Come on, zio," Calisto demanded, pulling on Affonso's hand.

"All right. We'll go. I'll see you later, Cam."

"Sure, later," his mother echoed.

"I'm sorry for intruding on your lesson," Affonso said as he turned to leave.

Camilla laughed tiredly. "You've been intruding for his whole life, Affonso. Why stop now?"

Calisto finished the piece with a deep ache settling over his fingers and in his knuckles. It had been a while since he played something as difficult as one of his father's works. It wasn't long enough to make his hands hurt after playing, however.

It wasn't a physical pain.

It was emotional.

Far down in his gut, embedded in his bones, and woven into his very person.

It would never leave.

Calisto could forget about it for a short time. He could pretend like it wasn't there and use his distance and disinterest as a way to keep it at bay, but it always came back.

Those memories, ones of his mother that tied into her past with his father, were ones that Calisto tried to stay away from as much as possible. His childhood had been mostly happy despite his father having died, but it still tainted the edges of his memories with a dark, black color.

The resounding claps brought Calisto out of the daze he was in. Carefully, he slid the top back down over the ivory keys and pressed his hand on the glossy wood.

A thank you of sorts.

An apology, mostly.

Hopefully, his mother knew.

Standing, Calisto offered the Sorrento family and their guests a smile. "There, something for you."

"You're very good," Minnie said.

"Thank you."

"Who taught you to play?" Emma asked.

Calisto found her with his gaze, wondering if he should answer truthfully. "My mother. She loved the piano, and she wanted me to love it, too."

DONATI BLOODLINES: PART 1

Before anyone could question him further, Calisto excused himself for what he said was a bathroom break. Really, he just needed a second to breathe alone.

He was always alone now.

Calisto imagined that must have been how his mother felt, too. Even when she was holding him.

19.

Calisto

Lighting up a cigarette, Calisto inhaled a hefty drag and let the smoke soothe his frayed nerves. It wasn't like him to be so jumpy and anxious. He didn't know how to deal with the onslaught of confusion swirling in his mind.

The Mercedes stereo blasted hard rock into the car. Calisto closed his eyes, leaned back in the seat, and drummed his fingers against the steering wheel in time with the music. It was nothing like his mother had enjoyed. She preferred blues or jazz. Something with emotion soaking every note and lyric. Something she could dance to.

Calisto needed to get out of his head.

Opening his eyes, Calisto surveyed the house just four doors down. He had arrived a little late to the dinner, and no parking spots were left for him to use in the Sorrento family driveway. He'd parked further down the street.

He hadn't gone back into the dinner party before leaving the house. Twenty minutes had already passed. Calisto hoped no one noticed his absence and came looking for him. Wining and dining didn't hold his interest.

Not tonight.

Ducking his head down, Calisto took another puff off his cigarette, tossed it out the window, and then massaged his temples. At least he could say he was cutting back by smoking less of a cigarette at a time.

That was something.

Right?

A knock on the passenger side window nearly made Calisto jump out of his seat. He found a stony-faced Emma peering in through the darkly tinted glass. She folded her arms over her chest, waiting.

Sighing, Calisto unlocked the door. Emma climbed in without a word.

"Party over?" he asked.

"No."

"What are you doing out here then?"

Emma's gaze jumped to him in an instant, and Calisto could practically feel it cut into his soul. Her worry was as clear as glass to him. Maybe she had taken note of his desire to exit the dinner party after playing the piano.

Calisto didn't want her to worry.

Not about him.

He might like it too much.

"I could ask you the same thing," Emma said.

"I wanted a smoke."

"You said you were going to the bathroom twenty minutes ago."

"Don't you have your own business to look after?" Calisto asked, sharper than he intended.

Emma didn't even blink at his attitude. "Is it me?"

"Is what you?"

"Whatever is wrong with you right now, Calisto. Your nastiness and your irritation. Is it because of me and what happened?"

Calisto frowned. "No."

Emma cocked a brow, but didn't say a word. Just her look alone was enough to make him correct his statement.

"Not entirely," he said. "It's still none of your concern, Emmy."

"You should start calling me Emma. Might as well get used to it before we get to New York."

Calisto scoffed. "Why?"

"Because Affonso doesn't like Emmy."

"I told you already, you're sorely mistaken if you think I give a good goddamn what that man likes, *Emmy.*"

Emma smiled slyly, but turned her head away to where Calisto couldn't see her face anymore. "The party got loud after they moved from the dining room to the living room with more wine. I'm not in the mood to listen to drunk people tonight. I don't even think they noticed that I slipped out when no one was looking my way."

Calisto chuckled. "Bad girl."

"Thank you, by the way."

"For what?"

"Playing the piano and taking the attention away from me. I could have played, but I don't like to all that much. I used to practice and have recitals when I was younger because my father wanted me to. I didn't enjoy it."

"It's fine. Don't mention it."

Literally, he held back from adding.

Emma didn't let it go. "You didn't seem to like it much either."

"I—"

"But you play like a pro," she finished, cutting him with yet another one of her looks.

"As I said inside, my mother taught me to play when I was a boy."

"You're very good for someone who only played as a child."

"I never said that."

Emma glanced down at her lap. "When was the last time you played?"

"Shortly before I came out here. I tuned a piano for a friend of mine, and played a bit to make sure everything was perfect."

"Before that?"

"What are you digging for?" he asked.

Emma shrugged. "Curious."

"Well, stop it. There's nothing to find."

Nothing he was willing to share.

"I've never heard that song before," Emma noted quietly. "The one you played, I mean. Did you compose it?"

Calisto laughed. "No. I'm not that talented. I may understand how to play and be able to pick up a tune easily enough, but I can't write music."

"But it is an unpublished, unrecorded piece." Emma turned in the seat, watching him with a burning glint lighting up her green eyes. "I may hate playing the piano, but I do like to listen to it. And like I said, I've never heard that before. I was curious who it belonged to."

"My father," Calisto said, wishing his chest wasn't as tight as it was. "He composed the piece."

"And your mother taught it to you."

"Yes. What does it matter?"

"Curious," Emma repeated. "You never mention them. Not with any depth. And then I see you with the piano, treating it with kind hands, and I had to wonder about it all. It helped that Maximo mentioned he knew your father had played the piano before his death. I might have drawn a few conclusions."

Irritation simmered below Calisto's skin. "So, you assumed the piece had come from my family, came out here to pester me about it, and tricked me with a few questions to get me to admit to it? What is the point in that?"

Emma's smile faltered. "I just wanted to know more. I didn't mean to upset you."

"There's nothing to know. My father played, he taught my mother, and she taught me."

"Does it remind you of them?"

"Leave it alone, Emma. Please."

Emma nodded, and rested back in the seat with a soft exhale. "I used to dance when I was younger, and then when I was a teenager. Ballet, actually. My grandmother was a ballerina. My dad's mother, not my mom's."

"So?"

"So, I grew up on her knee learning about ballet, seeing pictures of her in her costumes and whatever else. I stopped dancing when I was seventeen."

Calisto looked over at Emma, taking notice of the way her lips turned down at the corners and her hands balled in her lap. "Why seventeen?"

"My father told me ballet was an unimportant goal for me in the end. I never really understood why he felt that way until the whole marriage thing came up. It makes sense now."

"Doesn't explain why you quit."

"My grandmother died," Emma said. "I don't know if you've noticed, but my family is very materialistic. Being wealthy and significant is more important to them than anything else. It was more important to them than giving me time and attention while I was growing up."

"Your grandmother gave that to you instead."

"Yeah. Ballet didn't quite feel the same after. I was happy to give it up. My father was happy I gave up on a dream he didn't support."

"Win-win," Calisto muttered.

"Apparently." Emma lifted a single shoulder like it didn't make a difference. Calisto could tell by the wetness coating her lashes that it made every difference to her. "Anyway, my point is that it's nice you're able to keep something close to you that reminds you of your parents without it hurting you. I wish I had the same thing for my grandmother."

"It does hurt me," Calisto said before he could stop himself.

He wanted to take the words back immediately.

Emma stilled in the passenger seat. "Then why play?"

To remember.

To punish himself.

To apologize.

"For a lot of different reasons," Calisto settled on saying. "But tonight, I played so that you wouldn't have to. You didn't seem comfortable. I didn't think you wanted to have everyone looking at you after what happened. It was a small sacrifice."

"But you hurt now," she said, seeming confused. "Don't you?"

"But you didn't have to."

For Calisto, that was all that mattered.

Turning his head, Calisto stared out the opened driver's window. He wondered if anyone had noticed that both he and Emma had left the dinner party without a goodbye. He supposed it didn't make a difference.

Calisto didn't mind Emma's presence disturbing his peace, either.

"Calisto?" Emma asked softly.

"Hmm?"

Her hand rested on his thigh, and Calisto jerked in the seat at the innocent touch. The problem was, her touch couldn't be innocent at all. Not with the way he currently felt, the things he had done, or the lines he had already crossed with a mighty "fuck you." He hadn't been expecting it, and he didn't even hear Emma move in her seat.

Calisto barely had the chance to spin around and face Emma again before her mouth pressed against his. It was soft at first, smooth like her plump lips, and then her fingers dug into his leg like she was demanding something from him.

He didn't know what it was.

Instinctively, Calisto wanted to push her away. He wanted to kiss her back, too. The crazy side of his brain won, the side that listened to his selfish wants and not his needs.

Or maybe he needed it, too.

Calisto didn't know.

But he did grab onto Emma's dress. He fisted the fabric around his taut knuckles, and pulled her a little closer. His tongue swept the seam of her lips, wanting more, needing to be deeper, seeking her heat and taste.

A little wouldn't hurt, right?

Just a little more.

Emma sighed a sweet sound, giving into his unspoken demand by parting her lips. Calisto took the offering for what it was, kissed her harder, and let his tongue war with hers until she was gasping for air. Pulling away enough to catch a breath, Emma tipped her head up and hummed.

Calisto couldn't help himself but lean forward and kiss her chin.

He was fucking stupid.

Why did she make him so *stupid?*

"I should go in and say goodbye," he heard Emma say.

Calisto was too distracted by the flimsy fabric of her dress in his hands. A little pull with just enough strength and he knew that the dress would rip. She was close, and he could grab her around the waist before pulling her into the backseat.

The windows were tinted.

No one would see.

A little more wouldn't hurt.

"Calisto," Emma said.

His name in her mouth sounded divine. He would bet his bottom dollar that it would sound even better if she was bent over something sturdy, stretched full of his cock, and screaming his name to the heavens.

"Calisto."

He met her gaze, unsettled and unsure.

"Yeah?" he asked.

"I should go in and say goodbye."

"You'll see them in New York."

Emma wet her lips, drawing in his attention to that pout of hers. "I meant for the evening."

Oh.

Calisto let her go.

Emma fell back into the seat with a shiver. "We're going to get in trouble doing this."

DONATI BLOODLINES: PART 1

"Trouble" wasn't a good enough word for what would happen to them both if someone even whispered about what had already happened. Calisto chose not to correct Emma.

"You have to know what this is for there to be something," Calisto murmured.

And maybe if they didn't label whatever it was, it wouldn't exist.

It was ridiculous, sure.

Calisto didn't care. He was still trying to make sense of the mess he had now found himself in, a mess of his own causing. For a smart man, one who followed the rules and knew what was right and what was wrong, Calisto was sure proving how fucked up he could be.

Or rather, how fucked up he truly was.

Broken, maybe. Calisto knew what made him this way—callous, reckless, and selfish. He had learned as a young man that when a bed was made, it was made to lie in.

Emma caught his stare again, holding strong. "We shouldn't do this, Cal."

"No, we definitely shouldn't," Calisto agreed.

Calisto knew that they probably still would.

It wouldn't lead to anywhere good.

It couldn't.

• • •

Unbelievable.

Calisto stared down at the notification lighting up the screen of his phone.

Flight USAir B-2473 to New York, New York canceled due to weather conditions. All flights will be rescheduled and updates provided. We're very sorry for the inconvenience, and hope to have more information soon.

The sky above Las Vegas was as clear as it had ever been. The same couldn't be said for New York, apparently. A blizzard that was expected to miss the state changed direction in just enough time to cover everything in a good three feet of snow. It also ended up causing the cancelation of every flight going into or out of New York.

Damn.

Calisto hadn't counted on this happening. His bags were packed and waiting at the penthouse door along with Emma's four-piece luggage set. This wasn't good at all. He expected to be in the air in two hours. He wanted the distance that New York would provide him to clear his fucking head of Emma Sorrento and the nonsense Calisto had going on.

Now he couldn't do that at all. His damned penthouse apartment, the one he had been using, was emptied and then had been filled by a new guest with reservations. That left Calisto with Emma's apartment to stay in, or he could grab them a hotel closer to the airport.

A pressure landed on Calisto's shoulders, pushing him down under the weight. It was like the world was conspiring against him. Shrugging the heavy feeling off, he dialed a familiar number and put the phone to his ear. Three rings later, Affonso picked up the call.

"I heard," Affonso said the moment he answered. "They expect the storm to pass in a day and have flights coming in within two days."

"Saves me the time of explaining," Calisto muttered.

"I'm sure everything will run smoothly and on time when you get here. The dress Emma purchased arrived today, so let her know for me."

Great.

"Will do, *zio.*"

"And it's appropriate, I should add. Thank you for that, Cal."

Calisto's brow furrowed. "You looked at her dress?"

"Why not?"

"Because it's her wedding dress, Affonso."

"It's just a dress, my boy. I couldn't let the girl wear just anything. I had to make sure it was okay."

"Then what in the hell did you send me in with her for, if you were going to look yourself?" Calisto demanded.

"Your attitude is strong today. Awfully touchy, are we?"

Calisto snapped his mouth shut. "No, not at all."

The sound of running water drew Calisto's attention to the back hallway of the penthouse. The place was mostly empty, and had been for a while. Emma had said she wanted to jump in the shower before they left to catch the flight. Knowing she was just a short stride away, naked and wet, did not help Calisto's little issue of keeping a distance and a clear head.

It didn't help his still semi-hard cock, either. It wouldn't go down. It hadn't gone down since he'd felt her body, made her come, and he was left, still wanting more.

"I'll let Emma know about the dress."

"This flight mess has you stressed. I can hear it in your voice. Don't worry about it, Cal. Everything will be fine."

Affonso was wrong.

Nothing would be fine.

His uncle didn't have a clue.

• • •

"Just give me a few minutes to get dressed and we can go," Emma said from behind Calisto.

"Don't worry about rushing," Calisto replied without turning away from the windows. "The flights to New York are canceled for today, and maybe tomorrow, too. A blizzard came through and practically shut the state down."

"Oh."

"Yeah. You'll get one more night in your bed. I'll take the couch."

Emma didn't respond. Shooting a glance over his shoulder, Calisto watched as Emma turned away and walked back in the direction of where the bathroom was located. She had a towel wrapped around her figure, and had left her damp hair to hang in waves down her back. His gaze traveled over the curve of her waist that was accentuated by how tightly the towel was pulled, and the swell of her ass that swayed as she walked.

She was all natural. All of her. Calisto's fingers twitched, wanting to feel her warm, smooth body under his palms and taste her clean skin with his kisses and tongue.

Why did it have to be her?

Why did Emma—the one woman that was off-limits—have to be the one that finally made him take notice and want something?

You're not going to do this, he told himself.

Not with her.

"Calisto?"

Emma's sweet call of his name, all innocent and quiet, made Calisto snap out of his daze. He lifted his gaze from her backside to her eyes. She had stopped walking and was looking right at him.

Calisto couldn't even feel ashamed to be caught staring.

Beautiful things deserved attention.

Emma was incredibly beautiful.

"You don't have to take the couch, Cal," she said.

Calisto swallowed hard. "Don't do that. Don't put that out there, Emmy."

"Maybe we can just … get it out. It might work. One night, Calisto. And then we forget it ever happened. You get what you want, and I get to pretend for a night that things could be different. What will it hurt?"

Everything.

DONATI BLOODLINES: PART 1

Calisto didn't know how to explain that to Emma. His thoughts were silenced when Emma let the towel slip enough to showcase her naked side and still damp skin. Under thick lashes, she watched him from the shadows.

The offer was there.

Offers were meant to be taken.

Once might not be enough.

His self-control was gone.

"Don't do that," Calisto said again, one last time.

Emma let the towel drop even more. "I just did."

Fucked.

They were so incredibly *fucked*.

Calisto's restraint wavered, and he stepped forward.

Closer to sin.

Closer to his next mistake.

It was bad, but it had to be good.

He knew it was wrong.

It still felt *right*.

20.

Calisto's hand snagged Emma's wrist the moment she stepped into the bedroom. Emma didn't even get the chance to turn around and face him before he pulled her into his chest, drove his hand down her stomach, and yanked the towel away.

Emma sagged into Calisto's arms when his hand slipped between her legs. He didn't say a thing, not one word. His other hand palmed her ass while he started kissing her skin everywhere he could kiss.

Air cut through Emma's teeth in a hiss as he stroked her bare sex with two fingers. She knew what his hands could do to her, but she wanted to feel something thicker, longer, and harder fucking her.

"Just tonight," Calisto rumbled from behind her.

Emma nodded. "Yeah."

"Fuck it out."

She laughed, breathless and unsure. Her body was already singing, wanting this man.

"It's stupid, I know," Emma mumbled, tilting her head back to rest on Calisto's shoulder.

"It is."

Emma was pushed away from Calisto before she could say another thing. Confused, she spun on her heel to face him, only to find he was pulling at the buttons of his dress shirt, and working the zipper of his pants at the same time. Calisto kicked off his pants, keeping his gaze on Emma all the while.

Something dark was in his eyes.

Something hungry—*starved*.

Emma knew the feeling. She hoped that this one night with Calisto would serve to get rid of whatever craziness was wrong with her. She needed it to go away.

They couldn't *be*.

Calisto's shirt hit the floor. "You're fucking beautiful, Emmy."

Her mouth went dry when he shoved his pants down. His erection strained against his boxer-briefs, thick and heavy.

"Am I?" she asked.

"You won't be told nearly enough by him, I know it. I just wanted to let you know."

Emma wet her lips, her heart thundering loudly. She was naked standing there in front of him, but she didn't have the slightest urge to cover up her body or the imperfections he might be able to see. Why should she, when he called her beautiful, and sounded so entirely sincere that it almost hurt to hear it?

"Don't make this sweet," Emma told him.

Calisto met her gaze, his eyes a wild-black and burning. "I don't want to use you, Emmy."

"I don't need or want sweet, Cal. I don't want it to linger like it would if it was like that. Don't do that tonight."

"Okay."

Calisto shoved his boxer-briefs down, and his cock was freed to his hand. He fisted his length with quick, firm tugs, drawing Emma's stare down to his dick. Her stomach clenched with need. She watched as he bent down and pulled a foil packet from his discarded pants pocket. Quickly, he opened the condom and rolled it down his length without hesitation. He took two long strides, let go of his cock at the same time, and grabbed her face in his hands.

Emma took a single breath before his mouth was crushing down on hers. His teeth nipped against her lips, making her skin sting. His fingers bit into her skin, promising and wicked. She let him own her with his kiss, feeling his tongue dance with hers, taking away her air while he sought more of her heat.

"I bet you're wet for me," he mumbled against her mouth. "You're shaking already."

The huskiness of his voice was a drug.

So damned addictive.

"Fuck me," Emma demanded.

Just once.

It would all go away then.

Her feelings.

The craziness.

Her confusion.

It would go away.

Right?

Emma's thought process dropped off when she found herself spun around and shoved forward. Her knees hit the bed, and then Calisto was behind her. His hand buried into her hair and pulled with just enough force for it to hurt. His palms snapped against her inner thighs, forcing her legs wider.

It felt like fucking heaven.

"This is what you want?" Calisto asked. "*Mi vuoi?*"

She shivered. "*Sì.*"

"It doesn't have to be—"

"It does," Emma interjected quickly.

She needed it like this.

Hard.

Fast.

Even painful.

Making this into something different might make them into something different. Emma didn't need that, and neither did Calisto.

"Just fucking take me," Emma said, feeling his hands run over her ass.

Emma found herself flipped over in an instant. She barely had time to clear her vision and see Calisto above her before he fitted himself between her thighs. His cock was sliding through the lips of her pussy, and he flexed forward. She was wet enough that his cock found no resistance when he took her deep.

Her broken cry echoed.

Good *God*.

He filled her full, stretched her open, and it ached in the best way. He didn't give her time to adjust to his thick length before he was pulling out and thrusting right back in again. Emma's hands found his chest, her fingernails digging into his skin as she tried to find purchase.

She needed to settle, to breathe.

"*Cazzo Cristo*," Calisto cursed.

Calisto grabbed her waist and pulled her into him harder, reaching deeper. He didn't give her time to think. Not about what they were doing, the mistakes they were making, or what might come of it.

No, he just fucked her.

Skin on skin.

Teeth biting into her jaw.

Her fingers buried into his hair.

It was relief, sweet agony, and the desire for more, all rolled into one.

And it was perfect.

Emma wished it hadn't been.

• • •

Emma shivered as a fingertip traced lazy, loopy pathways across her naked shoulders. Following behind the soft touch was the press of lips and the pulse of breath washing over her skin. She nibbled on her bottom lip, trying to stay quiet and still as Calisto continued his silent exploration of her body.

Maybe he thought she was sleeping.

His touch, his kiss, was fucking exquisite.

It made her feel alive, but suspended in time. The simple stroke of his fingers and the whisper of his lips, were laced with his care and desire. It wasn't simply playing with her body, or enjoying the woman sharing a bed with him.

No.

His attention to her was worshipping.

Each caress. Every tiny breath.

His tongue lapping at her shoulder blade. His fingers raking over her skin.

Emma's body betrayed her when she let out a shaky sigh filled with the sound of her pleasure and need for more. Calisto shifted closer to her under the sheets, close enough that his chest melded against her back as his hand roved over her side to her stomach. The long, thick length of his cock rested heavily along the swell of her ass.

"Do you know how soft you are?" she heard him ask.

Emma swallowed hard, her words lost when his hand snaked between her thighs. She couldn't think of how to respond when his fingers began to explore under the sheets.

Gentle swipes of his digits circled her clit again and again. His cock grinded into her backside, and by the way it felt, she suspected he already had a condom on. She could feel her slick arousal smear to her thighs when his hand cupped her sex as he pulled her into his groin. Then, his attention was back on her clit, rubbing, pressing, and promising release. She shook in the bed, knowing her tenderness was a result of the fast, hard fucking from the night before.

This was nothing like that.

It was sweet.

It was blissful.

It wasn't rushed, demanding, or broken. She could breathe this time, feel everything he did, and it was enough to make tears gather in her eyes. She wasn't supposed to have him like this, soft, sweet, and attentive. It wouldn't make things any easier when it came to an end, but Emma couldn't make herself tell Calisto to stop.

Not when she felt like this.

She was hot, wet, and so damned *sensitive*.

Her clit throbbed from the attention.

"So soft," Calisto murmured into the crook of her neck. "All over, Emma. It's fucking addictive. I want to keep touching just to see if there's a single part of you that doesn't feel like silk underneath my hands. What the fuck did you do to *me*?"

Nothing, she wanted to say. What could she do to a man like him? She was just a woman. One that didn't belong to him.

Emma whined low when Calisto's fingers pushed into her sex as deep as he could get them. Widening her legs just a little bit allowed his palm to rub along her clit as he thrust into her pussy over and over.

"Oh, my God," Emma whispered. She twisted in his hold, feeling him move with her. The sensations running through her nervous system, the orgasm that was all too cloying but just out of reach, was teasing her. It was too much. It wasn't nearly enough. "Please don't stop ... *please.*"

"And this," Calisto ground out behind her. "*This*, Emma, *cazzo Dio*. All your little noises, and your trembling. You're doing this for me and I shouldn't like it at all but I goddamn well do."

Emma sucked in a sharp breath when his teeth buried into her shoulder. She squirmed in his hold again, seeking to find more of his body on hers and rolling her hips into every plunge of his fingers.

Calisto's mouth found her skin with kisses that burned her from the inside out. His free hand drove into her hair and held tight as his lips kissed a path over her cheek, jaw, neck, and her shoulders. She could feel his tongue strike against her skin, tasting her, while his fingers just kept fucking her to a racing orgasm.

"You didn't want sweet last night, Emmy, but you said nothing about this morning."

She couldn't stop moving, turning in his hands,

pressing back into his cock and his mouth.

More.

She needed more.

"God, *Calisto.*"

Breathless, spun, and high.

That's what Emma was.

Somehow, Emma found herself on her knees. Calisto was still wrapped around her with his fingers tied up in her hair, his kisses painting her skin with his private worship, and his fingers working her pussy harder than ever. She was slick, tender to the touch, and raving fucking mad with the stinging bliss just beyond her reach.

He made her crazy.

Why did he have to be the one to do that?

Emma cried out when she felt the loss of Calisto's fingers from between her thighs. Her desperation quickly melted into a low moan when his cock slid between the wet, fleshy lips of her pussy and filled her full with one smooth push.

"Jesus," Calisto breathed into her neck. "You're so good under me, *mia dolcezza*. So good."

Tears dampened Emma's lashes all over again.

He felt so much better than good.

Insane, even.

Deep in her soul, it hurt, too.

Emma shuddered, and fisted the bedsheets. "Why does it have to be like this?"

Calisto's body moved in slow, unhurried strokes. His fingers dragged down her skin, lighting her body up with sparks of pleasure. "I don't know."

"It shouldn't be this good," she mumbled.

"It shouldn't," he agreed, his tone husky and dark in her ear. "Just let me make you come, Emma. Just a little more, okay? One more time. Let me do that. I want it."

She needed it.

"Please," she said, backing into his next thrust.

Calisto groaned heavily. His hand found the back of

her neck, holding her down. Emma let him use her, fuck her harder until her throat was dry and she couldn't do anything but simply feel.

It was wonderful.

Messy, stupid, and beautiful.

She came hard, shouting his name, and hurting on the inside. His come painted her back not five seconds later.

Apparently, she had been wrong. He wasn't wearing a condom. Through her panting and lost senses, Emma didn't care. Calisto mumble words that made no sense. She tried to focus on what he was saying, but his voice was muffled into her neck.

"I would if you were mine," she heard.

Barely.

Emma blinked, feeling tears slip from her eyes. "Would what?"

Calisto's hand tightened in her hair. His tugged her head sideways, giving him access to her cheek and mouth. His kisses peppered her face, taking away the fresh tears and the new ache with every press of his lips. When he found her mouth with his own, Emma felt owned by the possessive swipes of his lips and the demanding strikes of his tongue against hers.

"Keep you," he said against her mouth. "If you could be mine, Emma. I think I would keep you."

But she wasn't.

So he couldn't.

Emma said nothing.

Five minutes later, when Calisto rolled her over to her back and spread her legs wide, Emma let him fuck her again. She sucked his fingers clean while he grabbed her jaw, forced her to watch him above her, and fucked her until she was raw all over.

One more time, he said, like he had earlier. *Just a little more.*

One more time should have been enough.

It wasn't.

• • •

"Miss Sorrento?"

Emma glanced up at the unfamiliar voice, only to find a man around her age waiting with keys in his hand.

"That's me," Emma replied.

She looked behind her, wondering where Calisto had gone to. Despite sitting beside one another on the plane, he had gotten lost in the flood of people as they began to exit at the terminal.

Where was he?

"I'm Carter," the man said, bringing Emma's attention back to him.

"Nice to meet you."

But what did it matter?

"Affonso sent me to pick you up," Carter said, shrugging. "He figured I could explain it to you as well as he can. I'm your bodyguard, your driver, and whatever else the boss needs me to be for you. We can grab your bags and head out. There's a dinner at the Donati family home, and you don't want to be late."

Emma frowned. "Who is driving Calisto?"

"Cal left his car at the airport when he flew out to Vegas. I imagine that's what he's taking back to his place."

His place.

A coldness settled over Emma's heart, layering it in ice.

They had happened.

They were done.

Her and Calisto, it was what it was.

New York was the line, she realized.

Calisto had drawn it.

"I didn't know Affonso was having a dinner," Emma said, wanting to get away from her thoughts. "He didn't mention anything about one."

DONATI BLOODLINES: PART 1

"Last minute thing. His daughters got in from boarding school a day earlier than expected. The weather cleared up. What he wants, the boss gets. You ready?"

No.

She would never be.

"Sure," Emma said.

"New York isn't Vegas, so you might want to put on your coat."

Emma didn't bother listening.

She couldn't get any fucking colder than she already was. The ice in her veins was cold enough to freeze hell.

Carter started walking away and Emma followed behind him without saying a word. Out of the corner of her eye, a familiar form caught her attention.

Calisto leaned against a wall with his suit jacket dangling from his fingertips. He watched her, unashamed but as impassive and aloof as he had been that very first day.

Masks were meant to be worn.

His was like stone.

Raising his hand from his side, Calisto waved two fingers in Emma's direction before he dropped it back in place.

Like it hadn't even happened.

Like they hadn't happened.

Emma wished it were true, but she couldn't forget. The familiar glint in Calisto's eye, taking her in and looking her over from afar, said that he couldn't forget, either.

New York should be their line.

Emma didn't think it would be.

• • •

Affonso's daughters were beautiful creatures with eyes made of fire. When their father wasn't looking, they glared across the table at Emma like she was the worst thing to grace their presence.

Michelle, the youngest, barely spoke two words when she had been introduced to Emma earlier. The oldest, Cynthia, sneered her hello and then walked on past her soon-to-be step-mother with the disinterest of most teenagers.

Out of all the things that Emma knew would be difficult when she became the wife of Affonso Donati, his children's rejection was the hardest. They had grown up with another woman as their mother, someone they loved and adored.

It was not Emma.

She couldn't fill whatever holes they had.

"Where is Calisto?" Cynthia asked her father.

Affonso stopped eating at his spot from the head of the table. Peering down the way at his oldest daughter, Affonso shrugged like he didn't give a damn. "The flight probably tired him out. I'm sure he'll be around to take you out for dinner at that place you like so much."

Strangely, Emma's heart warmed at the knowledge that Calisto was mindful to spend time with his cousins. He certainly didn't have to, but it was nice to know that he did.

"He promised," Michelle said, a whine in her tone.

Affonso cocked a brow at his youngest daughter, silencing whatever else she might say in an instant. The rest of the table quieted as well.

Emma had been quick to notice how the men surrounding Affonso at his dinner table weren't all that different from the men who surrounded her uncle and father at their dinners. The Don was the most important man in the room. His voice was the only one that needed to be heard when he was speaking. Attention was mostly focused on him unless he directed it elsewhere.

Affonso was a king to them.

He wasn't Emma's king.

Her introduction earlier as she joined the dinner had been to the point, and over before she realized it. A setting was already placed for her at the table, along with a chair for her to sit at Affonso's side. Her things were upstairs, waiting for her to unpack.

She hadn't even explored the house yet.

Leaning over, Affonso said quietly, "You have your own room, for now. That's where I had your things put."

Emma nodded, thankful for the space. "Thank you."

"After the wedding, you'll move into my room."

Anxiety thrummed deep in Emma's chest. She managed to keep it hidden.

"Yes, Affonso."

No one seemed to notice their exchange.

"Daddy?" Michelle asked.

Affonso gave his daughter a passing glance. "What, Michelle?"

"We don't have to call her mom, right?"

The entire table quieted of chatter almost immediately. A few utensils dropped from the hands of the guests, clattering on the table. A throat cleared down the way, but Emma couldn't gain the courage to see who it was. She didn't know who most of the people were, anyway.

Embarrassment settled in Emma's stomach, and a pain followed right behind. The girls looked at her like she wasn't meant to be sitting where she was. Their mother had probably owned the spot before Emma had taken her place there.

I'm sorry, she wanted to tell them.

The girls wouldn't understand.

She didn't want to take their mother's place. She hadn't asked for any of this. The marriage, the wedding, and her spot as their step-mother was not of her choosing.

Emma didn't want to hurt them.

Affonso sighed. "Michelle, now is not the right time to be asking that sort of thing. You know better, hmm?"

"But it's important," Michelle argued in all of her

fourteen-year glory.

"Michelle—"

"I won't call her mom," the girl interrupted fiercely.

Cynthia snickered at her sister's side, but kept her gaze down on her plate. At sixteen, Emma expected more issues from Cynthia than Michelle. She was closer to Emma's age, after all. Apparently, Michelle had other plans.

Affonso waved his fork at his youngest daughter. "Go."

Emma straightened in her chair, confused.

Michelle's face fell, crestfallen. "But, Daddy—"

"Go, I said," Affonso muttered. "Do not make me repeat myself, *ragazza*. You are crossing the line tonight with your attitude. I won't have you disrespect the woman I am marrying. Take your plate and eat in your room. Tomorrow, we'll see if you have changed your opinions at all."

"Affonso," Emma said quietly. "It's okay."

She ignored the way everyone turned to look at her, including Affonso's two daughters.

"She's just a girl," Emma added. "She doesn't understand, and she doesn't mean anything. She's just trying to make sense of how she feels."

Emma knew it was the truth.

"It does matter," Affonso replied in the most uncaring way Emma had ever heard. "And I won't stand for it."

Turning back to his daughter, Affonso waved his fork again.

"Go, Michelle," he told her.

Huffing, the girl stood from her chair, slammed it into the table with a bang, tossed Emma a glare, and stormed off. Emma held her breath, hurting for Michelle. She didn't deserve to be reprimanded and shamed in front of her father's people and her family, simply because she was a child who didn't understand what was happening.

DONATI BLOODLINES: PART 1

"I apologize," Affonso said.

Emma shook her head. "Don't. As I said, it's okay."

But it wasn't.

Michelle had every reason to dislike the woman who would take her mother's place in her life. And for that matter, Emma was not the perfect little queen that Affonso was trying to hold her up to be for these people.

He wanted Emma to be unsullied in their eyes. The perfect wife, his mob wife.

No shame.

She was dirty, more than Affonso could know. She had already broken the vows she had yet to speak when she laid down in a bed with his nephew. And then again when she fucked Calisto twice the morning after.

Emma was not good at all.

She wasn't made for this.

"Sorry I'm late," came a voice from the other side of the room.

Emma's heart dropped and her blood heated at the same fucking time. She forced herself not to look in the direction of Calisto's laughter as he greeted a man at the other end of the table. A chair scraped against tile as it was pulled out.

Apparently, he had come after all.

"Smile," Affonso demanded at her side.

Emma slid on her mask. All someone would need to do was look close enough to see what was really beneath the sheer falseness of her smile.

At the other end of the table, Emma found her lies staring her right in the face.

He smirked.

And winked.

Calisto Donati was her worst mistake, her greatest shame, and the one thing she still wanted more than anything. Emma could still feel him all over her, long after his touch and kiss was gone. In thirty days, her entire world had changed—he had changed her.

Emma had a feeling that if she played another game with Calisto, she would surely lose.

She had already lost once.

Wasn't it enough?

"Calisto," Affonso called out. "Where did you stay when the flight was canceled? You said the reservations for your room was over."

"I got another room for the night," Calisto said.

Lie.

"You didn't answer my calls after we first chatted."

"I was tired and fell asleep early."

More lies.

"You should have called me back," Affonso muttered.

Emma swallowed back her panic.

"I slept in and forgot about it," Calisto said simply, brushing Affonso off. "Then the airport notified me about the flight to New York and we rushed to catch it in time."

Another lie.

Calisto's falsehoods would be easy to unravel if Affonso looked into anything his nephew said. Thin lies were the easiest to see through.

Emma met Calisto's gaze again. The chatter at the table continued like nothing was amiss. Emma supposed to these people, nothing really was.

Calisto gave her another one of his sexy, knowing smiles. She didn't look away.

She couldn't.

21.

Calisto

The church smelled of burning incense. Calisto hated that smell more than anything. It lingered on everything it touched, his goddamn suit included.

"Father Day," Calisto said, knocking on the slightly open office door with two knuckles.

"Cal?"

Calisto smiled at the old priest's voice. He remembered spending Sunday after Sunday at this church when he was younger, hiding under the pews and ignoring every second of the sermons. When he had gotten old enough to know that was unacceptable, Calisto had taken a seat between his mother and uncle.

"Yeah, it's me. Do you have a minute?" Calisto asked.

"For you, my son, of course."

Calisto pushed open the door and stepped inside the small office. Father Day sat behind his desk, wearing his black ensemble and his white collar. Between his withered fingers, the priest held a small golden cross attached to a long length of black rosary beads.

"I didn't mean to interrupt your prayer," Calisto said quietly.

Father Day shook his head. "Nonsense, Calisto. I can pray at any time. He is always listening, as you very well know."

"So you say."

"So I know," the priest shot back.

Calisto chuckled. "You're right on the ball today, huh?"

"I always am. You're troubled."

There was no hiding from this man.

Calisto sighed, swallowed his nerves, and shoved his

clenched fists in his pockets. For the last couple of days, those very actions had been his repeated failsafe. When he felt confused, unsettled, or out of control; when he was too close to Emma and his thoughts wandered, he clenched his fists, let his fingernails cut his skin, and hid his shaking hands in his pockets.

It was easier than lying or hiding.

"Is it that obvious?" Calisto asked.

Father Day shrugged. "I have known you since you were just high enough to reach my knees. There is not much you can hide from me, Calisto. How long have I been taking your confessions or counselling you on personal matters when you needed it?"

"I started confessing at fifteen."

Smirking just a bit, the priest waved a finger at Calisto. "After your first time with a girl, I believe. You were not sorry in the least for your actions, but you knew the right thing to do was confess it. You couldn't quite say that you wouldn't do it again, however."

Calisto grinned. "That's just the Catholic in me, Father."

"Mmhmm. Sit, Cal."

He did as the priest demanded.

"I haven't seen you this month," Father Day said.

"I was out in Vegas for a while doing some business."

"You mean bringing back your uncle's paid-for bride. I know where the girl comes from."

Ouch.

Calisto sucked in air through his teeth. "Know about that, do you?"

"Affonso confesses, too. When people want things to happen in this church, on their time schedule, I demand their honesty on certain things. They know better than to cross the man who offers them the penance they crave in their darker moments."

"Yeah, well, that's where I was."

DONATI BLOODLINES: PART 1

"Pity," Father Day muttered, steepling his fingers in front of his face. "She's such a pretty, young thing and he's ..."

"Not," Calisto finished for the man.

"Hmm. You said it, my boy, not me. My place is not to judge."

"You could judge a little."

"I cannot," Father Day said in a murmur. "Tell me your troubles, Cal. Get them off your mind before they eat away at you. Remember last year, shortly before your mother died? That was an awful time for you. All that anger you let fester inside, and when she passed on, you nearly exploded with your guilt and grief. Don't do that to yourself again. You're far too good for that and you know it."

Calisto wished it was that easy.

"It's not the same thing," Calisto assured.

"How so?"

"I feel very little guilt for what I did this time, or, for that matter, what I didn't try to do at all. Maybe that's what bothers me—that I didn't try to stop myself, and that I have no remorse for taking something precious, something that didn't belong to me."

Father Day lifted a single brow high as he replied, "And do you wish to keep this thing; this thing that isn't yours, as you say?"

Calisto tried to stay quiet, but the confession slipped out. "*Sì.*"

"Why?"

"I don't know."

"That's not a good answer."

"There are a lot of reasons," Calisto said simply. "I'm not sure any of them would be worthy or good ones to move forward with. One is simply to hurt someone else, another is to feed my own selfishness, and others could be to build onto this complex I have festering in my head that I need to save something to keep it from being ruined like other things have been. I don't know, Father, because none of them matter."

"Because it isn't yours," Father Day said.

"Exactly."

"You know, Calisto, these roadblocks that pop up in our lives at the worst times and in the most unlikely of places are put there for a reason."

Calisto scoffed. "Really? And what is the reason for this one? Because believe me, it couldn't be worse than it is."

"It could," Father Day assured. "But God will not give you what He doesn't know you can already handle."

"That doesn't help."

"Because you're not listening."

Calisto blew out a frustrated breath. "In a month, I managed to break every rule I ever followed. I broke my oath to my *famiglia*, and I betrayed my uncle. My actions would defile the church, the vows that I believe in, and my faith. Did He really give me a barrier like this just to see me fail, Father?"

Father Day smiled softly. "Of course not, Calisto."

Then why did it feel like it?

"And," the priest added quieter, "you cannot blame God. He allows you to make your own choices, knowing that you are strong enough to handle the consequences of them."

"Even if it kills me," Calisto murmured.

It wasn't even a question.

Father Day glanced down at the rosary in his hand. "If it does, then He will be there to welcome you. You make your path, Calisto, and He will walk you through it."

"I don't know what my path is anymore, Father."

"You'll wander back to it, I'm sure."

• • •

Two days later, the church bells began to ring.

DONATI BLOODLINES: PART 1

At the very front of the church, Calisto sat at the end of the pew. His left ankle crossed over his right knee, and his chin rested in his hand. His gaze never left the altar where his uncle and the priest stood waiting, but his mind was somewhere else entirely.

A quiet room in Vegas.
Marble floors.
Breathless whispers.
White sheets.
Soft skin.
Morning light.
"I think I would keep you ..."
But she wasn't his.

Calisto reminded himself that he was obsessing over nothing—something he couldn't have. He was letting his confused thoughts tie strings with his emotions. This was exactly why he didn't attach himself to people. It always ended up ruined somehow.

He drew in a deep breath, needing the moment to calm the heaviness settling throughout his body. In his heart, his mind, and his chest, it was like a weight had suddenly been put there, taking him down under invisible water.

Clearly, he had not found his path yet.

He was still scrambling to keep from drowning.

"Beautiful day for a wedding," Ray said at Calisto's side.

Calisto passed his uncle's underboss a dismissive glance. "Mmm."

"You could show a little more interest in all of this, you know. Sit straighter and fucking smile, or something."

"I'm good," Calisto said under his breath.

Ray sighed loudly, but stayed quiet.

Calisto couldn't show any more interest in this sham of a wedding than what he already was. It had been an internal war just to get up on time, get his goddamn suit on, and show up at the church to take his seat.

A woman was being married today.

She didn't want to be married.

He knew the truth.

It ached.

Calisto clenched his fist on his knee. Shortly after, the wedding march began to play.

The doors to the back opened.

Calisto's chest got tighter than ever.

Somehow, he managed to stand like he was supposed to. Turning slightly, he found Emma and her father instantly. She was the only one wearing white, after all.

The veil she wore covered her face just enough to shroud her features. The sheer fabric trailed all the way back to the floor behind her and over the length of the dress. Lace hugged her curves, reminding him of how it felt to hold her in his hands, and to own those dips and swells.

A lump formed in Calisto's throat.

Emma wasn't smiling.

How could she?

This was a terrible day.

Calisto dropped his gaze as the father and bride-to-be started their slow walk up the satin-lined aisle. Tulle linked between every church pew, and a ball of white roses hung off the ends of each curled arm.

The closer Emma came to the front and Calisto's spot, the worse he felt.

He'd delivered her for this day. This was his penance for doing that to her when she didn't deserve it. The ache in his chest, the lead in his feet, and the wrongs he helped to make with her were all a part of the sentence he had to endure.

Emma Donati would be his punishment.

She wouldn't be as sweet after today.

She wouldn't ever be as happy as she had once been.

She would never be free.

Calisto would have to watch it all from the shadows, knowing he brought her to this.

So, he met Emma's gaze as she passed him by, arm in arm with her father, and didn't drop it until he no longer had a choice. He was quiet as she was handed over, familiar words were exchanged, and a new future was given to a woman who never asked for it.

Calisto didn't do a thing.

He couldn't, without hurting Emma in a new way. Not without putting her in danger, or worse, causing her to be shamed for their lies.

Hadn't he hurt her enough?

$$\bullet \ \bullet \ \bullet$$

"Another," Calisto demanded, waving his finger over the empty tumbler.

The bartender serving the wedding guests gave the glass a baleful look.

"That's your third glass in fifteen minutes, sir."

Was Calisto supposed to care?

He didn't.

"Another."

"Same thing?"

"Yeah."

The bartender poured another dirty whiskey and said, "Take it a little slower this time, or someone will be carrying you out of here tonight."

Maybe that's what Calisto was going for.

"Sure," Calisto said instead of voicing his inner thoughts. He picked the glass up, put it to his lips, and downed the four ounces of burning whiskey in one fast gulp. Putting the glass back on the bar top, he slid it to the bartender. "Was that slow enough for you?"

"I'm not pouring you another."

Calisto scoffed. "I don't want another."

Facing the crowd, Calisto leaned against the bar and rapped his fingers against the ledge. He scanned the crowd of people dancing in the bar. Affonso had decided to use one of his more upscale bars as the location for the reception. The place was packed, making Calisto feel more suffocated than ever.

These were his people.

His *famiglia*.

He still felt incredibly alone.

Calisto's gaze cut through the crowd again, zoning in on the one couple dancing in the middle. Affonso wore his usual pleased, sly smile with his hand holding Emma's and his other at her lower back. Emma had finally replaced her mask of nothingness for a thinly veiled smile that anyone with two brains cells could see was fake.

Nonetheless, she had done her thing. The cake was cut. The dances were had. She allowed Affonso to show her off, and smiled sweetly each time someone mentioned her new last name.

Calisto's chest started to hurt again. He turned to the bar, leaned over, and grabbed the bottle of whiskey when the bartender's back was turned. Pouring himself another hefty glass, Calisto slammed it back faster than his last one.

It burned all the way down.

It felt fucking sublime.

Creating his own pain was better than feeling the dull ache that just wouldn't let up. The sting in his throat from the whiskey was easier to focus on than the guilt eating away at him slowly.

"Cal?"

Calisto spun on his heel only to find his sixteen-year-old cousin standing behind him. Cynthia crossed her arms, and clicked her silver stilettos on the floor in a fast beat. Her pout and hard, brown eyes—eyes that matched his—said the girl was annoyed and getting worse by the minute.

DONATI BLOODLINES: PART 1

God knew his cousins were spoiled rotten. Affonso treated them like little queens, but he never gave them the right kind of attention. The kind that would teach them how a man should properly treat a woman in his life.

Calisto was left to that job.

"Hey, Cee," Calisto said.

"He made me wear a dress," Cynthia said, huffing.

Calisto couldn't help but laugh. "You look nice."

"I hate dresses."

"You sound like a brat."

"You look like ..." Cynthia failed to come up with something and scowled instead. "Shut up, Cal."

"I know you're not happy, but remember, Emma isn't here to try and take the place of your mom. You know that, right?"

Cynthia shrugged. "I guess."

"Then what's the problem?"

She glanced over her shoulder. Calisto followed her gaze only to find Affonso spinning his new wife out from his side, and then bringing her back again with a charming smile for the clapping people.

Calisto knew exactly what Cynthia's problem was.

"Has he danced with you tonight?" Calisto asked quietly.

Cynthia shook her head.

"Has he asked?"

"No," the teenager muttered.

"Then I will," Calisto said, pushing away from the bar.

He held his hand out for Cynthia to take, and his cousin's palm met his before she flashed him a shy, happy smile.

"Thanks, Cal."

"No problem. Pretty girls should be danced with. Come on."

Calisto led his cousin out on the dance floor, just a few feet away from Affonso and Emma. The slightly faster beat of the new song was more to Cynthia's tastes, so Calisto let her lead him into whatever dance she wanted to move to. His cousin's small smile turned into a brilliant grin, and he forgot all about the people and the not-so-happy fucking couple.

Family was important.

His mother taught him that first.

Calisto picked up the slack where his uncle failed with his daughters. If Cynthia wanted to dance, if she wanted some male attention to make her feel special for the evening, then Calisto would give it to her.

Better him than some random man filling a void.

As the song changed again, to a slow moving beat, Calisto drew his cousin closer for a waltz. Pink-cheeked and beaming, Cynthia poked Calisto in the chest.

"You should dance with Michelle, too."

"I will," he promised. "Do me a favor, huh?"

"Anything, Cal."

Calisto sighed. "Don't blame Emma for your father's lack of attention, Cee. I know she's the easy target for your resentment, and you think she's yet another thing for him to shower affection on while he forgets about you and your sister, but that's not the case. She is in no better of a situation than you."

"She's only twenty. That's what I heard people say."

"Yeah."

"Dad's almost fifty."

Calisto coughed. It was better for Cynthia and Michelle to draw their own conclusions about how Affonso's marriage to Emma came about. "Yeah."

"She seems kind of nice."

"She is," Calisto said quietly. "And I'm sure she would be happy to make friends with you if you tried a little bit."

Cynthia pursed her lips, still moving in the standard four steps of the waltz. "I'll try."

"Thank you."

DONATI BLOODLINES: PART 1

A few seconds later, a tap on Calisto's shoulder stopped his dance with Cynthia. Behind him, Affonso stood with a quiet, stony-faced Emma at his side.

"Would you trade me for a moment?" Affonso asked.

Calisto passed a look at Cynthia, wanting to make sure she was okay. The girl just shrugged.

"You could have asked her hours ago, *zio*," Calisto said, stepping away from his cousin and holding a hand out to Emma. "Fathers are the men who teach their daughters the most important lessons about love. Keep that in mind."

Before Affonso could respond, Calisto took Emma's hand and moved away from the somber father and daughter still staring at one another with a few feet between them. Calisto moved Emma to the middle of the floor, ignoring the softness of her skin as he spun her around to face him and put his hand on her lower back.

"That was nice of you," Emma said as they began to move with the beat. "Dancing with her, I mean."

"She's a good kid. Michelle is, too."

"I know. They're dying for affection, though. I can see it."

Calisto nodded once. "They are."

"Thank you for taking the time to give them some. When they're older, I'm sure they'll remember that you were the one who stepped up to care for them when it mattered the most."

This was too personal for Calisto. He wanted the topic to change, and soon.

"Can we, uh, dance and not talk?"

Emma frowned. "Sure."

Apparently, Calisto couldn't follow his own advice.

"You looked beautiful today."

She didn't respond.

Then, very quietly, Emma asked, "Was it hard for you today?"

Calisto's arm instinctively tightened around Emma. He didn't want to answer her. He wanted to pretend like there was nothing going on inside of him—that nothing had gone on between them.

"Was it hard, Calisto?"

"Incredibly so."

Emma laughed dryly. "Imagine how it felt from where I stood."

"I did, and it almost killed me."

"Hmm."

She didn't sound like she believed him.

Calisto didn't blame her.

"And I thought," Calisto continued, "for a second that maybe I should have let you run after I saved you."

"But you didn't."

"I didn't."

"Now here I am," she said.

"Here we are."

And what a fucking place it was.

"We can do this, right?" Emma asked. "Pretend like nothing happened."

"Nothing did, Emmy."

"Right. Nothing."

Calisto's mind screamed the truth louder than his words.

Something had happened.

Good and bad.

Something.

Calisto had a feeling that whatever had happened between him and Emma, it wasn't over just yet.

BIO

Bethany-Kris is a Canadian author, lover of much, and mother to four sons, a glaring of cats, and a pack of dogs. A small town in Eastern Canada where she was born and raised is where she has always called home. With her boys under her feet, a snuggling cat, barking dogs, and a spouse calling over his shoulder, she is nearly always writing something ... when she can find the time.

Find Bethany-Kris at her website www.bethanykris.com for more information, or links to follow.

Sign up to Bethany-Kris's New Release Newsletter here: http://eepurl.com/bf9lzD